Praise for *Discovering Peace*

"I loved reading *Discovering Peace* and could see myself in the story. I loved reading how all the voices in the adoption circle were included and the changes that can come in an open adoption. Loved this book. Thank you, Jen, for speaking out for adoption! Go, go adoption!"

Alison Lowe
CCLS / United for Adoption

"Jennifer Holt's *Discovering Peace* was a book I couldn't put down. I easily slipped into Ally and Livvy's world, because they are such easy characters to love. I enjoyed seeing the other side of adoption, what happens to the newly created family and the birth mom when the papers are signed. In *Discovering Peace* I enjoyed the alternating points of view from key characters. It wasn't just Ally and Livvy that needed to find peace. *Discovering Peace* is another triumph for Jennifer Holt."

Mindy Holt
Min Reads and Reviews, LDS Women's Book Review

discovering PEACE

Wishing you much peace and hope!

Jennifer Ann Holt
Nov. 2014

discovering PEACE

Jennifer Ann Holt

BONNEVILLE BOOKS ™
An Imprint of Cedar Fort, Inc.
Springville, Utah

ISBN 13: 978-1-4621-1413-9

Published by Bonneville Books, an imprint of Cedar Fort, Inc.
2373 W. 700 S., Springville, UT 84663
Distributed by Cedar Fort, Inc., www.cedarfort.com

LIBRARY OF CONGRESS CATALOGING-IN-PUBLICATION DATA

Holt, Jennifer (Jennifer Ann), 1977-
Discovering peace / Jennifer Ann Holt.
pages cm
ISBN 978-1-4621-1413-9
1. Birthmothers--Fiction. 2. Adoption--Fiction. 3. Adoptive parents--Fiction. 4. Man-woman relationships--Fiction. 5. Christian fiction. 6. Domestic fiction. I. Title.
PS3608.O4943593D57 2014
813'.6--dc23
2013041959

Cover design by Kristen Reeves
Cover design © 2014 by Lyle Mortimer
Edited and typeset by Melissa J. Caldwell

Printed in the United States of America

10 9 8 7 6 5 4 3 2 1

To Isabella, Tyson, and Jay
For bringing laughter, noise, love, and peace into my life

"Peace, be still."

MARK 4:39

BOOK ONE

CHAPTER ONE

Allison Campbell woke with a start. It was dark, and she struggled to orient herself. A young man with curly blond hair was fading from her mind. Ally closed her eyes and tried to force the dream to reappear, but the image wouldn't come into focus. After a moment, Allison let it go and sat up to look around.

The shapes of her bedroom were familiar shadows in the darkness, and Allison relaxed. She leaned against her pillow and rested her hands on her stomach. She struggled to swallow the ache as she touched the small bulge that remained after delivering her baby girl last month. She switched on her bedside lamp and picked up the pink and green picture frame that had arrived yesterday morning in a package from Michael and Olivia.

Ally studied Hope's little face. A face that was so familiar, yet already so different from the newborn baby girl Ally had given birth to. The soft blonde curls were the same, but her cheeks were filling out, and her eyes were no longer the newborn steely gray. They might turn out to be green. Ally fingered the locket that had become a permanent fixture on her throat. She opened the small gold heart and looked closely at the pictures that filled the inside frames. The first was herself holding Hope just a few hours after she was born; the second was Michael and Olivia. Ally felt the familiar burn of tears behind her eyelids and snapped the locket shut.

Ally resumed her study of the recent photo of Hope and allowed her tears to fall softly onto the glass covering her baby girl's face. She didn't regret her decision, and she was happy to have found Michael and Olivia and to know that they were Hope's parents. Ally knew that Hope would have all the love and care that any child could ever want. Ally's tears weren't for Hope—they were drops of her own pain. She missed her baby girl! She missed how it felt when Hope would move around inside her, stretching and kicking, trying to find some room for her growing body. Ally missed wrapping her arms around her pregnant belly and cradling and singing to her baby girl. She missed holding Hope and kissing her and feeding her and gazing at her beautiful, sleeping face.

A sob escaped, and Ally did the one thing she knew would help calm her. She rolled out of bed onto her knees and began to pray. She couldn't formulate words to describe her emotions, so she just opened her heart and mind to the feelings threatening to overwhelm her and pled with Heavenly Father to help her manage them. The gentle warmth began in Ally's chest and flooded through her body, not erasing her pain, but easing the burden and pushing back the anguish. She remained kneeling, savoring the warm glow and—as she had done so often over the last month—praying for the strength to move forward with continued hope and faith in the Savior.

Her prayer concluded, Ally looked at the bright green numbers of her bedside clock. Five thirty a.m. *Might as well get up,* Ally thought. *I don't think I can go back to sleep anyway.* She thought about reading her scriptures, as she had been doing every morning over the last few months, but her brain was still a jumble of emotions, so Ally decided to go for a walk to clear her mind first. She slipped off her pajamas and found a pair of sweatpants in the closet. She pulled a T-shirt and then a sweatshirt over her head and sat down on the floor to tie her shoes.

Ally had been relieved when her doctor told her she could

begin going for walks about a week after the delivery. She really wanted to run, but her doctor insisted that she wait until after her six-week checkup. What Ally was craving—even more than physical exercise—was the mental and emotional stress release that always came *with* the physical exercise.

She tiptoed down the stairs, stepping over the one step that always creaked, and headed out the front door. The crisp morning air felt good on her face as she started through the neighborhood. Ally had never really been a morning person, but she wasn't sleeping well since Hope's birth, so she'd been going for early walks before the sun came up and the commotion of the day began. She was amazed to discover how much she enjoyed it. That first morning, Ally had taken her iPod, as she always did when she exercised, but the battery died after just a few minutes, so she had continued to walk in silence. Without the interference from the music—or from traffic or other distractions—Ally began noticing the sound of the breeze through the leafless tree branches, the crunch of the gravel under her feet, even the sound of her own breath moving in and out of her lungs. She had taken time to look up into the sky and see the last few, brave stars shining as the edge of the horizon started turning from black to gray, signaling that morning was not far off. She liked it and had left her iPod at home each morning since.

Ally took a deep breath and the chilly March air burned her throat and stung her eyes, but she didn't mind. She walked and felt her mind start to relax. She could remember the hope and peace she had felt in the hospital that brought her the courage to place her baby girl in the arms of a mom and a dad who were sealed in the temple and who could give Hope everything that Ally couldn't have offered on her own.

Placing her baby for adoption had been the most difficult experience of Ally's life, but she had also felt the love and peace of the Savior more than she ever had before. The knowledge of Christ's love for her hadn't faded; it was the feeling of peace that now felt slippery and just out of reach. Often it was on the periphery of her life, where she could almost see and feel it, but not quite.

Ally smiled as she walked past Bishop Jenkins's house. He'd been so supportive through all of this, and Ally would always be grateful to him for that. He'd helped guide Ally to the Atonement, and he continually assured her that she was now free to move forward in her life. Just last Sunday he told Ally that all she had left to do was forgive herself.

Easier said than done, Ally thought as she picked up her pace. She knew that she'd caused a lot of grief for a lot of people. Her dad was trying hard to be supportive, and her mom had gotten to the point where she could accept Ally's decision to place the baby, but that didn't erase the pain she had caused them. At times Ally could see the anger behind her mom's eyes, and other times it seemed that her mom was too hurt to even look at Ally. She wondered if her parents could ever find peace in the wake of all this.

She thought briefly of Brandon, wondering if he even realized that the baby had been born. She hadn't spoken to any member of his family since the day she walked out of their house after Brandon's mom, Stephanie—on behalf of her son—had once again tried to convince Ally to have an abortion. She wondered if Stephanie knew the baby had come. This wasn't such a big town, and chances were good that Stephanie had heard about Ally having the baby and placing her for adoption. If so, she wasn't breaking the silence. Stephanie had promised Ally that she would not be involved or help in any way, and she was keeping that promise wholeheartedly. Ally had considered calling to let her know how everything had turned out, but so far she hadn't convinced herself this was the right thing to do. Maybe that was a chapter best left closed.

Ally continued around her usual loop through the neighborhood. She passed her own house and moved on for a second loop. This time around Ally tried to clear her mind. She concentrated on her breathing, expanding her lungs so that the cold air seemed to spread to every corner of her body. It felt good. As Ally approached her house for the second time, she noticed that the living room light was on, so rather than taking her usual third loop around, Ally went inside.

Ally's mom, Julie, was sitting on the sofa, staring out the front window. "Morning, Mom," Ally said. "I didn't wake you, did I? I tried to leave quietly."

Julie didn't respond at first and then blinked as if she were dragging her mind back to the present. "I'm sorry, Ally. What did you say?"

"I just said that I hoped I didn't wake you up."

"No, no," Julie replied, brushing the hair out of her eyes. "I thought I heard you leave, but I was already awake." She looked up and focused on Ally, really seeing her for the first time this morning. "Did you have a nice walk?"

"Yeah, it was okay. It felt good to get some air." Ally shrugged. "I wasn't sleeping either."

These words seemed to crack some carefully composed façade in Julie's mind, and she dropped her head into her hands and began to sob. "Oh, Ally, what have we done? What have we done! How could I have let you go through with it?" The words spilled through Julie's fingers with her tears. "I miss her! She is my first grandbaby. I can't sleep; I can hardly eat. And what's more, I know *you* miss her too!" Julie lifted her head, her wet eyes boring into Ally's, daring her to disagree.

Ally sat down on the couch and put her arm around her mom's shoulder. "Of course I miss her, Mom, but—"

"I knew it!" Julie jumped up from the couch and began pacing. "You're not sleeping well, either. I can hear you during the night, sometimes crying, sometimes shuffling around your room. And then I go in there this morning to see if I really heard you leave, and I'm faced with this!" Julie reached for something on the couch that Ally hadn't noticed and thrust it under Ally's nose. It was the photo of Hope that Michael and Olivia sent, the very one Ally was looking at this morning.

"There she is, *my granddaughter*, all happy and chubby, but she doesn't even know who I am. She doesn't even know who *you* are.

How is that okay?" Julie's hand was shaking as she held the picture frame out, and then she slumped onto the couch, in tears again.

Ally took a deep breath and turned to her mom. "Of course I miss her, Mom," she repeated. "*But* I also know—without any doubt at all—that I made the best decision for Hope. I know that I made the decision that Heavenly Father wanted me to make. And even though it's hard, harder than anything I can imagine," Ally paused and wiped the tears that were flowing down her cheeks, "I also know that this was the right decision for me." Ally's heart warmed as the Spirit echoed the truth of her words. "No, Hope doesn't know me right now. And I haven't decided if she ever will or not. But as soon as she is old enough to understand, she will know *about* me. She'll know how much I love her. How much *we* love her." Ally put her hand on her mom's knee. "She'll know that the Lord handpicked the most perfect, special parents for her, and that when He whispered to my heart who her family was to be, she'll know that I loved her enough to listen."

They sat in silence for a few moments, tears streaming down their faces. "And she'll know," Ally finished, "that *I* had wonderful parents who taught me to follow Heavenly Father's will, even when it seems impossible." Silence surrounded them as Ally waited for a response. Slowly, Julie moved her hand onto Ally's knee and gave a gentle squeeze. She didn't speak, but offered a small smile as she stood and walked back to her bedroom. It wasn't the reaction Ally was hoping for, but at least it was a start.

CHAPTER TWO

Olivia Spencer sat in her new rocking chair, humming to the little pink bundle in her arms. She never grew tired of watching her daughter sleep. *My daughter.* Olivia smiled as she thought the words. *My daughter, Hope.* She leaned forward and kissed Hope on the forehead. Her tiny eyebrows crinkled at the touch and then relaxed. Olivia squeezed her into a hug and then raised Hope's head up to rest on her shoulder. Olivia loved the feel of Hope's soft curls against her cheek and the smell of pink lotion and baby powder. It had taken years to bring Hope into her family, and now, after only a month, Olivia couldn't imagine life without her. It seemed Hope had always been her daughter, had always been part of her life. Olivia's full-time job as a nurse at the hospital was a distant memory, and she was cherishing every moment with her sweet baby girl.

Olivia's thoughts turned to Hope's birth mom. Ally had given them a daughter. Olivia smiled and shook her head. Their shared experience had created a special bond of love and gratitude that she hadn't anticipated. Although they had spent only a few hours together in their whole lives, Olivia loved Ally and would always think of her as a special part of their family. Ally was still unsure of how much contact she wanted to have with them, and for the time being, they were all content for their involvement to be in the form of letters and pictures.

Olivia looked up at the pastel butterfly clock that hung on Hope's bedroom wall. It was five a.m. She would be able to go back to bed and sleep for a few more hours before Hope was ready to get up for the day . . . or she could just sit here and continue rocking her. Olivia smiled at herself as she struggled over this decision, as she did every morning. In the end, she decided that today she needed the sleep more, and that there would be plenty of time for rocking and cuddling and loving during the daylight hours. She reluctantly stood up and gave Hope one last kiss on top of her head before laying her down in her crib. "I love you, Hope," she whispered as she tiptoed out of the room.

Olivia slipped into bed, trying not to wake her husband, Michael. As she pulled the covers up, though, Michael rolled over and put his arm around her. She snuggled into the warmth of his chest and he smiled when he said, "So, you opted for sleep this morning? I was just starting to think that rocking our daughter"—his smile broadened over the word—"was going to win out once again."

"It was a close race," Olivia whispered, "but I was pretty worn out yesterday, so here I am."

Michael chuckled and started running his fingers up and down Olivia's arm. It was nice, and Olivia felt herself easing into sleep. Just before she nodded off, she heard Michael whisper, "Sleep well, my Livvy. I love you." She smiled and was asleep.

The sun was sneaking between the slats in the window blinds when Olivia woke up. She stretched and rolled over, then jumped up when she saw that it was nine thirty. Hope was usually awake by now! She had to push back the fear as she ran down the hall to Hope's bedroom and darted through the open door. Hope was lying there, as peaceful as ever, her little chest moving up and down with each sleeping breath.

Olivia laughed at herself and wondered how long it would be before she stopped running in to check on Hope at every little noise and flying down the hall in a panic if the baby overslept a bit. Her friend Heather had told her that after a while she would quit being so anxious about each little thing, but that you never quit worrying about your kids. That was part of being a mom. Olivia stood watching Hope for a few more seconds, reassuring herself that she was, in fact, fine. Then, since the baby was still asleep, Olivia decided to treat herself to a nice, unhurried shower.

As Olivia walked into her bedroom, she noticed a note on Michael's pillow. Olivia knew he had already left. The high school where he taught biology and coached football started at eight thirty. He always kept quiet if Olivia and Hope were still sleeping, but he had never left a note before. Olivia picked up the folded piece of notebook paper and read.

> *Livvy,*
>
> *I was watching you sleep this morning and just wanted to tell you how much I love you. You are an amazing mom to Hope and a wonderful wife. I love you now more than ever. I can't wait until I get home to my two girls tonight. I love you!*
>
> *Love, Michael*

Olivia was smiling as she turned on the hot water in her shower. It had been a long road to get to this point in their marriage, but everything was going so well right now. She had worked hard to overcome the sadness and anger that consumed her through the years of infertility while Michael had watched helplessly. There had even been a time when Olivia wondered if their marriage could survive. But once Olivia had made the commitment to find out what Heavenly Father's will for her life was and then follow it no matter what, hope and faith had entered her life again. Followed closely by her very own little Hope. Olivia smiled again as she put Michael's note down on the counter and got into the shower. It was a miracle.

CHAPTER THREE

"Mom, Dad, can we talk?" Ally felt like she'd been saying this to her parents a lot over the last year. "Don't worry. It's no big deal," she added.

Ally's dad, Steve, folded his newspaper and put it on the floor next to his recliner as her mom came in from the dining room to sit on the sofa. They both wore masks of calmness, but Ally could read the worry behind their eyes. She felt as though they had been watching her so closely since Hope was born, waiting for her to . . . to what? Ally wasn't sure. Waiting for her to break down? Waiting for her to mess up? Ally felt confident that she would never get herself into a bad situation again, and she could feel her strength and determination grow every day as she prayed and read the Book of Mormon. Bishop Jenkins had promised her—and she felt the warmth in her heart confirming its truth—that if she consistently obeyed the basic principles of the gospel, she would have the Spirit with her to warn her, protect her, and help her make good decisions.

"What is it, Ally?" Steve asked. "What did you want to talk to us about?"

"Well, I've been doing a lot of thinking." Ally noticed her mom glance sideways at her dad, as if to say, *Here it comes.* Ally shook it off and continued. "I've been thinking that instead of taking my deferred acceptance to college—"

"No." Julie interrupted. "I've been worried that this was going to happen." She was bobbing her head up and down, eyes frantic. She turned to Steve. "Didn't I tell you this was going to happen? She's going to let everything go now. All her plans for the future—" Julie's voice cracked and her hands were shaking, but Ally tried to tune it out. She didn't want to get upset.

Ally couldn't really blame her mom for not trusting her right now. She just hoped that eventually her mom would be able to forgive her.

"Mom?" Julie was so caught up in her emotions that she didn't hear. "MOM!" Julie stopped and spun toward Ally. "Mom," Ally said and took a deep breath. "Just listen to me for a minute, then you can have your say."

Steve put his hand on Julie's arm. She pressed her lips together and nodded. "Go ahead."

"I'm still going to college. It's just that, well, I've really been feeling like I should go to BYU instead. The only problem is that the application deadline for fall semester was February 1st. So I won't be able to start school at the end of August. The deadline for winter semester isn't until October 1st, so I could still apply to start school in January."

"Ally," Steve began, "do you really think that the *only* problem is that you missed the fall semester deadline?"

Ally was surprised that it was her dad who questioned her. Maybe she'd misunderstood. "What do you mean?"

"Ally, you're a smart girl. You've definitely got the grades and test scores to get into BYU, but aren't you forgetting something?"

Ally shook her head and forced her teeth to unclench. "Forgetting what?"

"I'm not trying to upset you. I'm really not. I'm just . . . not sure. . . whether you'll be able to go there. The honor code is pretty straightforward."

Ally closed her eyes and then opened them, meeting her father's gaze. "I know about the honor code, Dad, but this is something I need to pursue. I just wanted to give you guys a heads-up that I might be staying until January." Ally took a deep breath and looked at her mom. "If it's okay with you two."

"Well, I don't have a problem with any of this, as long as you're still going to college," Julie said. "There's a nursing program at BYU, isn't there?"

Ally smiled. Her mom was trying to smooth things over. She was trying to help. "Of course, Mom. A really good one too. I've checked it all out. Believe me, I'm not giving up on myself or my plans. I'm just really trying to figure out what direction will be best."

Steve shrugged. "What do I know? I'm just the dad." He attempted a smile. "But go talk to Bishop Jenkins first. I don't want you setting yourself up for a disappointment. If he thinks it's all right, then I certainly won't stop you."

Ally waited in the hallway next to Bishop Jenkins's office door. She couldn't help but think back to the day, almost a year ago now, when she was waiting to go in and tell him that she was pregnant. It seemed like a lifetime ago. She was a different person now. More mature, for one thing. More humble, for another. Less judgmental and more loving. "Hmm," Ally said out loud just as the office door opened.

"Hmm, what?" Bishop Jenkins smiled and reached out to shake Ally's hand.

"Oh, I was just thinking," Ally said. She went in the office and sat down in one of the chairs across from the bishop's shiny desk.

"About what?" Bishop Jenkins asked as he sat down opposite her.

"About how different I am now than I was this time last year." Bishop Jenkins smiled his crinkly-eyed smile and nodded, encouraging Ally to continue.

"I'm not happy about the mistakes I made, but I feel like I've learned a lot and that I'm a better person now than I was before."

"You are, Ally." Then he added quickly, "Not that you weren't a good person before you got pregnant." Now it was Ally's turn to smile.

"But that's the amazing thing about true repentance," he continued. "Ally, your heart has been changed. You turned to the Savior and gave Him everything. Your pain, your pride, your mistakes, your heartache, your trust, and your love. You did whatever He asked of you, no matter the sacrifice. Of course you feel like a different person." He stopped, deep in thought. "You know, I counsel with a lot of adults, and they're still trying to learn those lessons. The thing is, to learn them, you can't just go through the motions. You have to really work at coming to know the Savior and understanding our Father's will for your life. It's something that we're all working on, every day. You're just a little ahead of some of us. The key is to continue on, to stay close to Jesus Christ, and to keep doing the little things every single day that will bring His spirit into your life."

Ally was already glad she had come. She always felt such love and peace when Bishop Jenkins talked to her. She knew that he was speaking from experience and that he was doing the very things he counseled her to do.

"You probably had something you wanted to talk about, though," he continued. "And here I am talking away. Now it's your turn."

Ally laughed. "Well, there is something I wanted to ask you." She was suddenly nervous. What if he told her to forget it—that BYU was out of the question? Brigham Young University was occupying most of her thoughts lately. She felt so strongly about it. What if he told her no?

"I can see your mind spinning out of control, Ally," Bishop Jenkins said. "Go ahead and tell me what's going on. It's okay."

"Yeah." Ally fidgeted in her chair. "So I've been thinking a lot about where I should go from here."

Bishop Jenkins smiled and didn't say a word. Ally liked that about him.

"I've been feeling like I should change my plans a bit." Ally found herself looking for a reason to stall, but couldn't come up with one, so she continued. "Well, I just feel that . . . I would like . . ." Bishop Jenkins raised an eyebrow.

"Bishop, I want to go to BYU. I'm just not sure if that's possible, or . . . or . . . what's so funny?" Bishop Jenkins was chuckling. Ally swallowed the rest of her thought and ducked her head. Was going to BYU really a laughable idea?

"Oh, Ally," he began after the laughter died away. "You had me concerned. You looked so worried."

"I was worried. I *am* worried. Why did you laugh?"

"I'm sorry about that, Ally. I'm just relieved. You looked so scared. I had no idea what you were about to tell me."

"Oh, okay," Ally managed. "So . . . what about BYU?"

"Well, weren't you at the top of your graduating class?"

"Yes."

"And I suppose you did well on your ACT test?"

"Yeah. I got thirty-two."

"And I remember you graduating from seminary."

Ally nodded.

"Well, then, I'd say you've got a very good chance of getting in."

Ally rolled her eyes. He'd entirely missed the point. "But, Bishop, what about the honor code?"

"What about it? Is there something going on that I don't know about?"

"No, but what about the stuff that you *do* know about?"

Bishop Jenkins sighed and shook his head, all trace of laughter gone. "You have repented, Ally."

"I know, but—"

"No buts. You have fully and sincerely repented and the Lord has forgiven you. You are as clean and worthy as anyone else who will be applying. Probably more clean and worthy than some."

"There's a form you'll have to fill out," Ally pressed.

"I know that, Ally," he said. "I've been the bishop for a while now and have helped several people apply to the Y," he added.

"So you would be okay about recommending me to go?"

"Absolutely." Bishop Jenkins rubbed his nose with his thumb and forefinger, and then looked Ally right in the eye. "There's something else I know."

"About the honor code?"

"About the honor code and about the gospel and about life in general."

Ally leaned forward.

"None of it is about what we've done in the past. It's about what we're doing now—today—to be the very best person we can be. To follow the Savior and do what He asks of us."

Ally sniffled and Bishop Jenkins passed her a box of tissues. "It's time for you to forgive yourself, Ally. Stop looking back."

"I'm working on that." A tear escaped the corner of her eye and Ally brushed at the wetness on her cheek. "I feel so bad about how hurt my parents are. Especially my mom." Ally looked down and smoothed her skirt. "I caused their pain. I should somehow take it away."

"You can't," Bishop Jenkins said softly, but with enough force and feeling that Ally looked up to meet his eyes. "No matter what you do, you can't take away their pain. And what's more," he continued when Ally opened her mouth to interrupt, "it's not even your job and it's especially not your responsibility to heal them. You have repented. You've made a loving sacrifice—a sacrifice that most people in this world will never be able to fully understand—because that is what Heavenly Father asked you to do. You've told your mom and dad how sorry you are. You have made things right with the Savior. Your part is over. Now it's up to them."

"I just wish there was something more I could do."

"I understand that, but there's not. Your parents are good people, Ally. They'll be okay."

"Dad will, and Mom's trying, but she's still so upset."

Bishop Jenkins was quiet for a moment, and then he said, "Sooner or later, Ally, your mom will get tired of holding on to the hurt. It might be a few weeks or it might be many years, but if she wants to feel better and she keeps working at it, that day will come. And when it does, the Savior will be ready to take all of the hurt and anger from her, and she'll be healed. But that's *her* responsibility. Her choice. Not yours. Do you understand?"

Ally nodded and she really did understand. "If nothing else, I guess I *have* learned that each of us has to choose to be happy and that the only real happiness comes from choosing to turn our will over to the Savior and follow Him."

Bishop Jenkins's eyes crinkled up again as a smile spread across his face. "I couldn't have said it better myself, Ally. Now, what do we need to do to get started on that college application?"

CHAPTER FOUR

"Wake up, Mommy!" Michael kissed Olivia's ear as he settled Hope next to her on the bed. "We've been up for *hours*—okay, maybe just half an hour—making you breakfast on your big day!"

Olivia breathed in the scent of her baby girl, mingled with strawberries and waffles. She also caught the scent of roses. She savored the moment before opening her eyes.

"Happy Mother's Day, Livvy!" Michael was beaming, and the gleam in his brown eyes made Olivia laugh. "That's just the sound I was hoping to hear."

Michael leaned forward and kissed her again, this time on the forehead. Balancing a breakfast tray in one hand, he began rearranging the pillows into a backrest. Olivia sat up. Michael bowed as he adjusted the tray on her lap. Hope swatted at the vase of red roses on the corner of the tray, so he picked her up and stood grinning at his wife.

Olivia leaned forward and inhaled the sweet smell of the roses. "They're beautiful." She smiled.

"Just like you," Michael said.

Olivia turned her attention to the food. "I assume there are some waffles underneath all of this cream and strawberries?" she teased.

"Of course there are!" Michael shifted Hope over to the other arm. "I just happen to know that the strawberries and cream are your favorite parts, so I gave you extra!"

Olivia took a big bite and closed her eyes as the strawberry burst in her mouth. "Mmmm. So good," she said before she had even swallowed. Michael watched her take a few more bites in silence. He bounced Hope up and down. The movement had become so natural that it seemed he didn't even realize he was doing it.

Olivia looked up at them, wiping the cream from the corners of her mouth. "I've dreamed about having a Mother's Day breakfast in bed for years." Michael smiled and Olivia continued. "This is even better than I hoped it would be." The tears spilled over onto her cheeks, and she brushed them aside. "Thank you, Michael."

"You're welcome, Livvy. I'd hope I wouldn't disappoint you."

Olivia grinned. "Nope. It was worth the wait."

Michael caught Olivia's eye and reached out to touch her fingers. "So?" he mouthed, poking his thumb toward the front of the chapel.

Olivia shrugged. "It's fine," she whispered. The Mother's Day program was going on, but Olivia was focused on feeding Hope. She smoothed the delicate pink dress she'd bought last week for Hope and tucked a few of the baby soft curls behind the big, pink bow in her daughter's hair. Olivia smiled at how intent Hope was on drinking her bottle. She sucked the few remaining drops of formula from the nipple, then looked up at Olivia with a milky smile. Olivia's breath caught. *Life doesn't get any better than this.*

For the first time in years, all the talks about mothers didn't hurt Olivia's heart at all. Even when one of the speakers mentioned that giving birth is an integral part of the mothering experience, Olivia decided she wasn't going to let anything ruin this day and chose to ignore the comment. *What does she know anyway? I'm your mom, and I love you.* Olivia lifted Hope to her shoulder and began patting her back.

When the meeting ended, Olivia stood with Hope in her arms as the young men passed out the traditional Mother's Day flowers. She smiled as one of the boys handed her a small, potted petunia, and she paused to enjoy the feeling of finally belonging. *I'm a mom!* Michael put his arm around her as she sat down.

"You know, Michael," Olivia said. "Mother's Day is the best!"

"I agree." He smiled. "Hey, there's Sister Roberts. I'll go remind her about coming over for dinner this afternoon."

"I'm glad we invited her again this year."

"Me too. I wasn't sure you would want her to come over now that you can celebrate Mother's Day as a mom."

"Well, last year was great, and she really enjoyed it too. Besides, she has nowhere else to go today." Olivia bent down to gather up the diaper bag. "I think it's the start of a nice tradition. Something we can do every year."

"You are amazing," Michael said. He squeezed Olivia's hand before he let it go and then walked off after the elderly Sister Roberts.

Olivia glanced down at the bench to make sure she wasn't leaving anything behind and then turned to find herself face-to-face with Sister Ellis and her oversized corsage. The flower conglomeration brushed Hope's head as Sister Ellis leaned in for an awkward hug.

Olivia hadn't said more than a few words to Sister Ellis since last Mother's Day when she had finally had enough of the "helpful suggestions" on ways to get pregnant. It had felt so good to tell Sister Ellis to mind her own business and leave them alone. Olivia smiled at the memory. Then, because Sister Ellis was just standing there, staring at her, Olivia finally said, "Yes?"

"Well, Olivia," Sister Ellis said, clearing her throat, "I wanted to tell you happy Mother's Day."

"Thank you."

"I hope you've been enjoying your day so far?"

"Yes, I have."

"Did Michael bring you breakfast in bed and the whole nine yards?" Sister Ellis was getting warmed up now.

"I've had a wonderful day. Thank you," Olivia replied as she tried to walk on by. Sister Ellis reached out and touched Olivia's shoulder, stopping her.

"I'm glad you have a baby now," she added.

Olivia started feeling bad about treating her coldly. Maybe Sister Ellis was trying to be nice. Olivia smiled. "Thank you, Sister Ellis."

"Yes, I'm happy that it worked out for you, and Hope sure is a pretty little girl." She tilted her chin up and looked down past the end of her nose. "But I don't know what kind of woman would *give her baby away.*"

Olivia was stunned. Sister Ellis patted her shoulder and turned to walk away, but now it was Olivia's turn to reach out and stop Sister Ellis.

"Well, I'll tell you," Olivia began. "I'll tell you exactly what kind of a woman would *place her baby for adoption.*" Her voice was shaking, but Olivia was glad she wasn't crying. "A woman who is so loving and unselfish that she is willing to sacrifice everything that she wants in order to give her baby a home and a family. A woman who allows her own heart to break so that she can be sure her baby's heart remains whole. A strong and selfless woman who it is my privilege to know and love."

Sister Ellis was silent. Her mouth fell open and her head jerked back. Olivia hitched the diaper bag higher over her shoulder and walked past Sister Ellis with a smile.

Allison rolled over and fumbled with her cell phone until she hit the button to shut the alarm off. She closed her eyes and thought about going back to sleep. No one would wake her for church today. In fact, if she wanted to stay in bed the whole day, no one would bother her or even question her motives. It was, after all, Mother's Day.

Ally wasn't sure she could face Mother's Day. Yesterday, however, had been a good day. Since placing Hope, Ally had learned that the Saturday before Mother's Day is Birth Mother's Day. She smiled. Her family had definitely been supportive.

First thing on Saturday morning, her seventeen-year-old brother, Charlie, came into the flower shop where she had started working and bought a small, but pretty, bouquet of flowers. When she asked who they were for, he just smiled. After work, she arrived home to find a homemade sign hung up on the mantle of the fireplace that read, "Happy Birth Mother's Day, Ally!" Charlie passed her the bouquet of flowers and said, "These are for you!"

Emma and Elsie, her thirteen-year-old twin sisters, gave her hugs, and Emma said, "We made the sign. Do you like it?"

"It's great! Thanks, guys!"

Ally's dad swallowed her in a huge bear hug and even her mom came over, kissed her cheek, and wrapped her arms around her.

To top it all off, her mom had pointed to the dining room table where a small package was waiting for her. The family all gathered around as Ally opened it and unwrapped a beautiful necklace with a flat, round piece of shiny silver that had the words "I Can Do Hard Things" engraved on it, and a pink crystal on the chain next to the small medallion. They all became teary-eyed when she unwrapped a framed, finger-painted picture of four flowers. The blossoms of each flower were a tiny hand- or footprint. There was an envelope containing a few pictures of Hope, curly-headed and bright-eyed as Olivia pressed her hands into the paint and then onto the paper. They all laughed and smiled and wiped their eyes as they looked through the photos.

The last picture stopped the laughter. Ally's lips parted, and she pulled the photo closer, studying it carefully. Hope's face was in the center. On one side of her, Michael's face was pressed close, and on the other side was Olivia, also squeezed in tight. It looked like Michael was holding the camera out in front of them, trying to take a picture of all of them together. Olivia had blue finger paint smudged on her nose, and Hope had some on her chin. They were all laughing.

Ally traced her fingertip softly over the paint on Olivia's nose, around Michael's smile, and then slowly over Hope's face, lingering on her laughing mouth. "This is why I did it," she whispered. "This is why it's okay."

As the memory faded, Ally sighed and reached for her nightstand where she had set that photo when she went to bed last night. She looked at the three smiling faces and had to smile herself. She thought of the new necklace shining in her jewelry box and rolled out of bed. "I *can* do hard things," she said and grabbed her bathrobe as she headed down the hall for a shower.

CHAPTER FIVE

Olivia was sitting in her backyard in six inches of water that covered the bottom of the little blue blow-up swimming pool they had purchased at the start of the summer. She was having a great time. Six-month-old Hope sat on Olivia's lap, laughing as she waved her chubby little arms around, throwing splashes of water up into their faces. It was August and hot, and playing in the pool had become their afternoon ritual. Olivia turned Hope around so that she was facing her, and they played a splashy game of pat-a-cake, which was one of Hope's favorites. At "toss it in the oven," Olivia scooped Hope up and lifted her into the air and then squeezed her tightly to her chest. Hope wrapped her little arms around her mom's neck and nuzzled in for a hug.

"I love you, Hope," Olivia whispered in her ear. "Mommy loves you."

"Here are my girls," Michael said as he stepped out the back door and onto the patio.

"Hey, it's Daddy!" Olivia said. She lifted Hope out of the pool and wrapped a colorful beach towel around both of them. "I wasn't expecting you home yet."

Michael wrapped one arm around his wife while Hope reached for the other one. Michael snuggled Hope into his free arm. "Well, practice ended, and I realized that I have already watched all of the game film we have on West High. Since we still have a few weeks until our opening game, I decided to come home early and help get things ready for Kevin."

"I'm glad you did," Olivia said. Their social worker, Kevin, would be coming by later in the evening for the final home visit before they could finalize Hope's adoption. By law, you had to wait six months after the placement before an adoption could be finalized. This was not to wait and see if the birth mom changed her mind, as many of their friends had asked them. Once the relinquishment papers had been signed, she couldn't come back and try to get the baby. Rather, it was to be sure that Michael and Olivia were happy with their decision and were, in fact, being good parents. In this case, tonight's visit was merely a formality and in just a few weeks' time, Hope's adoption would be finalized in court, and then Michael and Olivia could take her to the temple to be sealed.

"I can't believe it's been six months since Hope was born," Michael said. "Time has gone so fast!"

"I know what you mean," Olivia agreed. "But," she said turning to Hope, "look how big you've gotten!" Hope was grinning and squealing now. She always knew when her parents were talking about her. "You're growing into such a big, beautiful girl . . . of course it's been six months."

"And just wait," Michael broke in with a smile. "Just wait until you get to come to the temple with Mommy and Daddy. You're going to look so pretty in your white dress." Hope laughed and buried her head in her dad's shoulder.

"I can't wait for that day, either," said Olivia. "It will be such a relief to know that she is sealed to us. That she is ours forever . . . no matter what."

"That reminds me," Michael said, shifting Hope into his other arm. "I've been thinking a lot about something and want to run it by you to see how you feel about it."

Olivia nodded. "Okay, I'm listening."

"Well, I was wondering what you thought about maybe inviting Steve and Julie to come to the sealing."

"Ally's parents?"

"Yeah. Maybe even Ally . . . if she wanted to."

"I'm not sure, Michael," Olivia said. "From what Ally's letters have said, Julie is still having a bit of a struggle with all of this. I don't want to make them feel obligated to be here if they don't want to be." Olivia's forehead crinkled up like it always did when she was thinking hard. "Still . . ."

"Still, what?" Michael asked.

"Well, it might be helpful for Julie to see us all together. See how happy Hope is. See how much we love her." Olivia was nodding to herself. "That's not a bad idea, Michael. But we better think about it carefully and pray about it before we decide."

"Good idea," Michael said. "Now, what do you think about inviting Ally? I know she won't be able to come *inside* the temple because she hasn't been through yet, but do you think she would like to see Hope on her special day?"

"I don't know," Olivia said truthfully. "She wasn't sure she wanted any contact at all in the beginning . . . but she does seem to be enjoying the letters and pictures we've sent and has even sent several letters to us." Olivia stopped and Michael knew she was thinking again. "I just don't want to make things any harder for her. I mean, if she wants to put all of this behind her, I don't want to keep dragging her into it."

"I don't want to do anything that will bother Ally, either," Michael said. "I think we could invite her but make it clear that it's her decision, and that our feelings won't be hurt either way."

"You know, I'm surprised that I'm going to say this," Olivia began, "but I would actually really like to see Ally. I think it would be nice."

"I know what you mean," said Michael. "Well, it sounds like we know what we want to do. Let's pray about it for a couple days and make sure we feel good about it then."

Olivia nodded. "Meanwhile," she said, "let's go get ready for Kevin to come."

ೋ ೋ

The doorbell rang at 6:30 p.m. sharp. "Hi, Kevin. It's good to see you," Michael said as they shook hands. Kevin followed him into the living room.

"Hi, Olivia." Kevin smiled and sat down on the brown recliner Michael had offered him. Michael sat next to Olivia and Hope on the sofa.

"And look how big you've gotten!" Kevin said to Hope as she ducked her head behind Olivia's arm.

"Yeah, she's really grown," Olivia agreed. "I just can't believe it!" Hope peeked over at Kevin, and Olivia said, "Can you say hi?"

Hope considered for a moment, then turned and waved a pudgy hand at Kevin and flashed her best dimpled smile before curling up in her mom's arms.

"It looks like she's doing terrific," Kevin said with a laugh.

Michael nodded. "She is."

"Is she up to date on all of her immunizations and having her regular trips to the pediatrician?" asked Kevin.

"Yes," Olivia said. "Her doctor says she's growing and developing perfectly. She's in the sixtieth percentile on height and the seventy-fifth percentile on weight, so we've got one healthy little girl."

"Well, she's just as cute as she can be." Kevin added. "And how are you guys doing? Is being a mom everything you thought it would be?"

"Honestly, it's a lot more work than I imagined," admitted Olivia. "But it's also so much better than I ever dreamed."

Michael nodded. "Yeah. I never knew I would be able to love someone as much as I love Hope. I can't believe that I was ever concerned about not being able to love a baby that Livvy didn't give birth to."

"It's pretty neat how that works, isn't it?" Kevin said.

"It really is," said Michael. "I know that she's meant to be our daughter, and we're just so glad that she's here."

"Do you miss working at the hospital, Olivia?" Kevin continued.

"Not at all," Olivia replied. "I've waited so long for my baby that I'm just trying to enjoy every second. Besides," she continued, "I've started going in one or two evenings a month, to fill in here and there . . . just to keep my license current."

"Oh?" Kevin asked. "I didn't realize you were going back to work."

"I'm not 'going back to work.' It's a few hours in the evening here and there. It's only when Michael is here, and Hope usually doesn't even know I've gone because she's already in bed." Olivia's voice trembled just a bit. "My old boss called and wondered if I would like to fill in once in a while if they were in a jam. It's only a time or two a month, and I'm not obligated to go in. I can say no any time." Olivia's face was flushed. "Besides, although I'm not planning on working again until Hope—and any other children that we might have—are grown, I figure that you never know what might happen, and it certainly can't hurt anything for me to keep my license current . . . just in case."

"That sounds good. Like you've really thought it through," said Kevin.

"Yeah, we really have. It's working out great," Michael said.

Kevin only stayed for a few more minutes. "Well, it looks like everything is going super well here. I'll finish up all of the paperwork on my end in the next day or two, and your attorney will be contacting you within a week or so with a court date. Congratulations!" He smiled and shook each of their hands on his way out the door.

Michael could tell that Olivia had something on the tip of her tongue, but she didn't say anything until after she had fed, burped, and changed Hope, and rocked her to sleep with a few songs. He was sitting at the kitchen table going over the playbook for his high school football team when Olivia stormed down the stairs.

"I . . . am . . . so . . . mad . . . right . . . now!" Olivia was on the verge of tears, something that usually happened when she was angry, but that Michael hadn't seen in quite a while.

"I can see that. But why?" Michael was really curious. He had noticed her getting upset during Kevin's visit, but he couldn't figure out what was wrong.

"Why?" Her voice was rising. "Why?"

"Yes, Livvy. Why?"

"Because I can't believe," she said, throwing her hands in the air, "that he was criticizing me for going to work two times a month! He acted like I was committing some kind of crime or something . . . like I was leaving Hope alone while I went out partying instead of having her safely tucked in bed with her dad here while I go help out at the hospital!" She was really mad. "I'm a good mom," Olivia fumed, "and he has no business being all judgmental about me! I hate living under a microscope!"

Michael was confused. "Livvy, sweetie, I don't think that Kevin meant any harm." Michael was having a feeling of déjà vu. But Olivia hadn't freaked out like this in a long time. "It didn't seem to me that he was criticizing. A little curious, maybe, but he said that it sounded good. He said that you're a good mom and that Hope is doing great."

"Even if it *is* true that he wasn't criticizing, why should I have to explain myself to him?" Olivia was still upset, but her voice was calming down.

"You don't have to *explain* yourself to him, Livvy," Michael said gently. "It's his job to ask questions and see how we're doing and how Hope is doing and how we're all doing together as a family."

"But after everything we had to go through to get *qualified* for a baby—all of the interviews and questions and home visits and background checks—after all of that, you would think that they could trust us by now."

"It's not about trust, Livvy."

Olivia sighed. "I know it's not, Michael. I really do. It's just that his questions brought up all my old feelings of anger about it being so hard for us to have a family." Olivia shrugged. "I mean, why doesn't everyone who gives birth to a baby have a six-month visit from a social worker to be sure that the baby is being taken care of and is happy and healthy and growing? It's not fair."

"Livvy?"

"What?"

"It's not about being fair, either. It's just life. It's just reality. It's about making peace with the experiences we have here and being thankful for the blessings." Michael hesitated. "Besides, I . . ."

"You what?"

"Well, I just thought that you had worked through all of this. That you were okay about things."

Olivia pushed her fingers through her curls. "I thought so too. Once I stopped trying to push my own agenda and decided to do what Heavenly Father wanted, I just felt so much hope. I felt a clear path and direction for the first time in a long time. And then when Hope was born, I was so happy!" Olivia smiled through her tears. "I love her so much, it amazes me. I know that I couldn't love a baby that grew inside me any more than I love her. It's just that . . ."

"It's okay, Livvy. You can say whatever's on your mind," Michael prompted when the pause got long.

"I feel guilty saying it . . . even *thinking* it for that matter. Because I've been so blessed, and now I even have a beautiful daughter. I just, well, I . . . I feel bad for me." The floodgates opened and everything poured out. "I feel bad that I will never be able to announce to you that I'm pregnant, the way that I always used to imagine. I feel bad that I'll never feel that first flutter that tells me there is someone alive in there. I'm sad that I'll never shop for maternity clothes or put your hand over my belly to feel the baby moving or have an ultrasound and see the little profile. I'm sad that I'll never get to experience the miracle of giving birth." Olivia shook her head and wiped her face.

"It's weird, you know?" she continued after a moment. "I'm no longer angry or upset at all about not having a baby, because I *do* have a baby. I have the most beautiful baby girl in the whole world and I wouldn't trade her for anything! I guess I just feel a little sad for me, because I don't get to experience a pregnancy." Olivia stopped and squared her shoulders. "It's silly, I know, and I'll get over it. I'm really and truly happy with my life and everything that we've built together, and my anger really is gone. I just wish I could find some peace about this pregnancy thing. I don't want to feel a twinge in the back of my heart every time someone tells me they're pregnant."

Michael's mind was reeling. *I was so sure that adopting a baby would fix all of this! Especially since our daughter is so beautiful and amazing and we love her more than we could have ever imagined. I don't know what to say. I don't know how to help her. And I don't like it.*

"Hmm. No comment." Olivia forced a chuckle. "You're probably thinking that your wife is crazy, right?"

"No, no, not crazy." He smiled, not wanting her to worry about him. "I'm just afraid that I don't know how to help you on this one."

"I wasn't really asking for your help, you know." There was an edge to her voice. "Sometimes I just need to get stuff off my chest. I'll work through this." She molded her face into an uneasy smile and took Michael's hand. "Don't worry about me. I'm fine. Really."

CHAPTER SIX

"Ally, there's a letter on the table for you," Julie said as Ally walked in the door from work.

"Okay, thanks, Mom," replied Ally. "I'm going to go up and shower first. We had a huge shipment of sunflowers come in today, and they always make me itchy." Ally had planned on her job at the florist being short-term, just part-time to help out over Mother's Day and through the spring. Then she got her acceptance letter from BYU to start school in January. Once she knew that she'd be around for a while, the owner offered her a full-time position until she left. Ally had recovered from her pregnancy and decided that there was no reason to hang around the house until she left for school. So she took the offer and was happy to find something that she enjoyed doing.

"I usually enjoy it," Ally murmured under her breath as she headed up the stairs. "Except when I have to unload a truckload of sunflowers in the middle of the afternoon during the hottest part of the summer."

"And what's the matter with August?" Charlie asked, nearly crashing into her as he rumbled down the stairs. Charlie had always seemed more mature and insightful than many of the boys that surrounded Ally. He had also played a key role in getting Ally to really pray about the future of her baby girl and had been the first to support her when she had decided on adoption. Ally loved him a lot.

"Nothing's the matter with August itself." Ally grinned as Charlie raced by. "It's just the combination of the heat, the flowers, the unloading, and the sweating."

"Yeah, you've always been a wimp." Charlie laughed as he ran out the door. "See ya later!"

Once she was in the shower with cool water running over her, Ally stopped to think about the letter waiting for her downstairs. She knew it was from Michael and Olivia. Those were the only letters her mom specifically pointed out to her. Anything else, she just left on the dresser in Ally's bedroom.

"I hope they don't freak out," Ally said to herself. Ever since she had been accepted to BYU and started planning her move from southern Utah up to Provo, she had been worried about what to tell Michael and Olivia. Ally knew that they lived in American Fork, which was only a few miles farther north. That fact had not played into Ally's decision to apply to BYU. In fact, she hadn't even thought about it until she knew she was going. *Well, I'm not trying to step into their lives*, Ally thought. *I'm still not sure I even want to see them if I have the chance. Once I explain that to them, they'll be fine. I hope.*

Ally's mom had told her that it didn't really matter what they thought, and the reality was that it didn't. Ally knew she was supposed to be in Provo at BYU, but she still didn't want Michael and Olivia to be uncomfortable or to be wondering if she would be staking out their house every chance she got.

Ally rinsed the conditioner out of her hair and stood for a few more minutes letting the water stream over her head. "It'll be fine," she said to herself. "It *will* be fine."

Dried, dressed, and with her hair in a loose ponytail, Ally went to the kitchen for her letter. Sure enough, she saw "Michael and Olivia Spencer" written neatly in the top left corner. She tore open the top and pulled out two letters, each one folded carefully.

One of them had Ally's name written on the outside, and the other had Steve and Julie's names.

"Mom?" Ally called.

"Yes? What is it?" Julie answered, joining her daughter in the dining room.

"There's a letter for you and dad."

"For *us*?"

"That's what it says." Ally passed the letter across the table to her mom.

"Hmm. I wonder what this is about," Julie mused.

Ally smiled. "Just read it, Mom, and then you'll know."

Julie sat down at the kitchen table and unfolded her letter. Ally turned her attention to her own. As she unfolded it, three photographs fell out. One showed Hope dressed in a ruffled pink swimming suit in a little blow-up swimming pool. She was splashing and laughing. Ally couldn't help but laugh too. It looked like Hope was having a lot of fun! The second was of Hope sleeping in her crib. She was wearing purple striped pajamas and had her little thumb in her mouth. Ally brushed her tears back as she smiled and touched the sleeping face. She had sucked her thumb until she was five years old, and it had taken all of the threats and bribery her parents could come up with to get her to stop.

The last photo showed Michael and Olivia dressed in their Sunday best, sitting underneath a tree on the grass. Hope was in a sweet, little green dress with tiny pink flowers. She was sitting on Olivia's lap and holding Michael's hand. They were a beautiful family. Ally felt a jumble of emotions that she couldn't quite wrap her mind around. Love was there, definitely. Not only love for Hope, but also for Michael and Olivia. Gratitude for the wonderful home and life they were giving to her baby girl. Sadness at not having been a part of Hope's life for the last six months, and a lonely ache when she thought of not being the one that Hope ran to when she was tired or scared or hurt or happy or excited. She also had to acknowledge the excitement she felt about going away to college. That was closely followed by wondering if this should make her feel guilty. *No.* She decided in her mind. *First, I did what was best for my baby girl. Now, I need to do what is best for my life. And it's okay to feel excited about my future.*

Ally smiled down at the little family smiling up at her and then started to read the letter. Relief was flooding through her as she finished the letter and looked up to find her mom staring across the table at her, tears streaming down her cheeks.

"Mom! What's the matter?" Ally couldn't attach her mom's tears to her own feelings of relief.

Julie choked on a sniffle and then managed to say, "They want us to come to the sealing!"

"I know." Ally pointed to her own letter. "They told me. They want me to come too."

Julie continued staring at her daughter until Ally couldn't take the silence anymore. "Mom, why are you looking at me like that?"

"I . . . I just can't believe it!"

"Okay, but are those happy tears or sad tears?"

Julie crossed her arms on the table, dropped her head onto them, and began crying even harder. Ally reached across and put her hand on her mom's shoulder. "Mom, please say something. What can't you believe? Do you not want to go? You don't have to if you don't want to."

Julie raised her head. "It's not that. I *do* want to go. Of course I do."

Ally was getting confused. "Then what's the problem?"

"Okay," Julie said, wiping her eyes. "I'll tell you. Just don't get mad." Julie paused.

"Mom?" Ally pressed, while somewhere in the back of her mind she smiled, thinking that this conversation would usually be going the other way around.

"Well, it's no secret that I've been having a hard time facing your decision to place Hope for adoption."

Ally cocked her eyebrow. She had no idea where this was leading.

"But," Julie continued, "I've been working on that and praying for some of the peace and acceptance that you seem to have. I've also rededicated myself to reading my scriptures every day. It's just that . . ."

"What, Mom?"

"Well, things have been getting a lot better, and I can look at the situation and acknowledge that Hope is where she's supposed to be and that you are moving forward in the direction that you're supposed to go."

"Thanks, Mom. But I still don't understand all the crying."

"I still *really* want to see her," Julie said, shrugging. "I want to see Hope and give her a kiss on the head and just . . . I don't know . . . just *know* that she's really out there somewhere." Julie shook her head and rubbed her eyes again. "Crazy, I know, but I've been praying that somehow I would be able to see her again."

Ally couldn't believe it. She had no idea her mom had been going through all of that. "But, Mom, then you should be happy! You'll get to see her and you'll get to be in the temple with her."

Julie was nodding, but her tears were flowing hard again. "I guess we're never too old to be taught."

"What?" Ally hadn't expected that.

"I don't think I have as much faith as you do, Ally."

"Why do you say that, Mom? You're the one that taught me about faith."

"Because, Ally." Julie took a deep breath. "Because I've been praying that I could see Hope again for about a month now, but I didn't think it would happen. I didn't really *believe* that Heavenly Father would answer my prayer. And now . . ."

"And now He has," Ally concluded.

Julie nodded.

The two women sat in a comfortable silence for several minutes until Julie broke in, "But here I am going on and on about me, when I really should be asking how you feel about all of this. Do *you* want to go see Hope, Olivia, and Michael?"

"You know, it's funny," Ally began. "All this time I didn't really think that I wanted any more face-to-face contact, and lately I've been so stressed about how Michael and Olivia would react when they found out that I was moving to Provo." Ally smiled. "You're not the only one who's been praying, Mom. But I've been praying that when I told them, it wouldn't be awkward and that everything would keep going smoothly." She stopped and tucked her hair behind her ear. "This just feels like my answer. If they are inviting me to come and see them, I don't think they're going to freak out when they find out I'm moving closer. As far as seeing Hope?" Ally shrugged. "I still don't know how much contact I'll want in the future, but in this situation, I think I *do* want to see them. I think it will bring me a lot of peace to see the three of them walking out of the temple, sealed together forever. That's the biggest gift I wanted to give to Hope and I think I'd like to be there to see her receive it."

"You've become quite a woman, Ally."

"Thanks, Mom. I've had a great example."

CHAPTER SEVEN

"Oh look, Hope! There's a letter from Ally!" Olivia said as she pulled the envelopes from her mailbox. Hope reached out and swiped three letters from Olivia's hand and began waving them around in the air as Olivia carried her back into the house.

"I hope they're going to come up for the sealing. I think it would be nice to see Ally, Steve, and Julie again." Olivia unfolded Hope's fingers off the letters and tore open the one from Ally. There were two letters inside; one in Ally's handwriting, and a longer one in what must be Julie's. She started with Ally's.

Dear Michael, Olivia, and Hope,

Thanks so much for the pictures you sent! I especially love the one of Hope sucking her thumb. If she's anything like me, that's going to be a problem as she gets bigger! LOL! I think that I would like to come up when you take Hope to the temple. It would be nice to see you all again.

That actually brings up something that I've been wanting to tell you. I applied and have been accepted to attend BYU starting in January! I'm really excited about it and feel like that is where Heavenly Father wants me to be. I have been nervous to tell you, because I know that Provo is pretty close to American Fork, but I want you to know that I'm not doing this to try and move in on your life. I know that Hope is where she is supposed to be and that she was meant to be your daughter. I don't want it to be weird, and I don't want you to worry about me interfering in your life. Even though I would like to accept your invitation and come to the temple, I'm still not sure about contact after that. I just don't know if it will be too hard, you know? But please don't worry about me being involved in any way that you don't want me to be. I know that you guys are awesome parents to her. . . and if sometime down the road we all agree that a visit once in a while would be nice, I would only be there as a friend—someone who loves you all and wants you all to be happy.

Thanks so much for thinking of us, it meant a lot to me and it really meant a lot to my mom. She's writing a letter now, so I'll let her give you my parents' answer. Thanks again, and let us know when you have the temple date finalized.

Love, Ally

Olivia smiled as she set Ally's letter down. "BYU. Good for you, Ally!" she said to herself. She was a little surprised to find that she felt no anxiety over Ally moving so much closer to them. Ally's words had been so sincere that Olivia felt confident that everything would work out like it was supposed to.

Her smile faded just a bit as she picked up the pages of Julie's letter. Olivia had never received a letter from her before, and their interactions prior to this had been guarded at best. Olivia knew that Julie had not been excited about Ally's decision to place Hope for adoption, and she was curious to see what Julie had written. She unfolded the pages and started reading.

Dear Olivia and Michael,

I'm not quite sure where to begin, so I'll start by saying thank you for your invitation to be a part of your very special day at the temple. I must say that I never imagined that I would be in a situation like this. When Ally was growing up, Steve and I worked so hard to teach her about the gospel and about right and wrong. We tried to protect her and help her in any way we could. She was growing into such a beautiful and strong young lady.

I'll never forget the evening just over a year ago now that changed everything. The evening when Ally came home and told us that she was pregnant. I was angry. I'm now starting to realize that that wasn't the most helpful emotion, but in the moment, that was the truth. I was furious. I was angry at Ally for what she had done. Angry that she was now pregnant, and how that would affect not only Ally but also our entire family. Angry that Heavenly Father had not somehow stopped this from happening, and angry at myself for not having been able to stop her.

As the baby grew and Ally's waist expanded, I began to remember my own pregnancies and the excitement of bringing a spirit into the world. I also watched Ally grow and mature before my eyes as she faithfully met with our bishop and worked through the repentance process. As she talked about the sacrifices she was willing to make for her baby, I started feeling like we could make this work. It would be difficult, but we could pull through together. About this time, the realization set in that I was going to have a grandbaby, and I got excited. Sure, it wasn't exactly as I had imagined it, but we could help Ally. She would be all right in the end, and I WAS GOING TO HAVE A GRANDDAUGHTER!!!

Then came the day that changed everything . . . again. It was just after Christmas, and Ally was out walking in the snow. She had been gone for a while, and we were all starting to get worried. Steve had just walked out the front door to go find her when they came back inside together. Ally went upstairs to change her clothes and Steve called the family together, saying that Ally had something to say. I tried to be calm but was panicking inside. Then Ally dropped the bomb that she was going to place her baby girl for adoption. I am ashamed to admit that I was so caught up in my own feelings that I didn't even consider Ally's, and I got up and walked out of the room. The anger, which had never really healed but had only been pushed to the back corners of my mind, resurfaced with a vengeance.

We didn't talk much for several days, but I could see a peace in Ally's face that hadn't been there before. Even so, she did become frustrated as she looked through countless adoption files, trying to find the family for her baby. Honestly, I hoped that she would not be able to find anyone she felt good about, so that she would go back to her first plan and raise the baby herself. But I was with her at the computer the night she found your file. We had been there for quite some time and were just about to call it a night. I watched Ally's eyes light up as she looked at your photos and read the things you had written. I could see right away that she knew where her baby girl would be going. The peace came back to her face.

Once we met you both, Ally's resolve was firmer than ever. I know that I wasn't very warm or welcoming to you at that first meeting, and for that, I apologize. There is no excuse—I can only tell you that I was struggling and that I am still trying to learn and grow. When we met again in the hospital while Ally was in labor, I was no longer angry with you and had accepted Ally's decision, but I was still very sad about it. I wish I could say that all has been fine since the placement, but that sadness and turmoil in my mind still comes regularly. I have, however, been trying to work through these feelings and find the peace that the Savior offers. I have been turning to the scriptures more frequently, and my prayers have become more sincere, although my faith that they will be answered had not been fully restored. That is, until I received your letter.

You see, I had been praying that I would get to see Hope again. I felt that if I could just see her growing and healthy and happy, see the three of you together as a family, it would confirm to my heart that all is as it should be. I knew I had no right to ask this of you, but still I prayed for it—if only to prove to the Lord that He wouldn't answer my prayer. Does that even make sense? But then your letter came. As I read your offer to allow us to be with you in the temple when Hope is sealed to you, the Spirit covered me and flowed through my body more strongly than I have felt in a very long time. I felt the truth that my Savior does love me and that He does know who I am and where I am and that I am having a rough time. I felt the confirmation that Heavenly Father does answer prayers, and more especially, that He will answer my prayers. So, to answer your question, we would be honored to be at the temple to see Hope become a part of your forever family. I still have some healing to do and some things to learn, but I want to thank you for being the answer to a prayer that reminded me that we are not just down here on earth on our own trying to survive the experience. We have heavenly help from a loving Father and His Son that is available any time we are humble enough to ask for it. Thank you again, and we can't wait to see you!

Love, Julie

Olivia wiped the moisture from her eyes as she folded the letter and set it down on the table. She had never really taken the time to stop and think about how Julie would have felt watching her daughter go through this whole experience. It must have been heartbreaking. Without warning, peace and warmth flooded through Olivia and she felt the anxious feelings she had regarding Julie melt away. She was so glad to be able to glimpse Julie's side of the story and empathize with her feelings. She was also very thankful that Michael had been in tune with the Spirit and had suggested inviting them to the sealing in the first place.

She was definitely a little nervous now that she knew Ally, Steve, and Julie would all be there, but she was also excited to see them and was thankful that Ally seemed happy and was doing well. It would be a good day.

CHAPTER EIGHT

Ally heard the bell ring as the front door of the flower shop opened. "I'll be right out," she called from the back room where she was putting the final touches of baby's breath into a rose bouquet. She tied a pretty gold bow around the vase and carried it out to put in the cooler.

"That's beautiful."

Ally froze at the familiar voice, and her breath caught in her lungs before she even turned around to look into the blue eyes she could almost feel searching out her gaze. "Nothing compared to you, of course," he continued when Ally didn't respond. "I've always thought you were beautiful. Right from the first moment I laid eyes on you when I walked into biology our junior year of high school."

Ally finally managed to choke out, "Hi, Brandon."

"Hey, Ally." Brandon walked around the counter, took the vase of flowers from Ally's hands, and opened the cooler door to place them inside. When he looked back at her, she still hadn't moved. "My mom told me that she heard you were working here."

"Yeah, for a while." Ally pushed her fingers through her hair and then crossed and uncrossed her arms.

Brandon met her gaze and tentatively reached out to tuck a

lock of Ally's hair back to its place behind her ear. "Your hair is darker than it used to be."

Ally stepped away from his touch. "Yeah, it turned more brown while I was pregnant." She shrugged. "It's been that way ever since." She fidgeted with a stack of flyers on the counter.

"Why so nervous?" Brandon asked. "I'm still the same old me."

"Exactly," said Ally as she swallowed down the lump that was building in her throat. "You're the same old Brandon who told his best friend that she could either abort the baby she was carrying—which, by the way, was his—or go jump in a lake."

Brandon raised his hands to protest, but Ally didn't let him. She suddenly had a few things she wanted to say. "You're the same guy that I was willing to sacrifice everything for . . . willing to not go to school, willing to move to California, whatever it took to be a family with you and our baby, and when I offered you that and asked you to be there for me, you told me no and ran off to the coast!"

Brandon looked at the floor and said nothing.

"So forgive me," Ally concluded, "if I don't run right over and throw my arms around you."

They stood in silence while Ally tried to get her emotions back under control. She was so focused on calming her breathing that she didn't notice the tears forming in Brandon's eyes until he looked up and found her face. "I know."

This was not the response Ally was expecting. "You know?"

"I know I was stupid and that you have every reason to hate me. It's no excuse, but the only explanation I can give is that I was a scared kid and I didn't want to risk my football scholarship and my future." Brandon shrugged his shoulders. "Anyway, I was just home for a few days, and I wanted to come say hi and tell you that I'm sorry."

Ally didn't know what to say. She hadn't anticipated an apology. She had to admit that she *had* been wondering about him. How he was doing . . . whether he even cared that the baby had been born. Maybe she was even worried about him. He had made a few appearances in her dreams at night, and although she could never remember what they were about, she always awoke from them feeling anxious.

Brandon continued. "I'm sorry that I left you to deal with everything on your own." He paused and wiped his eyes. "I heard it was a girl . . ."

"Yeah. She is beautiful." Part of Ally still wanted to punish Brandon for turning his back on them, but she had already made her peace with the situation, and she knew that digging up her old grudge wouldn't help anyone. Brandon had come to try and make things right in the only way he knew how. She would let him. After all, after having felt the power of forgiveness in her own life, how could she deny that gift to him?

Brandon nodded. He smiled, and Ally noticed that his eyes were damp. "Of course she would be . . . with you as her mom."

Ally blushed. "She has your curly blond hair, and her nose is just like mine."

"Mom says that you gave her up." There was confusion behind his eyes.

"No. That's not how I see it. I gave her a family. I gave her a home. I gave her more than I could offer her. When I placed her for adoption, I gave her everything she deserves."

"Do you miss her?"

"Every day."

"Do you wish . . . things would have turned out . . . differently?"

Ally sighed. "There's no use thinking like that, Brandon. Things are what they are. But to answer your question . . . no. Would we really have been happy together? Raising a baby that neither of us was ready for? Me trying to live a religion that you don't believe in?"

Brandon shrugged. "I've missed you," he said. "I've missed my best friend."

Ally finally reached out her arms and wrapped Brandon into a hug. "I've missed you too."

They held each other for several minutes. Brandon's arms were bigger, slightly more muscled than Ally remembered, but they felt familiar. Even though they had only been intimate together that one night, Ally felt the memories of all the time they had shared in this moment. She cleared her throat and stepped back, out of his arms.

"So do you want to see a picture of her?"

"You have one?" Brandon seemed surprised.

"Sure. Michael and Olivia send me pictures and a letter at least once a month. Here, I've got several in my purse."

While Ally unzipped her purse, Brandon asked, "Michael and Olivia? They're . . ."

"They're Hope's parents," Ally finished for him.

"You named her Hope? I like it."

"Actually, Michael and Olivia named her, but they asked what I thought about it, and I loved the name *Hope*. It just seemed perfect for her." Ally looked up and smiled as she showed him the first photo she had recovered from her purse. "This is me and Hope shortly after she was born."

"Wow," Brandon said reverently. "She's so tiny, and, and . . ." His voice cracked and he shook his head.

"And what?"

"Well, look at you. You're just glowing!"

"It *was* pretty amazing." Ally smiled. "Painful. More pain than a jock like you will ever know about." She punched his arm. "But absolutely amazing."

Brandon looked at the photo for several long seconds. "I should have been there," he said softly. Then he looked up at Ally. "I'm really, really sorry that I wasn't there for you."

"Thanks," Ally said, reaching out to touch his arm. "That means a lot to me, but really, it's okay." She shrugged her shoulders. "I don't know why things happen the way they do, and I've quit trying to figure it all out. But I do know that Hope is where she is supposed to be, and that's good enough for me." Brandon had looked down at the floor, so Ally ducked her head also, forcing him to meet her eyes. "Do you want to see the rest of these pictures?"

He nodded, and Ally handed him the photo from Mother's Day—the one with Michael, Olivia, and Hope's faces all squeezed in together. "They look really happy," Brandon said. "And Hope *is* beautiful, just like you said."

"They are happy," Ally added. "Michael and Olivia are wonderful people. Michael's a high school football coach."

Brandon's head popped up. "Really?"

"Yep. He had heard all about you." She paused, watched Brandon digest that information, and then continued. "Olivia's a nurse."

Brandon shook his head. "Just like you want to be." His voice held a note of wonder.

"Yeah, and she loves playing basketball too. That's actually how they met. Olivia was playing in a basketball game." She laughed. "Apparently, she got a little sidetracked as she noticed Michael walk into the gym, and the ball hit her in the face. Gave her a bloody nose!"

Ally handed the final picture she had in her purse to Brandon, who was still smiling at the image her words had created in his mind. It was the most recent picture she had received: Michael, Olivia, and Hope sitting together under a tree all ready for church.

Brandon's smile faded, and he quickly brushed at his eyes as he touched the small face with the blonde curls that matched his own. He studied the picture for a full minute, and Ally was content to let the silence continue. It was Brandon who finally broke it with a whisper.

"I'm really glad you didn't listen to me about having an abortion, Ally." He straightened up and composed his face. "I didn't even stop to think about who it was that we would be destroying." His gaze flickered back to the photo one more time. "They look like a great family. Good job, Ally." He put one arm around her shoulder and squeezed.

Tears blurred Ally's vision, and all she could say was, "Thanks,

Brandon." He let go of her shoulder and started to hand her the picture.

Ally surprised herself by asking, "Do you want to keep it?"

"Really?"

"Yeah. If you want it."

"You know, I think I *do* want it . . . if it's really okay with you."

"Sure. You should have a picture of them." Ally wiped her eyes and found a smile. "After all, Hope is part of you too."

Brandon nodded. "Thanks, Ally. You've treated me way better than I deserved."

"Well, maybe I've been a little worried about you." Ally shrugged again. "It's really okay. Hope is going to have an amazing life."

Brandon nodded. "And you?"

"Me?" The question had caught Ally off guard.

"Yeah, you. Are you going to be okay?"

Allison thought of moving on, going off to BYU, becoming a nurse, maybe having a family someday. "I am," she said. And for that moment, she knew it was true.

CHAPTER NINE

It was already hot on the late-August morning when Michael and Olivia pulled into the parking lot at the Mount Timpanogos temple. Olivia felt like her heart was about to pound right out of her chest.

"I don't know why I'm so nervous," she said. "I thought that after the court hearing was over and Hope was legally ours, I would be able to relax a little."

"Do you wish we wouldn't have invited them?" Michael asked.

"No," Olivia replied. "I know we're doing the right thing for our situation. I just don't want Ally, or her parents, to be disappointed in us."

"Disappointed?" Michael suppressed a grin. "What are you talking about?"

"Well, what if Ally sees us and thinks we're not doing a good job? What if she regrets the decision she made? What if we can't find anything to talk about? What if coming here makes her feel worse?"

"Whoa, whoa, whoa, Livvy." This time Michael allowed himself to smile. "Take a breath and calm down." He gently turned her cheek so she was looking straight at him. "Olivia Spencer, you are an amazing mom. Ally knew that you would be, and it will comfort her heart to see, firsthand, that she was right."

Olivia started to protest, but Michael put his finger over her lips to stop her. "As for not having anything to talk about, look in the backseat at your daughter."

Olivia's emotions finally overflowed when she looked at Hope buckled in her car seat surrounded by a sea of white ruffles, eyes closed, peacefully sucking her thumb.

Olivia nodded. "You're right." She took a deep, calming breath. "This is going to be a terrific day."

As they walked toward the temple, Hope rubbed the sleep from her eyes with pudgy fists and blinked in the bright sun. They were planning on meeting Ally, Steve, and Julie outside. They reached the front doors, and while Olivia was fussing with the headband and flower in Hope's hair, making sure each curl was lying just right, Michael was squinting in the sun, his eyes sweeping the parking lot.

After a few moments, Michael touched Olivia's arm and tipped his head toward three people getting out of their car. Allison no longer had the baby bump that Olivia still carried in her mind, and without it, she walked with more ease and grace than Olivia remembered, but there was no mistaking her. She was a step ahead of her parents and seemed to be urging them to move faster as she occasionally looked over her shoulder at them. As they got closer, Olivia could see that Steve looked at ease, while Julie appeared as nervous as she, herself, felt.

Olivia was trying to get a good look at Ally's face, searching for any sign of resentment or regret when Ally looked up and caught her eye for the first time. A smile lit up Ally's face and Olivia's fears took a backseat as Ally first quickened her pace, then couldn't contain herself and broke into a jog to cover the final twenty yards that separated them. She threw her arms around Olivia, who shifted Hope over to her hip so she could accept Ally's embrace without squishing her daughter.

"Hi, Olivia! It's *so* great to see you again!" Ally's welcome to Olivia was so warm and sincere that her lingering fears were laid to rest, and Olivia found herself squeezing Ally in return.

"I'm so glad that you could make it, Ally," Olivia said and realized that she meant it. Hope had ducked her head under Olivia's arm during this commotion and ventured to poke it out once Ally had stepped back and turned to say hi to Michael.

Olivia fluffed one last curl and straightened Hope's white flower again. Then Michael turned Ally around and said, "There is someone who's very interested in what's going on here, isn't there, Hope?"

When she heard her daddy say her name, Hope looked up and, for the first time in six months, Ally came face-to-face with the baby girl she had given birth to.

"Hi, big girl," she said softly to Hope. "You've gotten so big!" Ally reached a tentative hand forward. After Hope glanced at Olivia, who smiled and nodded, she reached out her hand as well, and their fingers touched. Ally's eyes were shining, but no tears fell as she said, "Can I hold you?"

Olivia leaned Hope into Ally's arms. A look of concern flickered across Hope's eyes and she turned back toward Michael and Olivia, who were now standing side by side.

"It's okay, Hope," Michael said. "This is Ally. We've told you all about her."

The sound of Michael's voice, as well as the sight of her mom and dad looking so happy, comforted Hope, and she turned back to examine the person now holding her. Ally smiled. Hope searched Ally's face and then reached a chubby hand up to touch the white flower in her own hair.

"Yes, you have such a pretty flower in your hair," Ally agreed. That was good enough for Hope and her face lit up with a two-toothed smile.

Steve and Julie, who had been standing back watching the greeting unfold, now stepped forward. Steve embraced Olivia, and she said, "We're so glad you could come! It's great to see you again."

Steve stepped back and returned the smile, "Thank you for inviting us." He leaned closer and softly continued, "This really means a lot to us. *All* of us."

Michael shook Steve's hand. "Well, it's special for us too."

Ally was contentedly murmuring to Hope, who was now smiling and laughing and being as charming as ever. Julie was watching the scene with moist eyes but didn't seem to know what to say.

Olivia moved around Michael and Steve, who were already talking football, and slipped her arm through Julie's to lead her a few steps away. "Thanks for coming, Julie. I'm sure the past six months have been very difficult at your house." Julie nodded but seemed to relax. "I can't pretend to know how you feel, but now that I have a daughter of my own," Olivia's voice caught, "well, I think I can just begin to imagine what you must have been going through watching your daughter struggle."

Olivia cleared her throat and wiped her eyes. She wanted to say this. "I don't know whether it will help you feel any better, but I want to tell you that Hope has brought more happiness and joy and love into my life than I ever knew was possible. Michael and I love her even more than we thought we would. She filled the hole that my heart had become." They were both crying now, and Olivia put both arms around Julie in the first hug they had shared. "Thank you, Julie. Thank you for raising such a wonderful, brave daughter. Thank you for allowing her to make her decision to place her baby, even when it was so hard for you. And thank you for loving Hope. A child can never have too many people who love her."

Julie held onto Olivia for several moments, but when she let go, she was smiling. "Thank *you*," she whispered. "You weren't under any obligation to ever involve me in Hope's life again," she said, hesitating, "and after the way I acted, I wouldn't have blamed you if you didn't want to have anything to do with me. And yet . . ." Julie shrugged and looked around in wonder. "Yet here we are. Together. At the temple. And I get to watch Hope be sealed to her mom and dad for time and all eternity. I get to see that she's happy and healthy, and I get to see *you* as her mom." Julie wiped her eyes. "It suits you, you know . . . being a mom."

Olivia didn't know what to say. She wasn't sure she could get the words out even if she *did* know what to say. So she just gave Julie another hug, and let the peace of the moment do the talking.

❧ ❧

Because it was so hot, Ally opted to wait just inside the front doors of the temple in the waiting room, rather than walking around the temple grounds as she had planned. So, after making their way inside, Ally gave Hope back to Olivia and watched as her parents, and the little family who she loved so much continued on into the temple together. The elderly lady at the door smiled sweetly at Ally and showed her into the waiting room. It was quiet and peaceful, and Ally picked up a copy of the Bible that was on one of the chairs and settled in to read.

Time passed quickly as she read the account of the Savior's life and ministry. Maybe it was because she was here in the temple, maybe it was because she was alone here in this beautiful room, maybe it was because she read, uninterrupted, for about an hour, but as she came to the familiar passages about His sufferings, death, and Resurrection, she was enveloped in the same peace that had filled her soul the night before she relinquished her rights as Hope's mom and placed her in Olivia's arms. The peace that Ally had known was there, but had been unable to fully find again since that night, once again surrounded her.

Tears poured down Ally's cheeks as she remembered the feeling that had come as she watched Michael and Olivia walk out of her hospital room carrying Hope—that not only was Hope's life in good hands, her own was too. The nagging guilt she had been harboring about being excited to go to school was washed away as the Spirit confirmed to her that she was indeed following the path the Savior had planned for her, and that it was okay to be excited and happy about her future. Ally felt comforted once again to know that Hope was where she should be, and that at this very moment she was—in a literal way—joining her *forever* family.

Ally closed her eyes, intent on soaking in this moment, so that she could remember the peace, love, and hope she was now feeling.

Feelings she knew came straight from her Savior, Jesus Christ. As the moment passed, Ally offered a silent prayer of thanks to her Heavenly Father for His love, His caring, and most of all, His Son.

A few minutes later, Michael and Olivia came into the waiting room carrying Hope. Ally smiled at the three of them beaming across the room at her. It was as though even Hope sensed, on some level, the significance of what had taken place. Before Ally knew it, she was swept up in a group hug and the four of them held tightly to each other.

"Thank you, Ally," Michael said. "Thank you for giving us a family." Ally could only nod. They held on a few seconds longer, and then Michael stepped back and put his arm around Olivia.

"Everyone else is waiting outside," he said. "Your parents are visiting with our families."

Ally nodded. "Okay."

Michael continued, "Olivia's brother and his wife are here, as well as her parents, who just got home from their mission last month, and her grandma. My parents also flew into town, and one of my sisters and her husband were able to make the trip out."

"Okay," Ally said again. She wasn't sure why Michael was explaining all of this to her.

"Some of our close friends are here, as well," he added.

Olivia could see that Ally was looking puzzled, so she stepped in. "We just don't want you to be uncomfortable. We'd love for you and your parents to join us all at our house for the afternoon, but most of the people out there will be coming over as well. If it's too much for you, we certainly understand, but . . ."

Olivia's voice trailed away because, now that Ally understood, she was grinning from ear to ear. "I'd love to come!" But then her forehead creased and a shadow crossed her face, "Oh, wait . . ."

"Yes?" Olivia urged when Ally didn't continue.

"I don't know if my mom will be comfortable with all of that. Let me talk to her first."

"Well, actually," Olivia said with a grin, "I already talked to her. She said that they want to come but would leave the decision up to you."

Ally laughed. "Well, it sounds like everything's taken care of then! Let's go!"

⁂

Michael checked the rearview mirror to be sure that Ally and her parents were still following them. It was just a short drive from the temple to their house.

Olivia reached over and gave Michael's hand a squeeze. "That was wonderful!"

"It really was," Michael agreed. "You know, I feel like an actual weight has been lifted off my shoulders now that Hope is sealed to us."

Olivia was nodding her head. She knew exactly what he was talking about. "It's the knowledge that no matter what happens, Hope is our daughter . . . forever."

"It's funny," Michael went on, "but I never really thought a whole lot about the sealing ordinance before we adopted Hope."

"What do you mean?"

"Well, my parents were married in the temple, and so it was always a part of my life; right from the day I was born. Then I had always planned on getting married in the temple, and of course," he gave Olivia a quick peck on the cheek, "that was a great day."

She smiled at him, a little unsure where he was going with this. Michael paused and furrowed his eyebrows. Olivia knew he was thinking carefully. When he started talking again, it was softer, reverent.

"I think I always took it for granted. I never realized the peace and safety and protection that specific ordinance brings into our lives, because I always had it. Until we adopted Hope, and she *wasn't* sealed to us."

Olivia understood. She squeezed Michael's hand. Was it possible that she loved him even more today than on the day they got married?

Michael shook the emotion from his voice. "Anyway, now I can feel—actually feel—the difference. Already. After fifteen minutes." He chuckled and briefly met Olivia's eyes before looking back at the road. "Is that crazy?"

"Well, if it is, we're crazy together, because I feel exactly the same way."

They all had a great afternoon, eating hoagie sandwiches and grandma's homemade potato salad. Ally loved Hope's room and smiled at all of the rainbows and butterflies carefully painted on the walls. She visited with everyone there and seemed at ease. Steve and Julie sat hesitantly on the couch at first, until Olivia's grandma claimed the seat next to Julie and started talking her ear off. Before long, they were all laughing together.

When it was time for Hope's nap, she was playing happily on Ally's lap. Olivia held out her bottle and Hope reached for it. Ally gave her a big squeeze and then passed her to Julie, whose eyes filled with tears. Hope snuggled next to Julie's chest and started drinking from her bottle. Olivia showed Julie to the rocking chair in Hope's bedroom, where she settled in to feed Hope and rock her to sleep.

Several hours later, and after everyone else had left, Steve reluctantly stood up from the couch. "I'm afraid it's time for us to hit the road. It'll take us several hours to get home and I've got work tomorrow." He grinned as he continued, "I also want to make sure that the house is still standing after Charlie and the girls have had the run of the place since early this morning."

Julie stood too, taking Steve's hand. "Thank you *so* much for inviting us. It was a wonderful day!"

Michael shook Steve's hand and Olivia gave Julie a hug. "We're so glad you came. We really are. We'll have to get together again . . . if you want to."

Julie smiled. "I think that would be nice, if you're sure. We don't want to intrude at all. You've got a beautiful family, and

Hope is so lucky to have you as parents." She smiled at Hope, who was snuggled against Olivia's shoulder. "I must admit, though, it would be great to see you all once in a while."

"We'll plan on it," Michael said.

They headed out to the car and left Ally to say her good-byes.

"Thanks again," Ally said. "It really was a great day. I'm so glad that we got to be a part of it."

"So are we," Olivia said. She hesitated for a moment and then added, "I know that you said you're not sure how much contact you want from now on, but I want you to know that, once you get moved to Provo for school, we'd love to see you every now and then." Michael nodded and Olivia continued, "You could come over for Sunday dinner once in a while or something."

Ally took a step back and looked at the little family that she had helped create. Michael had his arm around Olivia's waist and she was leaning into him just a little. Hope was resting her head on Olivia's shoulder, almost ready to drift off to sleep again, and her blonde curls were mingling with Olivia's soft brown ones. It looked so . . . *right.* She thought back to her morning in the temple and remembered the feeling of peace that had flooded through her.

Hope was with her family. She was with the people who were meant to be her mom and dad. Ally was sure of it. There was so much love between them, and Ally felt blessed to share a little part of that. She finally knew what she wanted to do.

"Well, at first I thought it would be too painful to see you three together. I thought it would be really hard to watch you, Olivia, being Hope's mom." Ally tucked her hair behind her ear and then looked up and smiled. "But I was wrong. It has been so amazing watching the three of you together and seeing how much you both love Hope and feeling the love and concern you have for me. If anything, it has made me feel better. Now I'm more certain than ever that Hope is in the right place and the right family, because I've seen it firsthand."

Olivia's eyes were shining, so Michael spoke. "We're really glad you feel that way, Ally."

"So, if you're sure you don't mind," Ally continued, "I'd love to see you once in a while after I get moved up here. Not to try and move in on your life, or check up on you, or try and take control, I just . . . well, I had a wonderful day today, and I think it would be really fun to get to know all three of you better. I would love to be your—and Hope's—friend."

"That sounds wonderful, Ally," Michael said. Olivia smiled. It seemed he had taken the words right out of her mouth.

BOOK TWO

CHAPTER ONE

Shanelle tried to ignore the movements of her two-year-old son, Joey, on the couch next to her. Her head hurt, and he would be up crying soon. Crying for breakfast. She sighed. Her own stomach rumbled as she looked up at the kitchen cupboards. The doors were hanging off all but one of them. She could only see a few empty bottles of cheap booze.

Joey stirred again and she laid her hand on his tight black curls. "Shh, shh, shh, baby boy. There ain't nothin' to eat when you wake up, anyhow," she whispered. Shanelle tried to slide over to give him more room, which earned her a stab in the ribs from one of the broken springs poking up through the cushion. She started to curse but thought better of it. No need to wake up her younger sisters, Laura and Josie, who were sleeping on the flimsy mattress a few feet away in the corner. "At least we got us a place to sleep," she mumbled to herself.

The three girls shared not just this sleeping space but also a mother. None of them had ever met their respective fathers, but that was no big deal. Most of her friends didn't know who their fathers were, either. Shanelle also had two older half-brothers somewhere, but no one had heard from them since before Joey was born.

She looked down at her son and smiled. Even as a toddler, he looked so much like Benjamin with those long eyelashes that brushed at his cheeks while he slept. At the thought of Joey's dad, her eyes filled with tears. *If only his stupid cousin hadn't cheated those thugs on that drug deal, they wouldn't have killed him, and Benjamin wouldn't have gone out two nights later for revenge.*

Shanelle shook her tears away. It had been one year, four months, two weeks, and five days since that night. There had been a big party going on that Benjamin had promised to join after "showin' those jerks a lesson," but when Shanelle answered the pounding on the door with Joey on her hip and saw Benjamin's best friend, Marcus, standing there covered in blood with his eyes as big as beer bottles, she knew her life would never be the same.

Her mother had told her it was all for the best; that Benjamin never would've stuck around anyway. "Least since he's dead, you can pretend he mighta stayed," she said with a shrug. "I guess you and Joey be movin' back in with me." And that was that.

Shanelle eased off the couch, careful to avoid another stab from a rogue spring and shivered in the cold February morning as she started rummaging through the mess of leftover debris covering the grimy kitchen counter. *Hopefully it starts warming up soon,* she thought as she uncovered half a bag of potato chips and a couple of pieces of beef jerky. She set these offerings down between her sisters' heads, hoping they would wake up and eat them before her mother and whoever she had been partying with last night stumbled out of the only bedroom. Chances were good the girls would get them. The laughing and drinking and yelling and fighting hadn't stopped until a few hours ago. Her mother probably wouldn't emerge until well after noon.

Shanelle thought about waking Josie up. It was important that she eat something. She was fourteen now—younger than she herself had been when she got pregnant with Joey at age fifteen—and had told everyone a couple weeks ago that she was pregnant, although she didn't know how far along she was or who exactly the father might be. It didn't occur to Shanelle to be upset with her half-sister. That was just life. At least twelve-year-old Laura wasn't giving them another mouth to feed . . . yet.

In the end, Shanelle decided Josie needed the sleep at least as much as the stale breakfast, so when Joey started fussing, she quietly scooped him up, wrapped his tattered blue blanket around him, and slipped out the door.

⁂

Shanelle knocked softly on Audrey's door. Audrey slept in the living room with her three kids, so with any luck, she wouldn't wake anyone else up. Audrey was about twenty, two years older than Shanelle. Because of her three children, she got more government help than Shanelle did. Maybe she had something Joey could eat.

"Hey, girl, what are you doin' here so early?" Audrey mumbled as she peeked out the door and tried to smooth down her greasy blonde hair.

"Sorry, but Mama took my card and spent everything that was left on it, and me and Joey don't have nothin' to eat."

"Girl, you gotta quit lettin' your mama take food outta your baby's mouth."

"I ain't lettin' her," Shanelle said as she stepped into the light and pushed her many long black braids out of her face. Audrey grimaced when she saw her neighbor's bruised and swollen expression. "Sometimes I ain't got no choice, ya know?"

Audrey paused as if listening carefully, then whispered, "All right. Hang tight for one second." She closed the door, but didn't let it latch and then reappeared a moment later with a handful of change.

"Here, go get that baby some food. He ain't lookin' so good." Audrey paused and looked everywhere but at the battered face in front of her. "But, see, this is all I can do. Jordan showed back up last night, and you know he don't want me seein' no one."

Shanelle nodded. Audrey was only friendly to her when

Jordan—the father of her oldest kid—wasn't around. "Thanks, Audrey. I owe you one." Joey started to fuss and Audrey moved to close the rusty green door.

"Hurry and get outta here." Audrey's eyes were nervous. "I think I hear him wakin' up." She paused when the door was nearly shut. "Remember, don't come back again, least not 'til I come see you and tell you he's gone."

Shanelle trudged down the four flights of metal stairs that separated Audrey's apartment from the street and wrapped Joey up a little tighter in his old fleece blanket to keep out the cold wind. "Come on, buddy," she said softly. "Let's see if we can find you some food."

CHAPTER TWO

Ally fingered the silver "I can do hard things" necklace that she had worn nearly every day for over a year and a half now. In the background, her microbiology professor was droning on about something. Usually Ally enjoyed this class, but she just couldn't concentrate today. Her mind was far away—in time and distance. Today was February 14, Valentine's Day, but Ally wasn't thinking about romance. Instead, she was back at the hospital in her hometown two years ago, giving birth to Hope.

Wow. How can it have been two years already? She could still remember the scene so clearly—Hope, still slippery and wet, blonde curls stuck to her head, being wrapped in a blanket and placed on Ally's chest. Her mom had cut the cord, and Ally had cried at the sight of the perfect, beautiful miracle that she had helped create.

When Ally signed the papers and placed Hope in Olivia's arms, she had known that she was doing the right thing, and she felt peace at that knowledge, but she had been sure the emptiness in her own heart would never go away. It was funny how, yet again, life had taken an unexpected twist. Ever since she had started at BYU just over a year ago, she had spent some time nearly every month with Michael, Olivia, and Hope. There were still times when Ally missed Hope, but the fact that she got to see her and play with her and realize over and over again that Hope was in the right family and was happy and healthy and growing brought more healing to Ally's heart than she would have thought possible.

On top of that, Ally's life was moving along in a great direction too. She had started school last January and spent the first semester living in the dorms. During that time she did all the regular "dorm" stuff, including eating in the cafeteria, watching basketball games in the common room, getting ice cream from the Creamery, and hanging out with friends until midnight and only *then* starting on her homework that was due the next morning. She had even joined in on the BYU tradition of tunnel singing a few times.

When the semester ended in May, Ally moved into an apartment off campus and continued taking classes through the summer. In the fall, several new roommates moved in, and the six of them got along just fine. Two of her roommates, Shaylan and Holly, were going into nursing as well, and she was starting to get close to them. Ally had also started working at the florist shop just north of the campus proper. It was a great, low-stress job that Ally enjoyed. Her BYU ward was good, but there were times when she missed Bishop Jenkins. No one in Provo knew about Hope, and for the time being, Ally wanted to keep it that way. She wasn't ashamed; she was just trying to move forward, and she wanted to be treated like a regular girl. Her roommates knew she had some friends in American Fork that she visited now and then, but that was all that had ever been said.

Ally loved being at BYU. She loved everything about it. Her testimony was growing and her spirit was getting stronger every day. She was so glad that she had listened when she was prompted to change her plans and come to BYU, and that Bishop Jenkins had convinced her that she could and should apply.

She had even started dating. She tried to keep it all laid back and fun, but there had been one guy, James, who kept trying to convince her that they should "take their relationship to the next level."

"What does that even mean?" Ally had asked in exasperation one evening.

"Well, you know," James had stammered, "that we should only date each other and see if we're right for each other and if we should get married."

Ally tried hard to keep a straight face. After all, James was a nice enough guy, and she didn't want to hurt his feelings.

"Shouldn't that just kind of happen on its own?" Ally had responded. "I mean, if we were supposed to be together, then gradually we would stop wanting to date anyone else, and we would end up only dating each other." She smiled to soften the blow. "I just don't think it's something we need to plan out and analyze."

"Well," James had continued, slightly frustrated. "I've been home from my mission for two years now, and it's time for me to start *planning* and *analyzing* how my future is going to come together. I'm just trying to find out if you are interested in being a part of that."

Ally was dumbfounded and once again tried to pull out her poker face. After all, they had fun together, but she and James had only been on five dates. She liked him okay, but now she was feeling like he had a checklist, and "find a wife" was the next thing to be marked off. She chuckled to herself; she would have to graciously decline.

"I'm sorry, James, but I just don't know you well enough to be able to make a decision like that today."

"I've already invested quite a lot of time into this relationship," James responded, looking hurt. "If you're not interested, I need to find someone else who is."

What? Ally couldn't contain it anymore, and a small laugh escaped her lips. "I won't waste any more of your time, then," she said. "You'd better find someone else."

James nodded solemnly and turned to walk away. Ally managed to wait until he was driving away before she burst into laughter.

She smiled at the memory. Most of the other guys Ally had gone out with, though, had kept it fun and simple, and that was just how Ally liked it. She just wasn't ready to get serious with anyone, and she wasn't sure she ever would be. Ally still didn't know how to explain Hope to a future boyfriend.

Ally was nudged back to reality by Shaylan, who was sitting next to her. "You look a million miles away," she said with a grin, "so I've been taking notes for both of us, but now I have no *idea* what he's talking about. You better start listening, so you can help me figure it out later!"

Ally smiled at her friend and gave her necklace one last rub. She would be going over to the Spencers' house for Hope's birthday party tonight, so she really did need to focus on this microbiology right now.

"What were you thinking about, anyway?" Shaylan whispered.

"I'll tell you later," Ally responded. And she was starting to think that maybe she really would.

Olivia hugged Ally when she answered the door later that evening. "Come in, come in," Olivia said as she closed the door behind Ally. "Michael is with Hope at the park, so I could get everything decorated."

Ally took in the now-familiar living room filled with colorful balloons, streamers, and a poster board hanging above the mantle with "Happy 2nd Birthday, Hope!" written in pink marker and crayon-drawn balloons decorating the edges.

"Everything looks great, Olivia! Thanks for inviting me."

"I'm glad you could make it." Olivia gestured to the sofa and they sat down. "How's school going?"

"Good. I really like my microbiology class, and my anatomy class is very cool! I'd heard horror stories from everyone about how awful it would be." Allison laughed. "But I really do love it. It just makes sense to me."

"I always loved the anatomy classes," Olivia agreed. "There

was definitely a ton of memorization, and the tests were super difficult, but it was just so fascinating."

Ally nodded. "So, any news from Family Services about a second baby?"

"Nothing," Olivia answered. "Our file has been approved and active for over a year now." She shrugged. "We're doing everything *we* can. Sometimes I worry that people will get tired of us telling everyone we know that we are trying to adopt, and if they know anyone who is considering placing a baby to send them our way."

Ally nodded again. It was hard to know what to say.

"Oh," Olivia continued, "you've got to see these cute family pictures that my friend Heather just took to put on some new pass-along cards."

Olivia walked into the dining room and opened the top drawer in the desk that sat in the corner.

"Those are the cards to give to people that have your email address and the web address of your adoption profile on them?" Ally asked.

"Yep. That way if they know someone who is considering an adoption plan, they can just give them our card and all of our information is right there." Olivia handed Ally a small stack of pictures. "Anyway, Hope has grown so much in the last year that we decided to make new ones."

Ally looked through the photos while Olivia was putting the finishing touches on Hope's fairy-themed birthday cake. "Wow, these are really good," Ally said. "I love this one of the three of you in front of the pond, and . . . also this one of you snuggled together reading a book to Hope. Of course," Ally said, laughing, "I might be biased. One of the main things about you guys that caught my attention was the photo of you and Michael reading together."

"I really like that picture too," Olivia agreed. "I love how Hope is grinning up at Michael. You can sure tell she loves her daddy."

"Yes, you can." Once again Ally was reassured that Hope was exactly where she should be.

Ally handed the pictures back to Olivia. "Well, good luck. I'm sure it's hard to wait."

"Thanks," Olivia said. "It *is* hard to wait. Our social worker keeps telling us that we shouldn't be *waiting,* we should be *finding,* but"—Olivia grimaced—"whatever you call it, it still feels an awful lot like waiting to me." They were both laughing when Michael walked through the door with Hope following close behind.

"Hi, Livvy. Hi, Ally," he said and gave Olivia a quick peck on the cheek.

"Hi, Mommy," Hope said as she gave Olivia a big, slobbery kiss.

"Hi, sweetie. Look who came for your party."

"Ally!" Hope squealed and ran over to give Ally a hug.

"Happy birthday, Hope," Ally said and handed her a brightly wrapped package.

"I open it now?" Hope asked, looking at Olivia. Every time Ally came over, she was amazed at how much Hope was growing and changing. She was talking even better than the last time Ally had visited.

"Sure, Hope, you can open it now," Olivia answered.

Hope immediately pulled off the light purple bow and stuck it right on the top of her head. Then she proceeded to very gently unwrap the present, being careful not to rip any of the wrapping paper. Ally laughed. "That's just how I open presents," she said. "It drives my dad crazy!"

"We wondered where she got that from," Michael said with a smile.

"Baby! Baby! Mine own baby!" Hope had gotten the paper off the soft, cuddly baby doll and was hugging it fiercely. "See, Mommy? See?"

"I can see your baby, Hope. She's very pretty. What do you tell Ally?"

"Thank you, Ally," Hope beamed and gave Ally one more hug before she ran down the hall to show the baby her bedroom.

"That's great, Ally," Olivia said. "She loves it."

ൟ ൟ

The party was a lot of fun. Ally enjoyed seeing Olivia's parents and grandmother again, and Michael and Olivia's friends Heather and Greg were there with their four kids. They sang, then clapped when Hope blew out her candles, and they had cake and ice cream with a few spills from the kids thrown in for good measure.

The grown-ups sat visiting in the living room while Hope showed Heather's kids the new doll that Ally had given her and the tricycle that was her mom and dad's gift. After a while, Ally reluctantly announced that she'd better head home, because she and Shaylan still had to figure out the day's microbiology assignment. There were hugs all around, and Ally kissed Hope on top of the head and said, "I'll see you in a couple weeks, kiddo."

"'Kay. Bye, Ally!"

Ally headed for the door and, to her surprise, Olivia's grandma stood up and followed her. "I need to stretch my legs for minute," she said. "I'll walk you to your car."

Ally got a little nervous, but Grandma Anna—as she had taken to calling her—had always been so sweet that she tried to tell herself there was nothing to worry about.

They got all the way to the curb and Ally's little green Volkswagen bug before Grandma Anna said anything. Then she took Ally's shoulder and turned her so they were facing eye to eye. There was nothing but love behind those wrinkly, smiling eyes, and Ally relaxed.

"You're a good girl, Ally."

"What?" Ally was caught off guard. "Oh, thanks, Grandma Anna."

"No, you really listen to me." Her old silvery-blue eyes seemed to peer right into the depths of Ally's heart, where the lingering doubts about her future and whether anyone would accept and love her after finding out about Hope stayed hidden.

"You're a good girl, Ally. You have brought love and laughter into Michael and Olivia's life. You believe in Jesus Christ and know that He loves you. You have sacrificed and cried and hurt and cried some more. And now, you are starting to heal."

Tears sprang to Ally's eyes, because she knew Grandma Anna was right. She had been searching for peace, but also, in a way, trying to avoid it. It felt like a betrayal to Hope for her to truly be at peace and moving forward.

"Let that healing come, Ally. Hope doesn't want you holding yourself back. Allowing healing and peace," she paused, "and *love* back into your life does *not* mean you're being unfaithful to Hope.

Ally was crying now and could only nod. Grandma Anna wrapped her time-worn, loving arms around her and concluded, "And anyone who rejects you based on your past experiences is someone that you don't need in your life anyway."

Grandma Anna stepped back and gently wiped Ally's tears. "We love you, Ally. We all do, and there are lots of other people waiting to love you as well. Just give them the chance."

"Thanks, Grandma Anna." Ally sniffed. "I'll try and remember that." Grandma Anna smiled and waved once more as Ally drove away deep in thought.

CHAPTER THREE

Shanelle jumped at the loud knock on her front door. It was late, and she was trying to get Joey to sleep, but Laura was in the corner watching their tiny old television set, and Joey was much more interested in what was going on with *The Late Show* than in going to bed. Shanelle hesitated. Her mother wasn't here, but she wouldn't knock when she got home . . . unless she had lost her key again. It could be Josie, but Shanelle doubted it. Late as it was, it was still too early for her sister to be coming home.

The knock came again, and this time Laura looked up too. Shanelle handed Joey to her and moved cautiously to the door. "Who's there?" she demanded.

"It's me, Marcus. That you, Shanelle? Let me in." His voice sounded slightly slurred, but not angry, and after all, Marcus had been Benjamin's best friend, so Shanelle unbolted the various locks and quickly ushered him in.

His eyes were red-rimmed and blurry, and Shanelle knew right away that Marcus was drunk or high, or maybe both. He threw his arms around her and started shaking. It took a second before Shanelle realized that he was crying. This had happened just once before, almost a year ago. It had been about six months after Benjamin was killed, and Marcus had gotten good and plowed. But for whatever reason, instead of numbing his emotions, it had heightened his pain and sense of guilt for having seen Benjamin get stabbed multiple times and then watching him bleed to death in his arms. He had been too scared and in shock to do anything else.

Shanelle caught Laura's eye and looked meaningfully at Joey and then at the couch. Laura nodded. She would watch Joey and try to get him to sleep. Shanelle knew from many past experiences that when people let their willpower be taken over by a substance, they became unpredictable, and she wanted to put a little space between Marcus and her baby boy. Knowing it wasn't safe to be outside just hanging out this time of night, Shanelle moved Marcus into the one bedroom that occupied the back half of their tiny, square apartment and shut the door. He slumped onto the bed and continued crying.

He finally took a shuddering breath and looked up to meet Shanelle's eyes. Immediately, she wished he hadn't, as the haunted look of despair was something that Shanelle recognized, and it scared her. That was the look of the utterly hopeless. Of someone who was so tortured by the past that they had lost the will to go on. She had seen it on the face of a girl that she only knew casually, yet it had still been a shock when the paramedics had come to take away the body. And she had seen it on the face of her mother's younger sister, who had lived with them up until Shanelle was ten. In that case, Shanelle was the one who walked in on the body, with the empty pill bottle on the floor and the bottle of booze still clutched limply in her aunt's lifeless hand.

They hadn't seen much of each other since Benjamin had died, but Shanelle would do whatever it took to keep Marcus alive. She couldn't handle another death. Not right now, especially if there was any way she could prevent it.

Shanelle walked over and sat down on the squeaky bed next to Marcus. He dropped his head on her shoulder and she held him, rubbing his back and murmuring comforting words into his ear. After a while, the shaking stilled and Shanelle gently brushed the tears from his cheeks, still cooing, "Shhhh, shhhh. It'll all work out," the way she did when Joey would cry.

Before Shanelle realized what was happening, Marcus was kissing her. Hesitantly at first, then hungrily. Shanelle momentarily paused, thinking about the fact that she hadn't been with anyone since Benjamin had been killed. Then Marcus was kissing her again, rolling her over onto the bed. She hesitated again, but maybe this was what Marcus needed to get his mind right, to make it through the night alive. *And after all,* she thought as she gave in, *it has been an awful long time.*

Three months later, Shanelle was certain. She had only seen Marcus a couple times since the night they had sex, and their relationship was the same as it had been before. For about a month, Shanelle had wondered if he even remembered their encounter, but then he had said something in passing about if they should "get together" again. So he did remember. Shanelle told him she didn't think it was a good idea, and he let it drop. She wondered what he would say when he found out she was carrying his baby.

Shanelle was out walking, hoping to run across Marcus. She was glad the warm weather was here. This was the time of year she liked best: Late May. Warm enough that Joey could just be in a pair of shorts, but not so hot that they were all miserable yet. She looked down at her son, who was toddling along beside her. He would turn three in August. She shook her head. *Where did the time go?* He was skinny and a little smaller than the other boys his age. Shanelle knew he wasn't getting enough to eat, because she could see every one of his ribs as he bent over to study a line of ants. But she was doing the best she could.

She hoped she could find a way to do a little better once this baby arrived. She wanted to be a good mom, but as she looked around at the dirty streets, the rows and rows of apartment blocks, and the countless people just hanging around smoking and drinking, she felt doomed to failure.

❧ ☙

It had been almost a week since Shanelle started really trying to find Marcus. She wasn't overly concerned. It wasn't uncommon for someone to just be gone for a while. She knew he would turn up sooner or later. And she was right. She finally ran into him while she was hanging around outside the gas station hoping that someone would offer her and Joey something to eat. Marcus came striding up but paused when he saw Shanelle standing there.

"Hey, Marcus. I been wantin' to talk to you."

"Hi, Shanelle. I'm kinda in a hurry."

"This'll only take a minute."

Marcus sighed and rolled his eyes. "Whaddaya want?"

"Well, I'm pregnant."

"So?"

Now it was Shanelle's turn to sigh. "I'm pregnant, and you're the daddy."

"You sure?"

"Course I'm sure." Shanelle shook her head. "I ain't like my sister."

"Okay."

"That all you got to say?"

"Look, Shanelle, I already got a kid I don't ever see." He shrugged. "I guess one more don't make much difference."

Shanelle nodded. This was about what she'd expected. "Just thought you should know."

Marcus had already turned and was walking through the convenience store doors. Shanelle touched his shoulder, and he turned around. "You got some money so me and Joey can get some food?"

"Sorry. This ain't my money. I'm just the only one old enough to buy beer who's sober enough to come." He chuckled.

Shanelle watched Marcus through the big glass windows. He grabbed a case of beer, paid for it, and then walked out the door without even a sideways glance at her.

❧ ☙

By late afternoon, Shanelle was getting desperate. It was the end of the month, and no one had money left on their food cards. Joey had started whimpering beside her over an hour ago. She had to do something. She couldn't just stand here and let her baby cry. Besides, she was starting to feel dizzy. Shanelle hadn't eaten more than a bite or two for the last couple days. She had been giving every scrap of food she could come up with to Joey, which still wasn't much. They needed to eat.

Shanelle waited until she could see that the clerk was busy helping a customer and had two more people in line.

"Joey, you just sit here and be real quiet and still, and I'll go get some food. Okay?"

Joey nodded his little head and Shanelle took a deep breath and slipped through the door. A quick glance at the clerk told Shanelle that he was still preoccupied with his customers and she quietly made her way to the end of the aisle that held the bread. She peeked over her shoulder and could see the back of Joey's head through the window. She turned and slipped a loaf under her shirt.

Shanelle closed her eyes and tensed momentarily, waiting for someone to see her, but nothing happened. She opened her eyes. The clerk hadn't noticed anything! She was about to turn and leave, when a jar of peanut butter caught her eye. Joey could sure use some peanut butter on his bread. She stood there staring at the peanut butter, absorbed in the debate going on in her mind. Finally, she snatched up the peanut butter and headed for the door without looking back. Her heart was pounding and her palms were sweating, but she was going to make it. She was going to make it! She pushed open the glass door and in two more steps she was outside.

"Joey, come on," Shanelle called in a loud whisper. She was walking in the opposite direction from where she had left Joey, but she knew he would follow. He always did. Shanelle didn't dare stop walking until she had reached the corner of the building and realized that Joey wasn't at her side.

She turned around to call him again, but the words froze in her throat. She had been so caught up in deciding whether to take the peanut butter or not, and then in making it out of the store without getting caught, that she hadn't even noticed the shiny black car with lights on top that had pulled up in front of Joey. She'd been inside when the officer got out and knelt down next to Joey to ask him if he was okay and did he know where his momma was. What Shanelle did see when she turned around was a tall policeman holding one of Joey's hands. With the other hand, Joey was pointing at her.

She tried to run, but Shanelle was rooted to the spot. She started to hear a weird wheezing sound. It took a second before she realized that the sound was coming from her. It felt like her throat was closing off and she had to gasp for air.

"Are you okay, ma'am?" the officer asked, taking a step toward her. "Is this your son?"

Shanelle tried to speak but couldn't. She just nodded her head as she forced herself to take a deep breath.

"Are you sure you're okay?" the officer was asking again. And this time he walked all the way over to her. "Do you need some help?"

Shanelle tried to clear her mind, calm her breathing. She had to *think*. But panic was swirling around the edges of her mind, mixing with the dizziness that was threatening to overwhelm her. And her heart just kept on pounding.

"Ma'am, maybe you'd better sit down for a minute. You don't look very good. Are you feeling okay?"

Shanelle faintly heard the words, but they sounded like an echo. Like she was sinking into a deep hole and he was at the top, shouting down to her. She started to slump and he half-caught, half-lowered her to the sidewalk.

"Joey," she whispered weakly. The last thing Shanelle remembered was feeling Joey's little arms grasp her neck. She leaned her head onto his and then darkness took over.

CHAPTER FOUR

Ally looked around at the empty study area of the Harold B. Lee Library. She liked being on campus during the summer. It was so much less crowded and definitely quieter. But her heart dropped a little when she realized that there was no one here *at all*. For the past week, she had been exchanging smiles with a cute guy who, it seemed, came to the library at the same time as she did to study.

She plopped her backpack down on the nearest round table and began poring over her physiology notes. Ally had finished reviewing the lecture notes and was reaching into her bag to fish out her book to double check a few things when a voice interrupted her.

"Is someone sitting here?"

Ally jumped slightly and then looked up into the dark brown eyes that she had spent the week admiring from across the room. She moved her backpack to the floor next to her and replied, "Nope, it's all yours."

She smiled and began flipping through the pages of her physiology book, trying to concentrate. She looked up once and smiled at him, noticing that his hair—which she had thought was light brown—actually had a definite reddish hue to it now that she was this close. He returned the smile and then went back to figuring some complicated-looking calculus problems. After another hour or so, Ally was finished with what she needed to get done but didn't want to leave just yet, so she started reading the chapter they would be going over in class next week.

A few minutes later, Ally's stomach rumbled loudly. She felt an embarrassed heat seeping up her neck and into her face and then the guy shut his book, gathered up his papers and looked Ally squarely in the face.

"I guess that's the signal that it's time for lunch," he said with a grin. Ally nodded, her embarrassment momentarily disabling her power of speech. "I'm really glad," he continued, looking down to shove his book, papers, and calculator into his backpack. "I'm starving. I've just been waiting for you to get hungry enough to start packing up, so—" He looked back up and caught Ally staring at him. She blushed and he smiled again. "So I could ask if you wanted to walk over to the Wilkinson Center and have lunch with me."

Ally hadn't been expecting that, and nervous butterflies immediately darted around her stomach. "Um, yeah, okay," she managed to get out. She bent down to pick up her bag and took a deep breath, willing herself to say something halfway intelligent. "That would be nice. There's only one problem."

"What?" he asked, a look of genuine concern flashing across his face.

"I don't generally eat with people when I don't even know their name."

He laughed. "Oh, well, that's an easy fix." He stuck out his hand. "My name's Scott McAllister."

Ally took his hand. His grip was firm. "I'm Allison Campbell."

"Well, Allison Campbell. It's nice to finally meet you."

"He's *so* cute!" Ally gushed to Shaylan and Holly. She was draining a pot of spaghetti noodles while Holly was heating up a bottle of Prego sauce and Shaylan was cutting up some cucumbers for their salad. "He's got these gorgeous brown eyes and this brown-ish, blonde-ish, red-ish thing going on with his hair that is really hot!"

"So, you liked him, then?" Shaylan kidded as she tucked her thick black hair behind her ear.

"I think that's *obvious,*" Holly replied with a giggle. Her white-blonde hair and pale blue eyes were a stark contrast to Shaylan's olive skin and almost-black eyes.

"My grandma would disown me if she knew I was eating store-bought pasta sauce," Shaylan said with a sad shake of her head.

"Oh, get over it," Holly teased as she dumped the sauce onto the pile of noodles. "We're busy students. We can't spend all day making the secret family recipe that your grandma brought with her from Italy."

"Okay, okay." Shaylan laughed. "But *no one* tells Grandma!"

The three friends filled their plates and then sat around the little square table in one corner of their kitchen. It was nice, now that their other roommates had gone home for the summer, they had the apartment to themselves.

"So are you going out with him again?" Shaylan asked Ally, bringing the conversation back around to Scott.

"Yep," Ally said in between bites of pasta. "Tomorrow night. We're going bowling and then out to dinner."

"So, you already told us how *hot* he is," Holly said. "Hopefully he was just as nice?"

"He was *more* than nice," Ally answered. "He opened doors for me, pulled out my chair for me to sit down, and even carried my backpack while he walked me back to my car."

Shaylan and Holly nodded. "But the best part," Ally continued with a grin, "was when his cell phone rang during lunch and he just reached into his pocket and hit the silent button without even looking at it!"

All three girls laughed as Shaylan said, "Well, that settles it. He's *definitely* a keeper."

"We'll see," Ally said nonchalantly. But her insides squirmed, and she wondered if maybe he was.

Two weeks later, Scott knocked on the apartment door to pick Ally up for their sixth date, including that first lunch together. She answered the door wearing a new pair of denim capri pants she bought especially for today and a fitted light-pink T-shirt. She had a brown zippered sweatshirt over her arm. Even though it was the end of June, once the sun went down it would be a little chilly in Provo Canyon.

"Hello, beautiful," Scott whispered as he wrapped his arms around Ally's waist and pulled her close.

"Hey, Scott," Ally replied as she laid her head against his shoulder. She really liked the way his arms felt around her, so strong and secure. He hadn't kissed her yet, and part of Ally was really hoping that tonight would be the night. The other part was scared stiff at the thought of kissing Scott. She hadn't kissed anyone since Brandon, and that had been over three years ago. There had been several guys who Ally had known wanted to kiss her, but she never gave them an opportunity. She hadn't been ready to stir up all of those emotions and let someone in like that. Until now.

Scott reluctantly let go of Ally and smiled down at her. "Ready to go?"

"Sure am." Ally was actually a little nervous. They were going to be meeting a bunch of Scott's friends tonight. Friends he had known for years. She was sure to feel like an outsider.

Her thoughts must have shown on her face, because Scott took her hand and said, "It's going to be fine. They'll all think you're great." He reached up with his free hand and touched Ally's cheek. "Just like I do." His fingertips lingered on her skin, and when Scott released her hand and gently wrapped his arm around her waist, pulling her close to him, Ally froze. She had been hoping for this moment tonight but wasn't expecting it quite so soon.

Scott felt her tense, and he paused, searching her eyes for the answer to the question that he was silently asking. *You've already decided to let him in, Ally,* she reminded herself. And she *had* imagined how it would feel to have her fingers in his hair, his lips on hers. She took a deep breath and leaned closer, allowing a soft smile to find its way to her face. That was the answer Scott was looking for, and he closed his eyes as their lips met. It was even better than Ally had imagined it would be.

The rest of the evening passed in a blur. They roasted hot dogs and marshmallows over a fire, and then someone started telling scary stories. Ally usually didn't care for silly stories that always, *always* scared her, but it was fun tonight. Having Scott by her side with his arm around her shoulder made all the difference. In the middle of a particularly tense story, the wood in the fire popped loudly and Ally jumped. They both laughed and Scott wrapped his arms around her, chasing the fight-or-flight adrenaline away and replacing it with a cozy warmth.

When Scott walked Ally to her front door later that night, he wrapped his arms tightly around her. This time he didn't hesitate before he kissed her, and the emotions that swirled up inside Ally took her breath away. She hung onto him for a few moments, savoring the closeness. Then Scott backed away, gave her one little peck on the cheek, and whispered, "I'll see you tomorrow," before getting in his car and driving away.

Ally unlocked her front door and slipped into the apartment. Shaylan and Holly were already in bed, but they had left a light on in the kitchen for her. She leaned her back against the wall and slid down to a sitting position. She couldn't stop smiling.

"So, are you going to tell me what we're doing today?" Ally asked, resting her left hand on top of Scott's right as he drove his pickup truck onto the freeway. They had seen each other every day for the past six weeks, and the closeness was very comfortable. "And why we had to get up so early?" Ally yawned. The sun was just beginning to peek over the mountains that formed the eastern border of the valley.

"Okay." Scott grinned. "I know the perfect spot for watching the Days of '47 parade in Salt Lake." He stifled a yawn of his own. "The only problem is that you have to get there pretty early."

"Oh, that's right," Ally said. "Today's the twenty-fourth of July. Pioneer Day. I totally forgot."

"Forgot?" Scott shook his head in mock sadness. "I'm not sure that's acceptable, Miss Campbell."

Ally laughed. "And why not, Mr. McAllister?"

"Because," Scott continued, "the twenty-fourth of July is *only* the best day of the whole summer!"

"Oh, really?"

"Yes, really," Scott teased. "Parades, water balloons, barbecues, rodeos, fireworks—"

"Okay, okay," Ally conceded. "You're right. The twenty-fourth is the best day of the summer."

"And this one will be the best Pioneer Day yet," Scott added.

"And why's that?" Ally was still teasing, but Scott suddenly became very serious.

"Because I'll be spending it with you."

Ally leaned her head on Scott's shoulder and smiled as he wrapped his arm around her.

Scott hadn't exaggerated. They were on the front row of the parade route, and it was a lot of fun. They waved and clapped and cheered, and whenever Ally caught Scott's eye, he would lean over and give her a quick kiss. Ally would have been content to stay right there all day, but the parade ended, and soon they were making their way through the crowd, Scott holding both of their folding camp chairs in one hand, and clinging tightly to Ally's hand with the other.

They watched a fun matinee performance of the famous "Days of '47 Rodeo." They laughed at the rodeo clown and oohed and aahed along with everyone else at the bull riders. Ally couldn't help but think of Bishop Jenkins and smile at the memory of the story he had told her from his own bull riding days.

The rodeo ended and Scott took Ally to a fancy downtown fondue restaurant. Ally had never been but had mentioned to Scott on their second or third date that she thought it would be a fun place to eat. He had remembered. The hostess seated them, and they were enjoying dipping various breads and vegetables into the gooey pot of cheese in the center of their table when everything changed.

At first, Ally didn't notice the group of four girls walk in and get seated at a booth across a wide aisle from them. She vaguely heard their laughter and chatter, but she was too wrapped up in watching Scott to take any notice of them. After a few minutes, though, she noticed that Scott kept sneaking glances at the table full of girls and then shaking his head and laughing.

Finally, Ally could take it no longer. "Do you know those girls?" she asked carefully, not wanting to accuse Scott of repeatedly focusing on a random group of girls while he was on a date with *her.*

"What?" Scott asked, whipping his eyes back to Ally. "What did you say?"

"I asked if you know those girls," Ally repeated. "It kind of seems like you do."

"No," Scott answered with a big grin, his eyes darting over at them again. "No, I don't."

Ally was getting annoyed now. "Then why do you keep looking at them?"

"Isn't it *obvious*?" Scott asked.

"Well, I guess they are cute and young," Ally answered, with tears welling up in her eyes.

"What?" Scott said again. "No, I mean look at that blonde girl on the end."

Ally glanced over but didn't see anything out of the ordinary. She shrugged.

"Look at her closely, Ally, and listen to what they're saying, and you'll see what's so funny," Scott prompted again.

Ally set down the wooden skewer that she had just used to stab a chunk of bread and turned to fully face the table of girls. She hoped they would keep up their conversation and not notice her staring at them. She looked carefully at the girl that Scott had pointed out. She was pretty, with her long blonde hair pulled back in a ponytail. Ally guessed that she was about eighteen. Ally pulled her gaze back from the girl's face, taking in her whole body, and suddenly, dreadfully, she realized what Scott was staring at—what he thought was so funny. Ally found herself wishing that he *had* been looking at them because he thought they were cute or because one of them was an ex-girlfriend or something. This was much worse. The girl was pregnant.

Ally tried to play it cool. "Scott, it's not nice to laugh at pregnant women." She gave him a little smile, hoping that would be the end of the discussion.

"But did you notice," he went on, "she's not wearing a wedding ring."

Ally could feel her chest constricting, like a giant snake was squeezing the life and energy out of her. "Well, maybe her hands are too swollen to put it on," she said weakly, desperate for this conversation to end.

"Come on, Ally," he said, "I've been listening to her go on and on about how she doesn't know what she's going to do or if her boyfriend is going to leave or what." He shook his head. "I mean, how dumb do you have to be to get knocked up?"

Ally squared her shoulders before looking Scott in the eye. "That wasn't nice, Scott. You don't know her. You don't know anything about her. She certainly doesn't need you laughing at her."

"Hey, don't get mad at me. *She's* the one who screwed up."

Ally tried to take a deep breath, but that imaginary snake around her chest was squeezing too tightly. She couldn't seem to get any air.

"Why do you care, anyway?" Scott asked.

"I just think she's going through enough stuff right now without random strangers laughing at her."

"Whatever," Scott said.

I can't believe this is happening, Ally thought. "Maybe she made a mistake," she said, "but she's trying to figure out what to do next." Ally was getting upset.

"It sounds like she made a *huge* mistake." Scott chuckled.

"Okay, so what if she did make a *huge* mistake and now she's trying to figure out what to do? How does that give you any right to laugh at her or judge her?"

"I'm just saying, this wouldn't happen to a smart person." He nodded smugly. "Not to me, and not to you."

That was the deathblow. Ally lost the battle with the snake, and she couldn't seem to breathe at all. "I need some air," she said, rushing out of the restaurant, wiping the tears that had finally spilled onto her cheeks.

When Ally reached the freedom of the parking lot, she was finally able to breathe again, but the summer air was too warm to bring any real relief. Hot tears were dripping onto her shirt. She couldn't decide if she was more embarrassed, humiliated, or just plain mad. She felt like Scott had completely and utterly betrayed her. *He doesn't know anything about Hope*, Ally reminded herself.

He wouldn't be here if he did. Ally hated it when her internal voice pointed out things she'd rather not think about.

"Now what are you going to tell him?" Ally mumbled to herself. "You really made a mess out of that." She looked around the parking lot and found Scott's shiny, black pickup truck. She knew that she should probably go back inside and make up some excuse about why she reacted the way she did, but she just couldn't. So she lowered the tail gate of the truck and sat down on it to wait. *Is there any way to fix this?* Ally wondered. *Do I even want to fix it?* Ally wasn't ready to answer that question yet. When she thought about how she felt about Scott, and how he seemed to feel about her, she wanted to believe that he would change his thinking if she just told him about mistakes and forgiveness and love and Hope. But the nagging voice in the back of her mind kept repeating, *I don't know. You saw the look on his face while he was talking about that girl.*

Ally finally decided that she wasn't going to make any decisions tonight. It had been a long day, and she was tired. When Scott came out, she would just ask him to take her home, and she would figure all of this out tomorrow. She only waited a few more minutes before Scott came out of the restaurant looking as confused as Ally felt.

"What happened in there?" Scott asked. His soft, brown eyes reflected the hurt that Ally herself was feeling.

"I'm tired, Scott," she said. "Can we call it a night?"

"Okay, but—"

"I think it's best if we just go home and talk about this tomorrow."

Scott's face fell. Ally wanted to reach up and stroke his cheek, run her fingers through his hair, kiss him softly, anything to take the look of pain away, but then she remembered his words. *That wouldn't happen to a smart person. Not to me. Not to you.* And instead she got in the passenger door and buckled her seat belt.

Ally saw Scott shake his head, raise the tailgate, and rub his face before opening his door and climbing into the truck. Scott laid his right hand on the seat—an invitation. Ally crossed her arms. The forty-five minute drive home seemed to last for hours.

Scott knocked on Ally's door at ten o'clock on the dot. He was really hoping that whatever had happened last night at the restaurant would have blown over by this morning. Maybe Ally had just been emotional last night, or tired, or—he rolled his eyes—hormonal. He had never seen Ally act that way before and get so worked up about a perfect stranger. Scott just couldn't understand.

Ally answered the door in a faded pair of jeans and a BYU

T-shirt. "Morning," she said. She tried to smile, but it didn't quite come out right. Her eyes were red and puffy. She had been crying. For quite a while.

Terrific, Scott thought. *It didn't just blow over.* But immediately his mind switched gears, and he started to get worried. Why had she been crying? Was this it? Scott hadn't admitted it to anyone yet, but he was really starting to care about Ally, and he wanted their relationship to continue. Surely it wasn't going to end over something so stupid as laughing about a girl being pregnant and not married.

"Aren't you going to say anything?" Ally asked softly, breaking the silence.

"Sorry," Scott began, "I was just thinking." He forced a smile. "Are you okay?"

"Come on in," Ally said. "Shaylan and Holly went shopping, so we can talk here."

"Do you want to go out and get some breakfast?" Scott asked.

Ally shook her head and stepped back, motioning him inside. "No, I'd rather we had a little privacy."

"Okay." Scott had been confused since last night, but that feeling was slowly morphing into panic. *A private talk? That's never good.* He walked in and sat down on the couch, leaving plenty of room for Ally to sit next to him, but she sat to the side of the couch in an ancient recliner that had seen better days.

"I didn't sleep much last night," Ally admitted. "I had a lot to think about."

"Ally, if this is all about what I said about that girl, let's just forget it." Scott found himself talking fast, wanting to explain why this was all no big deal. "I'm sorry that I noticed that group of girls. I know I shouldn't have been making a fuss about them when I was on a date with you."

Ally nodded but didn't comment.

"Ally, I really like you. I think you know that."

She nodded again.

"I'm sorry. I'm sorry I noticed them. I'm sorry I pointed them out. I'm sorry I ruined our day." Scott had stood up and walked behind Ally's chair and put his hands on her shoulders. "Can you forgive me?"

"Scott." Ally took one of his hands in hers and led him around the side of the chair. He sat down on the arm of the couch and didn't let go of her hand. "Do you really think that is what I was so upset about?"

"Well," Scott began, "I did, but now . . ." He studied her face for a moment. "Now I'm not so sure."

"No girl likes her date checking out other girls"—Ally forced a weak smile—"but I really wish that's all it was."

Scott started to say something, but Ally held up her hand, stopping him.

"It really bothered me how judgmental you were about that girl, Scott. You had no problem laughing about her and her situation." Ally's voice cracked. "People make mistakes . . ."

"*Some* people."

"But not you?" Tears filled her eyes.

"Not like that." Scott watched Ally swallow hard. She was trying not to cry.

"I believe that anyone can make a mistake," she said. Scott shook his head, but Ally forged ahead. "Anyone can mess up, and it's not my place or yours or anyone else's to judge another person."

"Why does it even matter, Ally?" Scott crossed his arms. "I don't see why you're getting so worked up about this."

"It matters," Ally began softly, "because I really like you too."

"You do?" Scott uncrossed his arms and leaned forward, a grin sneaking onto his face.

"Of course I do." Scott tried to lean down and kiss Ally, but she put a hand on his cheek, stopping him.

"The problem is," Ally continued, "I don't want to get any more attached to you when—" Tears filled Ally's eyes, and she tried to blink them away. "When I'm not sure we have a future together."

"Ally, what are you saying?" Scott was shocked. "Are you seriously going to let this come between us?"

"Let me ask you one question before I answer that," Ally said. She took a deep breath. "Would you ever, under any possible scenario, consider having a serious relationship with a girl like the one we saw last night? Would you ever marry her?"

Scott exhaled sharply. This was so unfair! He and Ally had a really good thing going here, and now she was going to ruin it, all over some stupid girl that neither of them even knew. Scott had to force himself to be calm.

"Ally, I've been a good guy my whole life. It's not like I haven't had chances to do something stupid, even if it would have been fun, but I've always done the right thing." He threw his hands in the air. "I don't even know why this is an issue. I like you Ally. I like you a lot."

⁂

Ally froze. She knew they had a great time together, but this was serious. Because she liked him too. A lot. Scott stood and paced in front of the chair she was sitting in. Finally he turned and offered her his hand. Ally looked into his eyes. They were wet and more intense than she'd ever seen them. She reached up and took his hand. Scott pulled her to him. Before Ally knew what was happening, Scott was kissing her. His mouth was moving over hers with a passion that surprised her. He pulled her even closer to him and Ally wanted to forget everything except for this moment, now, here, with him. Much too soon, Scott stepped back and moved his hands to her shoulders. They were both breathing heavily.

"Ally, I think I'm falling in love with you. Please, can we just let this go? I'm sorry I ever said anything about that girl."

He looked so sincere. Could it possibly be true? *You could tell him. Maybe it will be okay.* Ally reached up and brushed her fingers along his cheek. "You didn't answer my question. Could you ever be with someone like her?" Scott opened his mouth to protest, but Ally cut him off. "Even if that someone was me?" Time froze for a split second before Scott stumbled backward like Ally had punched him.

"Wait." Scott rubbed his hand across his face. "Are you saying that you *are* like her?" Ally reached out to touch his arm, but he took a step back. "You have a baby?" His voice was soft. When she didn't immediately answer, he yelled, "You have a baby?" Ally jumped at the outburst, but she found her voice and matched the volume to his as her tears finally escaped.

"I had a baby. Yes. I had a baby. I was just like that girl you found so hilarious last night. Stupid me, got knocked up and had a baby."

Scott stepped back and looked her up and down. "Well, you sure put on a pretty great act."

"And what act is that?"

"All good and smart and . . . innocent." He spat the word at her. She shrunk back at his words. *Had* she tried to fool him? No. She stepped forward again.

"There's no *act,* Scott. Just me." She lowered her voice, but kept eye contact. "Just me."

They faced off, each lost in their own thoughts until Ally finally broke the silence. "So, now what?"

Scott chuckled, but there was no humor in it. "I never did answer your question."

"What?"

"Your question about whether I could ever be with a girl like her." He shook his head. "With a girl like *you.*" Something about the way he said it made Ally's stomach turn.

She nodded but didn't meet his eyes this time. "So could you?"

"No, Ally. I couldn't."

Even though she sensed they were coming, the words still stung Ally like a slap. She gasped and wrapped her arms tightly around herself as fresh tears spilled onto her cheeks.

"What about everything else you just said?" Ally demanded. "About falling in . . . in love with me."

Scott looked up and his tone was flat. "I was wrong."

He looked at her for a few more seconds and Ally wondered if he was going to say more, but then he turned and headed for the door. "Good-bye, Ally."

"Scott? Are you sure?" Ally choked out the words.

He looked over his shoulder, opened his mouth, and then shut it again. He watched her for a long moment and then responded, "I said good-bye, Ally."

The door slammed shut and Ally dropped onto the sofa, a sob erupting from deep inside her.

CHAPTER FIVE

When Allison opened her eyes on the early September Saturday morning, she could already hear Shaylan and Holly in the kitchen. She slipped on some jeans and a T-shirt and pulled her hair back into a ponytail before joining them.

"Look who decided to join the land of the living," Holly said as Ally walked in.

"Very funny," Ally replied. "I bought football tickets. I said I'd go to the games this year, so here I am."

"We just weren't sure if you would still come," Shaylan said.

Holly nodded. "You haven't done anything except school and work since you broke up with Scott."

"It's been over a month," Shaylan added.

"I know." Ally sighed. "And I'm sorry about that. I've just been trying to get my mind right, you know?"

"Um, actually we *don't* know," Shaylan replied, "because you won't tell us anything about what happened."

"I just haven't known what to say." Ally sat down at the table and reached her hand into the box of Life cereal that the other girls hadn't put away yet.

"But now," Holly prompted.

Ally laughed. It felt good. "But now I think I'm ready to

talk about it." She popped a handful of cereal in her mouth.

"About time!" Holly said.

"For sure," Shaylan agreed. "Except that if we don't get down to the stadium very soon, we're not going to get good seats for today's game."

"Right," Ally agreed. "Let's talk about it after the game."

"Fine," Holly conceded.

"Time to rise and shout!" Shaylan yelled as they hurried to their rooms to get ready.

Ally hurried to brush her teeth and find her BYU hoodie. "It's going to feel good to relax and have fun after everything that happened with Scott," she told her reflection as she straightened the ponytail in her hair. It still hurt to think about him, and she had even considered calling him a time or two, but she had heard the finality in his voice. Now that he knew the truth about her, he didn't want to be with her. She wasn't going to beg.

It was, however, way past time to tell Shaylan and Holly about Hope. Although LDS Family Services had birth mother meetings in Provo that she could go to, Ally had been unable to fit them into her busy schedule of work and school. She still kept in touch a little with some of the birth moms from her group back home, but it would be nice to be able to talk about something that was such a big part of her life to her new best friends. Ally didn't think they would judge her too harshly or belittle her decision to give Hope a family.

They were planning on going out to dinner after the football game. That would be a good time to tell them. It would be great to stop feeling like she was hiding this from them. She wasn't ashamed of her past and it was time to get it out in the open. Yes, definitely tonight.

They arrived five hours before the stadium gates were going to open, only to find that hundreds and hundreds of other students had also lined up early to get the best seats possible. Now Ally was glad that they had brought the blankets to sit on while they waited. Holly laughed. "Just like we expected."

Shaylan nodded. "Yep. Oh well, hanging out here will be half the fun of going to the games."

They folded their blankets and arranged them at the back of the line, saying hello to the group of girls seated in front of them. The girls nodded politely but went right back to their game of Phase 10, so Ally, Shaylan, and Holly settled into a little circle and left the other girls to their game.

"So," Holly began, looking pointedly at Ally. "What happened with you and Scott?"

Shaylan laughed at the look of shock on Ally's face. "Smooth, Holly. Real smooth."

"Well?" Holly continued, never looking away from Ally's face. "You said you were ready to talk about it."

Shaylan touched Ally's knee. "We've been worried about you, that's all."

"I actually do want to talk," Ally began, "but not here." She looked around. "There are too many people." Holly raised a curious eyebrow. "Basically, I told Scott some things about me that he—" Ally's voice cracked and she tried to swallow the lump in her throat. "Some things that he couldn't handle. When he realized that he would never marry me, he ended it." Ally shrugged and wiped the moisture that had appeared in her eyes.

"I'm sorry, Ally," Shaylan said. "I know how much you liked him."

"But what on earth could you have told him?" Holly asked. "It was clear how much he liked you."

Two guys joined the end of the line and smiled down at Ally, Shaylan, and Holly. "I'll tell you all about it later today," Ally said. "Now's not the time." She jerked her head in the direction of the new arrivals before grabbing the deck of UNO cards that Holly was fiddling with and starting to deal.

A few minutes later, one of the guys sitting behind them pulled two boxes of mini powdered sugar donuts out of his bag and tapped Ally on the shoulder. "Do you girls want some donuts?" he asked.

"No thanks," Ally replied. "I never eat donuts without milk."

"You're in luck, then," he said opening a little cooler that Ally hadn't noticed. "It just so happens that *I* never eat donuts without milk, so I came prepared." He smiled as he displayed his disposable cooler full of individual plastic bottles of milk, packed in ice. "They're ice cold," he continued. "Besides, we wouldn't feel right about eating in front of three beautiful ladies."

"Unless you were joining us," his friend added.

Shaylan laughed. "Okay, you talked us into it."

Ally shot a withering glance at Shaylan. She wasn't in the mood to make small talk with two random guys. But she did love powdered sugar donuts, so she reached in the box and grabbed two when it was passed to her. She was just about to pop one in her mouth when the instigator reached out his hand. "I'm Riley," he said.

Allison finally looked up and met his eyes. They were a deep, bright green, which was a stark contrast to his almost-black hair that somehow looked messy and very put together all at once. If she hadn't just gone through everything with Scott, Ally would have admitted to herself that she was attracted to him. As it was, she just balanced the donuts on her knee and shook his hand. "I'm Allison." She released his hand quickly and motioned to her friends. "This is Shaylan and Holly." Riley shook each of their hands and then introduced his friend as Damon.

Ally ate her donuts and cracked open a bottle of milk, content to let Shaylan and Holly take the lead on the conversation. She found that Riley was from Salt Lake City, just forty miles to the north. Damon was from somewhere in Tennessee. The two had met when they were companions on their missions to Sydney, Australia. They had come home two years ago within three months of each other and had been roommates ever since.

When Riley said that he had been a three-time state champion wrestler, Ally took notice of his broad shoulders and muscled arms. "So why are you here when BYU doesn't even have a wrestling program?" Holly asked.

"Well, I actually had a wrestling scholarship to Oklahoma, and I wrestled there a year before my mission." Shaylan looked impressed. Ally knew that Shaylan's brothers had wrestled; apparently Oklahoma was a good place to be a wrestler.

"So what happened?" Shaylan asked.

"Well, in my first match at the NCAA Tournament I got caught in a throw and landed funny. It tore my shoulder up pretty bad." He rubbed his left shoulder. "I already had my mission call and was planning on being gone for the next two years, so I had surgery on my shoulder, left on my mission, and decided to see what happened when I got home."

In spite of herself, Ally was listening now. Riley noticed her watching him and smiled at her before continuing. "Anyway, after being away from wrestling for a couple years, I realized that I didn't really miss it." He shrugged. "So I decided that if I didn't miss it, then there was no reason to devote so much time and energy to it." He laughed and popped a whole mini donut in his mouth. "Besides, now I can eat donuts whenever I want."

Everyone laughed with him, but Ally happened to catch Riley's gaze, and something about the look in his eye made her wonder if there was more to the story than that. *Why do you care?* She thought to herself. *As soon as we get through this line, you'll never see him again, anyway.*

They all ate a few more donuts, and even though Ally kept quiet and tried to ignore Riley and Damon, before long Shaylan had invited the boys to join them for a game of UNO. Riley squeezed in between Ally and Shaylan, and Damon settled himself on Shaylan's other side, between her and Holly. After a few hands, everyone was laughing and having fun. Even Ally had let her guard down and playfully punched Riley's arm when he played a Draw Four on her.

When the stadium gates opened, they put away the cards and gathered up the blankets they had been sitting on. Ally had enjoyed herself, but she would be glad to get into the game and away from Riley and Damon. It had been fun to hang out with them for a few hours, but there was no way she wanted anything to do with stupid boys right now. Not after the way things had ended with Scott.

Ally was jolted from her thoughts when she heard Holly say, "Hey, you guys should sit with us during the game!"

"Yeah," Shaylan agreed. "That would be fun."

"Hmm," Riley said, wrinkling his forehead in mock concentration. "Damon and I go to the game by ourselves, or with three fun, cute girls? That's a no-brainer!"

Damon was smiling, and a dimple appeared in his smooth, chocolate-toned cheek. "Sounds good to me."

"Ally?" It was Riley and he was looking straight at Ally with those emerald eyes. "Is that okay with you?"

"Me?" Ally tried to make her voice sound light and carefree. "I don't care." She was afraid it came out annoyed. "You guys do whatever you want."

Riley looked at her carefully while Holly gave her a discreet pinch on the arm, and a look that said, *Be nice.*

"If you're sure . . . ," Riley said, letting the question trail off.

"Of course she's sure," Holly interjected. "It'll be great!"

Ally forced a smile and nodded. Just because she wasn't interested in dating didn't mean that Shaylan and Holly couldn't have some fun.

The line moved pretty quickly once the gates were open, and before long Ally, Shaylan, Holly, Riley, and Damon were crowding onto the bleachers of LaVell Edwards Stadium. Ally took a deep breath. She'd forgotten how much she loved the smell of a football field. Unfortunately, that thought reminded her of Brandon, and how he was the reason she wasn't with Scott. Suddenly, all of the fun was gone from the afternoon. She ducked her head and could hardly bring herself to even watch the game. To make matters worse, every time she looked up, she noticed Riley watching her. His intent gaze unnerved her.

At the start of the fourth quarter, Ally couldn't take it anymore. She stood and brushed her way past her friends mumbling something about seeing them later at home. She almost made it out of the stadium before the tears arrived.

Holly and Shaylan arrived home to find Ally wrapped in a quilt on the couch staring blankly at some old movie she'd turned on.

"Sorry about today," Shaylan said.

Ally looked up. "It's okay. Not your fault, anyway." Ally shook her head. "I guess I'm still trying to work through everything." Shaylan and Holly looked miserable. Ally didn't want to be the reason they had a bad day. She squared her shoulders and smiled. "Did you guys have fun, though?"

Shaylan laughed and Holly blushed. "Holly did. Damon couldn't take his eyes off her. He's obviously interested."

"Do you really think so?" Holly squealed.

"Absolutely," Shaylan said.

"I hope so. With that curly black hair and those big brown eyes . . ." Holly sighed.

"He's *so* dreamy," Shaylan finished for her. Holly's face flushed crimson. "Come on," Shaylan continued. "You know you were thinking it."

Holly cleared her throat. "He was fun to be with and we had a great conversation." Shaylan eyed her closely. Holly couldn't contain a giggle. "And he *is* so dreamy!" Even Ally let a laugh escape at that. Holly ducked her head and put a hand on her burning cheek. "Do you really think I've got a shot with him?"

"Well, you've got the rest of football season to find out," Shaylan said.

"What do you mean?" Ally asked.

Shaylan glanced around the room, and finally Holly spoke. "We invited them to sit with us at the next game too." She reached out and put a hand on Ally's shoulder. "I really want to get to know Damon better, but I want you to come and have fun too." Ally looked up at her friend. "Pretty please?" Holly said, batting her eyelashes.

"Fine." Ally laughed. "I'll make the best of it."

"Oh good," Holly said. She turned to Shaylan. "Now you can give her the leftover pizza. Are we forgiven?"

Shaylan handed Ally a pizza box. Ally thought about being upset that they went out to dinner without her, but *she* had been the one to leave. Plus, pizza from The Brick Oven was her favorite.

"You're forgiven," Ally said. "I can't ever stay mad at you." She opened the box and ate a couple slices while Holly recapped all of the times that Damon had touched her shoulder or leaned over to whisper in her ear.

"They do seem like good guys," Ally admitted. *Then again, Scott seemed fabulous, and that ended up being a disaster,* she added in her mind.

Shaylan must have noticed the cloud roll across Ally's face and spoke up. "But you didn't get the chance to talk to us about Scott. Do you still want to?"

Ally glanced at Holly. She didn't want to put a damper on her excitement, but she was ready to get all of this out in the open. It was beginning to feel like she was hiding Hope from her two best friends. "Are you both sure you want to get all serious right now?" Ally asked, looking at Holly. "Because there's more to this than just me and Scott breaking up."

"Yes," Holly answered without hesitating. "The floor is all yours."

Ally smiled at Holly and then looked to Shaylan, who nodded. "We're sure," she said.

"Okay." Ally took a deep breath and fished something out of her purse. "It mostly has to do with the friends I go visit in American Fork."

Shaylan and Holly exchanged a confused glance. Ally noticed their puzzled expressions and said a silent prayer that these two girls were still her friends at the end of this discussion. She thought about her "I can do hard things" necklace that was tucked under her shirt at the moment and forged ahead.

Ally handed Holly the photo with tattered edges that she had just removed from her purse. "This is Michael, Olivia, and Hope Spencer."

"Cute family," Holly said, passing the picture to Shaylan. She nodded her agreement, and then Ally noticed Shaylan's eyes lingering on Hope's face. Even at two and a half years old, and although her eyes were a different color and her hair was curlier, Hope's features looked a lot like Ally's.

Ally knew from past experience that it would be easier to get this out quickly now that she had started. "So it's kind of a long story, but the short version is that during high school I was best friends with a guy named Brandon." Ally was pleased to realize that she could say his name out loud without feeling much pain. "Looking back, I can see that he was my boyfriend, although we never really thought of each other in those terms."

Shaylan nodded and handed the photo back to Ally, who smiled down at Hope's little face before continuing. "Anyway, on graduation night, one thing led to another and we ended up sleeping together." Holly's head snapped up, but Ally continued without giving her a chance to speak. "It just happened that one time, but once was all it took." Ally took a breath and turned so that she could see both her friends' faces. "I got pregnant."

Ally looked carefully at Shaylan and Holly, and although she saw shock and surprise in their eyes, and maybe a little sadness, there didn't seem to be any anger. "Anyway, Brandon was headed to California on a football scholarship, and he didn't want anything to do with a baby." She tucked a stray hair behind her ear. "After their initial shock, my parents were pretty supportive, and for most of my pregnancy I planned to raise my baby myself. I loved her before she was even born, and I knew that I was willing to make any sacrifice necessary to take care of her."

Holly and Shaylan hadn't moved. They were watching Ally closely, but Ally couldn't read their emotions. She just needed to finish her story. "The hardest day of my life was when I realized that the sacrifice she really needed from me was going to be the most difficult to give. She needed a mom *and* a dad who were sealed in the temple. So I decided to place her for adoption and give her a family." Ally nodded her head. "I can't speak for others, but it was definitely the right decision for me and for the baby girl I gave birth to.

"I was never planning on coming to BYU," she continued, "but after lots of meetings with my bishop and lots of prayer and soul searching I was ready to put my life back together, and BYU seemed to be the answer." The words were tumbling out now. This was the first time Ally had retold the whole story—from beginning to end—in one sitting, and it actually felt good. "I didn't know how much contact I wanted with Michael and Olivia, but they invited me and my parents to come to the temple sealing and it was amazing, so now I visit them almost every month. It's nice to see what a great family they are, and how Hope is thriving."

Ally finished and sat quietly, deciding to give Shaylan and Holly a chance to digest the information before anything else was said. It was Holly who finally broke the silence.

"Wow, Ally, thanks for telling us that. I always knew you were a good person, but I never knew how strong you are."

Shaylan was nodding her head, and to Ally's surprise, tears were filling Shaylan's dark brown eyes, making them shine. "You know my older sister Jasmine?"

"I remember you talking about her," Ally said. "She's, what, ten years older than you?"

"Thirteen," Shaylan said, wiping her eyes. "She's the oldest and I'm the baby of the family."

"That's right. I remember," Ally replied.

"Well, about fifteen years ago, Jasmine got pregnant and placed her baby boy for adoption. Adoptions were mostly closed back then, though." Shaylan stood and walked to the little bookshelf in the corner of their living room and grabbed a couple of tissues from the box on the shelf. "She still gets a letter and pictures once a year," she said, wiping her nose.

Ally barely kept her jaw from dropping, and then she felt tears coming to her own eyes, tears of gratitude for having been led to two such amazing friends who were loving and supportive and understanding.

"I never knew that, Shaylan," Holly said, sitting down in between her friends and putting an arm around each of them.

Shaylan handed Ally a tissue and she dabbed at the moisture leaking from her eyes. "I'll bet that was hard on you," Ally said. "I know my little sisters didn't handle it very well."

Shaylan nodded. "I wasn't very old, and I just didn't understand, you know?" They sat quietly for a few minutes, glad for the silent companionship.

"So have you seen Brandon since Hope was born?" It was Holly that broke the silence.

"Yes, and it actually went really well." Ally went to throw her soggy tissue in the trash can. "He told me he was sorry, and that he was glad I made the decision that I had. He even kept a picture of Hope." She sat back down next to Holly. "He's back in California now. He doesn't want to meet Hope yet, but he's glad to know she's happy and healthy."

"Do you still talk to each other?" Shaylan asked.

"No, not really. I mean, I could find out how to get in touch with him if I needed to, but we decided it was better not to have too much to do with each other." She shrugged. "We need to move forward, not keep looking back."

Holly's face suddenly dropped and she let out a gasp. The other two looked at her, surprised. "So did you tell Scott about Hope and that's why it didn't work out?"

"Oh yeah," Ally said. "I forgot this whole thing started with talking about Scott." Shaylan stood up and wiped her face with one more tissue, then threw the whole moist bundle she was holding into the trash.

Ally related the story of all that had happened at the fondue restaurant, from Scott laughing about the girl who was pregnant to Ally storming out and the long, miserable drive home.

"Maybe you should have told him," Shaylan said. "You know, given him the chance to rethink his opinions."

"He might have realized how wrong he is," Holly added.

"I did tell him," Ally replied. "He came over the next morning and we tried to talk things out, but when I told him that I had been in the same situation as that girl, he started yelling and telling me how I'd been putting on an act." Ally stopped and buried her face in her hands. She was crying again. "Then he told me good-bye and left." The words came out muffled through her fingers.

"Sorry," Shaylan said.

"Yeah. That's terrible," Holly agreed.

Ally looked up. "The worst part is," Ally began and then hesitated.

"What?" Shaylan and Holly asked together.

"Well . . . I guess . . . in some small way . . ." Ally's voice trailed off. The other two girls just waited for her to continue. "In a small way, I can kind of see his point. It was a stupid mistake, and I *did* know better." She shrugged. "I think any good guy would react the same way that Scott did." An awkward pause followed this admission.

"Ally . . ." Shaylan broke the silence, her voice much softer than usual. "You are an amazing person. It's like you told Scott. We all make mistakes, and none of us are perfect. You've felt the hope and love and forgiveness of the only One who can truly judge—our Savior. Now you need to forgive yourself."

"So I hear," Ally said with a self-deprecating laugh.

"Jasmine really struggled with that for a long time," Shaylan said. "And she had to forgive herself and move forward before she found any lasting happiness. And I learned, from watching her, that one of the miracles of the Atonement is that besides forgiveness, peace is also possible." She hugged Ally. "You've experienced forgiveness, now let yourself experience peace."

Ally nodded. "Thanks, guys. Thanks for being my friends." The words didn't seem to be enough to express all she was feeling, but when Ally saw the smiles and shining eyes of her two friends, she knew that they understood.

CHAPTER SIX

The next home football game of the season was a late afternoon game, and even though the September evenings had started to get cool, the sun was still out and it was pleasant as Ally and Shaylan walked from their apartment to LaVell Edwards Stadium. Holly and Damon were out for lunch before getting in line for the game and would be meeting them there. They had been out a couple of times already, and their relationship seemed to be moving along.

Ally and Shaylan settled into the line and, within minutes, Holly and Damon joined them. Riley arrived shortly after, and Ally was content to sit back and watch everything going on around her. She stayed out of the conversation but couldn't help but smile as the line started moving and they flooded into the stadium. As Ally walked out into the late afternoon sunshine, saw the team out on the field warming up, smelled the freshly cut grass mingled with popcorn, and felt the nearly palpable energy of the players and fans, she felt her heart quicken. She really did love football, and she was going to choose to have fun. Scott may have ruined her chances at having a relationship, but she was not going to let him ruin football season for her. For some reason this thought made her giggle, and Shaylan looked at her quizzically. "It's going to be a fun game," was all Ally said.

As they squeezed into their seats, Riley positioned himself to be sitting next to Ally. He smiled at her. She hadn't really looked at him all day because she didn't want to accidentally see that unnerving stare he'd given her last home game, but now as she really noticed him, she was reminded of how cute he was. His dark green eyes were sparkling as he sat down next to her, and by the way his shoulders filled out the navy thermal shirt he was wearing, she could definitely tell that he had been an elite college athlete. She smiled but then caught herself. *You're not going to get involved.*

"Good to see you again," Riley said with a smile. "Why are you trying so hard to ignore me? I promise I don't bite."

Ally felt her cheeks flush. "I'm not ignoring you," she lied. "Just excited about the game." She was saved from further conversation by fireworks and music that signaled the start of the game.

Before long, everyone was cheering and high-fiving. Ally couldn't remember the last time she'd had this much fun. At halftime, the Cougars were up by three points, thanks to a last minute drive and field goal.

Riley looked up and smiled at Ally's obvious excitement. "You look like you're having fun," he said, brushing his dark hair out of his eyes.

"I really am," Ally agreed. Her heart was still pumping from the adrenaline rush of the last score. Her cheeks were flushed and her eyes were shining. Her hair was spilling over the sides of the fuzzy blue headband she had slipped over her ears to keep them warm, and Riley couldn't keep his eyes off her.

"My dad loves college football, and I followed right in his footsteps," Ally said. "Actually, I love to watch *any* football."

"Oh, really?"

"Yeah," Ally said. "My best friend in high school was the star wide receiver and is playing college ball right now. I went to all of his games." *Oops. Too personal,* Ally scolded herself.

"Well, Ally," Riley began, "it might interest you to know that in addition to wrestling, I was also the quarterback for my high school football team."

"Were you really?" Ally couldn't tell if he was serious or just teasing her.

"Ouch, that hurt." Riley laughed. "Is it so hard to believe?"

Ally leaned back, appraising him with mock severity. "No, I suppose I can believe it, but I just couldn't tell if you were being serious or not."

"Well, believe," Riley said. "I still hold a few of the high school passing records for the state of Utah."

"So did you get recruited to play in college?"

"Actually," Riley said with a slight flush, "BYU tried to get me to come here." He shrugged. "I was also recruited by the University of Utah and Boise State University."

"What happened?"

"Well, my dad really wanted me to wrestle . . ."

"Oh, that's right," Ally said. "Oklahoma."

"Yeah, and when they offered a wrestling scholarship, I didn't feel like I could turn it down."

"But you didn't love wrestling in college?" Ally asked.

"Oh, I enjoyed it," Riley said. "It was a great experience, but one day I realized that I could take it or leave it, I didn't really care."

"So, why didn't you return to football after your mission?"

"Ah, now . . . that's what's known as 'the rest of the story.'" Riley looked down and brushed at an imaginary spot on his jeans.

"Hmm. I wondered if there was more to that story when you told it a few weeks ago."

"You were listening?" Riley asked with a laugh. "I thought you were too busy wishing we would go away and leave you alone."

Ally blushed. "Was I that obvious?"

"You kind of were," he admitted. "But when Damon saw Holly as we were walking up to the line, he insisted that he had to get to know her." He grinned. "I couldn't let him down."

"Well, I'm glad you didn't," Ally said. Riley raised an eyebrow. "Because it looks like Holly and Damon are off to a great start."

"What? Oh . . . yeah . . . I guess so," Riley spluttered.

"But you're changing the subject," Ally said. "What happened with football?"

The marching band had started their half-time performance out on the field, and without realizing it, Ally and Riley were leaning in closer to each other in order to make themselves heard.

"Well, I'm a leftie"—he wiggled the fingers of his left hand—"and I tore my left shoulder up pretty bad, and I skipped out on most of my rehab to head out on my mission."

The picture was forming in Ally's mind, and she found herself feeling sad for Riley.

"Anyway, when I got home and tried to start playing football again, my shoulder just couldn't handle it. I tried physical therapy for a while, but it became obvious that I wasn't going to be able to make it at the college level with a bad shoulder."

"Could you have gone back to Oklahoma and wrestled?"

"Oh, I don't know. Probably. I never really looked into it."

"I'm sorry, Riley," Ally said. "I'll bet that was really hard."

"I don't admit it very often," he said, "but it was. I was disappointed."

"So what did you do?"

"I got over it," Riley said matter-of-factly.

"Just like that?" Ally challenged.

"No, it took some time, but I felt good about coming here for school. I'm actually planning on going to law school, so this is a great place to be."

Ally thought about what Riley had told her as they silently watched the marching band finish their half-time show. As they were leaving the field, Ally spoke again.

"I'm surprised you come to the games."

"What?" Riley was caught off guard.

"I think it would be really hard to come and watch, knowing that you could've been the one out there that everyone was cheering for."

Riley smiled. "Yeah, I actually didn't come to the games that first year home from my mission."

"So you do have some human emotion in there, somewhere?" Ally teased.

"Of course." Riley said. "I was pretty mad, and I sat at home on Saturday afternoons feeling miserable."

Ally was nodding. "But after a while," Riley continued, "I decided that I could either lay around feeling sorry for myself, or I could move on with my life. I realized that if it was important in the overall plan for my life to play college football, I would be playing." He shrugged. "Apparently, my eternal progression didn't depend on me having that particular experience," he concluded with a laugh.

"And you've been coming to the games ever since?" Ally asked.

"Well, yeah." Riley answered. "I mean, I *love* football, and if I can't play, at least I can come watch and cheer." He shrugged. "Maybe someday I'll have a son that wants to play and I can help coach his team or something."

Ally realized that she was staring at him and scolded herself for being interested. It had been over six weeks since things had ended with Scott, and she hadn't so much as noticed another guy since then. She couldn't risk getting attached to Riley. Sure he had a great attitude about his own disappointments and trials, but he wouldn't understand Ally's, and she would just get hurt again.

When Ally resurfaced from her thoughts, she became conscious that Riley was watching her closely. He looked like he wanted to say something, but the third quarter had just started, and the BYU return man was making an awesome run. Ally just gave Riley a quick smile and then turned her attention to cheering. He followed her lead.

The truth was, Ally was hardly paying any attention to the game. She was much too focused on the reality of Riley's presence right next to her. She tried to ignore the way his shoulder felt pressing against hers, or the tingle that shot up her leg when Riley reached down for his drink and his fingers brushed against her pants.

It's no good, Ally kept reminding herself. *I'm not getting sucked in again.* She forced her mind back to the game. She was aware that Riley kept looking at her. Clearly he wanted to say something. At the end of the third quarter, he finally spoke.

"Hey, Ally?"

"Hmm?" Ally's eyes remained glued to the playing field, but her stomach was doing flips.

"I was just wondering if . . ." Riley paused and Ally jumped in, not wanting to hear what was coming next.

"What a game, huh?"

"What? Oh yeah." The light in Riley's eyes dimmed, but he tried to continue. "Anyway, maybe after the game . . ."

Ally faked a yawn and pretended like she hadn't heard. "These evening games sure wear me out. I can't wait to get home and climb into bed."

The yawn successfully smothered Riley's question, but Ally's heart groaned at the look of disappointment that he didn't quite manage to hide. Ally pulled the hood of her sweatshirt up over her head and tucked her neck down inside. Suddenly, the fun was gone, and she couldn't wait for the game to get over.

❧ ❧

The following week was an away game, but Holly had invited Damon and Riley over to their apartment to watch it. Ally answered their knock. Damon slipped inside to find Holly, leaving Riley and Ally standing together in the doorway. Ally tried not to look at Riley and she turned to head into the living room. Riley stopped her with a light touch on her arm.

He hesitated and then cleared his throat. "Look, Ally, I'm sorry if I made you uncomfortable last week at the game."

Ally was shaking her head, trying to dismiss this conversation. "Don't worry about it. It's not you—"

"Ouch." Riley chuckled softly. "The old 'it's not you, it's me' line." Ally blushed, but Riley pretended not to notice. "It's okay," Riley said, his emerald eyes forcing Ally to hold his gaze. "Let's not make this weird. I don't want it to be weird."

Ally was relieved. She did want to be friends with Riley. And it appeared they would be spending time together every Saturday through football season. They could at least have a good time together, even if she couldn't allow it to go any further. Ally nodded slightly, and now it was Riley's turn to look down.

"Just forget I tried to ask you out, okay?"

Ally forced a grin. She wanted to move past this. "Done."

Riley composed his face into a smile and looked up. "So . . . friends?"

"Friends," Ally agreed. "Now let's get in there before there isn't any pizza left for us."

⁂

"So it looks like everything turned out okay with Riley," Holly said after the boys had left.

Ally shrugged. "We're going to leave it at friends."

"Are you sure?" Shaylan pressed. "I thought I saw some sparks last week at the game." She grinned. "And even though he kept his distance today, he couldn't stop looking at you." Ally scolded herself for hoping that Shaylan's words were true. "There might have been a spark . . . last week," she admitted. "But you two know what's really going on. He wouldn't be interested if he knew about my history, so there's no use letting things start down a road that's just going to end with both of us hurting."

"You sound like you're trying to convince yourself," Holly suggested.

Ally shook her head. She was getting irritated.

"He clearly likes you," Shaylan added. "Just because Scott was a jerk doesn't mean that all guys will be."

"I just can't do it, okay?" Ally stood up and grabbed her purse off the counter. "I'm going to the store. We're almost out of milk. See you later."

The door slammed a little too loudly when Ally walked out.

CHAPTER SEVEN

Ally answered the door to find Riley and Damon bundled up against the flutters of snow coming down. "Come on in, guys," she said. "We're almost ready."

Ally shut the door behind them and briefly smiled at Riley before heading back to her bedroom to finish getting ready. They were heading to the fourth home football game of the season, and Ally, Holly, Shaylan, and the guys had fallen into an easy routine. Damon and Holly were solidly together, seeing each other every day. Since Riley was Damon's only roommate, and the three girls didn't see much of their other roommates, the five of them ended up doing quite a bit together.

Ally sat on her bed and slipped on a second pair of socks, before putting her brown snow boots on. She already had a pair of cotton leggings on underneath her jeans. She had been a little chilly at last week's game and wasn't taking any chances today. It wasn't quite Halloween, but it was already starting to feel like winter.

"Ready, Ally?" Shaylan hollered from the living room.

"Coming," Ally replied. She pulled her sweatshirt over her head, arranged the Cougar blue stocking cap down over her ears, and grabbed her coat, scarf, and gloves.

"Cute hat," Holly said as Ally walked into the room.

"Yeah," Riley added. "It looks good on you." He smiled. Ally felt the warmth creeping up her neck, and she dropped her glove so she would have an excuse to look down instead of at Riley. She was annoyed that her stomach got all fluttery when he smiled at her. They had gotten to be friends over the last couple months, but Ally couldn't afford to let it go further than that. She didn't want to be hurt again.

"Should we go?" Ally asked after picking up her glove.

"Definitely," Shaylan agreed. They walked out into the brisk air and headed toward the stadium. Holly and Damon lagged behind, absorbed in their own little world. Riley kept pace with Ally and Shaylan, but seemed content to keep quiet while they chatted about one of their upper division anatomy classes.

They arrived at the game and filed in with the rest of the students. Damon and Riley slipped into the men's room.

"Can I sit on the far end, please?" Ally asked, maneuvering past Shaylan and into the row first. "And you can sit next to me."

Shaylan grimaced at her.

"What?" Ally asked.

"I don't know why you keep trying so hard to stay away from Riley." Ally turned and glared at her. "Okay, so I do know why, but I think it's silly." Ally sat down in her spot but didn't respond. "He's an amazing guy, and it's so obvious how much he likes you."

"But he wouldn't if—"

Shaylan interrupted her and her voice was slightly raised. "Do NOT even say that he wouldn't if he knew about Hope."

Holly touched Shaylan's arm lightly. "I'm not sure that this is the best time to get into this," she said.

"Now's as good a time as any," Shaylan said. "I know that lately you only notice Damon." Shaylan smiled to soften her words. "So you don't see the way Riley looks at her like she's the most amazing person he's ever laid eyes on."

Ally blushed. "No, he doesn't."

"He most certainly does." Shaylan nodded emphatically. "And

you think he's not too shabby, either." Ally wanted to protest but couldn't. That part, at least, was true. "He likes you, Ally. A lot."

Ally opened her mouth, but Shaylan sat down and put a gloved finger on her lips. "And I think he always will, no matter what you tell him about your past."

They sat silently for a moment or two, before Ally burst out, "But what if he doesn't?"

Holly looked down, unable to find an answer, but Shaylan didn't waver. Her dark brown eyes bored into Ally's and she said, "Then he isn't worth having. Anyway, wouldn't it be better to know for sure than to miss out on something amazing because you were too scared to go for it?"

Ally's gaze was furious for a moment, and then it broke and she dropped her head. Shaylan had to lean close to hear her whispered words, "First Brandon, then Scott . . . I just don't think I can handle being rejected *again* any time soon."

Shaylan and Holly were spared a response by the arrival of Damon and Riley carrying five steaming cups of hot chocolate. Damon handed one to Holly and sat down next to her. Riley passed one to Shaylan. "Thanks," she said. He smiled but didn't sit down. After a slight hesitation, Shaylan slid over and made a spot for Riley between her and Ally. Ally didn't protest. She was trying to hide the emotion that had welled up in her eyes. Riley pretended not to notice while he sat down, and when Ally had control of herself, he handed her a cup of hot chocolate. As she reached for it, their gloved fingertips touched. Riley smiled and held onto her cup a moment longer than necessary. Their eyes met, and Ally wished that she wasn't thinking about how it would feel if their hands weren't covered by gloves.

Riley let go of her cup and took a sip from his own. "Should be a good game today."

Ally relaxed. She could talk football. "Yeah. A good option offense can be really tough to stop. BYU has had trouble with it in the past."

Riley nodded. "Yeah, but the past is just that. The past."

Ally was sipping her hot chocolate, and she nearly choked. "What?"

Riley looked at her curiously until her coughing subsided. "The past. None of that matters today." He took another sip and smiled. "That's the great thing about football. No matter what happened last week, or last month, or last year, it doesn't influence the outcome of today's game. It's all about how the players handle things today. Right now." He shrugged. "It's a fresh start every week."

The band started to play the Cougar fight song and Riley stood up to rise and shout with everyone else. Ally also stood, but her mind was reeling and she was glad that she had the hot chocolate as a distraction. She took a long sip and savored the way the warmth spread through her as she swallowed. Was Riley simply talking about football, or did he know more about Ally's situation than he was letting on? Ally ventured a glance at Shaylan who had overheard the conversation, but Shaylan shrugged and shook her head. She hadn't told him anything.

The game started and Riley showed no more signs of wanting to do any serious talking. In fact, he hardly said anything directly to her at all. They cheered when BYU played well, grumbled when things went wrong, and yelled when the officials made questionable calls, but they could easily have been two random people who happened to have seats next to each other in this giant stadium.

Ally chided herself for letting her imagination get the better of her sense, and for allowing Shaylan to put ideas into her head. Of course Riley had been talking about football with all that nonsense about the past not mattering and a fresh start. Shaylan was wrong about how he felt. Riley might have liked her at first, but she had shut him down, and he only thought of her as a friend now. And that's definitely all Ally wanted. She decided to quit stewing over every word and action and be friends. She tried to stop worrying about Riley's every move and motive, and to just enjoy the game.

With under a minute to go in the game, BYU was ahead by

four points and the defense stopped their opponent on a third and six. They had no choice but to go for it on fourth down, and the crowd went crazy. Everyone was stomping their feet and yelling. In the midst of the student section, Ally and Riley joined in on the jumping up and down and cheering at the top of their lungs.

The ball was snapped and the quarterback started running. He faked a pitch, but none of BYU's defensive players were fooled, and they sacked him for a loss. The game was over! The entire stadium erupted, and in the celebration, the guy seated behind Ally lost his balance and almost fell, catching himself against Ally's shoulder. His elbow smacked the back of her head, and Ally saw stars. The force knocked her into Riley, and their momentum forced them to the bench. Ally landed right in Riley's lap where he caught her and wrapped his arms around her protectively.

The embarrassed offender mumbled an apology that Ally barely heard. She felt her face warm as Riley studied every inch of her face. She couldn't bring herself to move.

"Are you okay?" he whispered.

She started to answer, but the words caught in her throat. His eyes were so sincere, so caring that she could almost believe that he was interested in her, and more important, still would be—even if he knew about Hope. Almost.

Her heart pounding, Ally tried to sit up. Riley loosened his arms a bit, but didn't let her go. "Is your head okay?"

Not trusting her voice, Ally just nodded. She pulled her gaze away from Riley's face and realized that everyone in the immediate area was watching her.

"Are you sure, Ally?" Shaylan said, frowning. "That looked bad."

"It's okay," Ally said. "I'm fine." She made a quick movement to sit up and found her nose inches from Riley's. He didn't move away. Instead, he slowly traced one hand up Ally's back, finally pulling her stocking cap off. His fingers moved through her hair as he gently found the lump forming on the back of her head.

The bleachers were as crowded as ever and the celebrating

continued all around them, but everyone disappeared as Ally absorbed the feel of his hands in her hair. "You'd better get some ice on this," he said. Ally nodded but couldn't find her voice. He searched her face for several more seconds before Ally cleared her throat and pulled away. Riley dropped his hand and passed Ally her hat. She quickly put it on and pushed her way through the mass of people, disappearing before Riley knew what was happening.

CHAPTER EIGHT

Olivia was busy putting all of the Halloween decorations away. She always went all out for Halloween, but not in the scary, haunted house way some of their neighbors did. She thought their decorations were cool, and definitely scary, but she liked more of a fun fall look with cute bats, witches, and jack-o'-lanterns. Hope agreed and had been carrying several of the decorations around for the past week playing with them. One witch, in particular, had become a favorite and now everything was packed except for it.

"No! I won't put her away!"

Olivia sighed. Hope would be three in a couple of months, but right now she was in the middle of the terrible twos. It seemed that everything was a fight these days.

"Sorry, Hope. Halloween is over and it's time to put her away until next year."

Hope clung tightly to the glass witch. "No!" Olivia reached down to take it from her and Hope jumped away shouting, "No, no, no, no, no!"

"Hope!" Olivia's raised voice caught Hope's attention, and Olivia scooped her daughter up and tried to pry the witch out of her hands.

"Mommy, no!" Hope squealed again and jerked her hand

back. The witch flew out of both of their hands and crashed onto the tile kitchen floor, exploding to pieces.

Hope started to cry as she yelled, "You broke her, Mommy!" Olivia fought her own tears back as she carried Hope down the hall to her bedroom. She set Hope down in her crib and said, "You need to wait here until I get that mess cleaned up."

Hope flopped down on her belly and started to cry even louder.

Olivia walked out of the room and stood staring at the shattered witch before bending over to pick up a few of the bigger pieces of glass. One of the pieces pierced Olivia's finger and she let go of it as a large drop of blood appeared. It didn't hurt, but it was more than she could take. Olivia grabbed a paper towel to wrap her finger in and sat down on the living room couch. She put her face in her hands and started to cry.

"No wonder God won't give me any more children. I can't even handle the one little girl I have."

They had been trying to adopt again for over two years now, and it was hard to be patient. A couple of her friends who had had babies around the same time Hope was born had already gotten pregnant and given birth again. Olivia was really working at being happy for them.

From the very first time Olivia held Hope in her arms, she'd known they were meant to be a family, and she loved her more than she had ever dreamed possible. It was also harder being a mom than she ever imagined, and she was starting to wonder if her parenting flaws were the reason that they weren't being blessed with another child. The fact that she had no control over the number of children in her family and when—or if—they might arrive was hard to swallow, and it made these moments of tears and tantrums that much more difficult.

"Mommy! You coming?" Hope yelled from her bedroom.

Olivia took a deep breath and wiped the blood from her finger. "Just a minute, Hope," she called. She found the broom and swept the glass into a pile, but she couldn't seem to stop her tears. As she dumped the witch rubble into the trash can she said, "I'm doing the best I can. That's all I can do." Then she washed her hands, wiped her eyes, and headed down the hallway to try again.

ↀ ↀ

A few days later Olivia was sitting on the couch reading a story to Hope when the phone rang. She reached over and answered the phone off the end table.

"Hello?"

"Hi, Olivia. This is Alex Tucker."

"Oh, hi Alex." Alex was their adoption attorney, but she couldn't imagine why he would be calling her. "What's up?"

"To be honest, Olivia, I'm not sure if it's anything."

"Ooo-kay . . ." *What does that mean?*

"Well, I met a young woman this morning who is planning to place her baby."

Olivia's heart jumped to her throat.

"But," Alex continued, "I don't know whether you and Michael would be interested."

Olivia swallowed hard and managed a reply. "What's the situation?"

"Well, she's from Chicago, and she is working with the Child's Heart adoption agency."

"Okay." Olivia had heard of them. They were a reputable agency.

"Apparently she was in rough shape in Chicago. She has a toddler who is currently in foster care, and she's trying to get him back, but she has to prove that she can provide for him." Olivia remained silent, so he continued. "She has to have an apartment and a place for him to sleep and a few things. Anyway, she's afraid that if she tries to raise the baby she's carrying, she'll never be able to do what the judge is asking, and not only will she not get her son back, but they'll also take the baby. So she chose a couple for her baby girl out here and is asking for living expenses for a few months to help her get back on her feet."

"Can we give her living expenses?" Olivia asked.

"Yes," Alex answered slowly, "but I would recommend getting it all approved by a judge." He cleared his throat. "She seems a little . . . unstable."

"What do you mean?"

"I would just caution you that—should you get involved—to go one hundred and ten percent by the book. By law, you are allowed to help with living expenses, even for several months after she gives birth, but be sure to get every expense approved by a judge so that she can't come back and say that you paid her for the baby. That could get a little sticky."

Olivia felt that he had sidestepped her question. "What do you mean she seems a little unstable?"

"When I met with her, she was extremely emotional and kept yelling at me, and she just keeps talking about her son, Joey."

"Okay." That didn't seem so weird for a girl in her situation. Then a thought struck Olivia. "But, wait, I thought you said that she picked a couple and that's why she's out here."

"She did," Alex answered.

"But then she didn't like them once she met them?" Olivia asked.

"No," Alex said and hesitated before answering further. "They decided they weren't interested in her baby."

"What?" Olivia couldn't believe that.

"Well . . ." Alex cleared his throat again. "Their exact words were, 'She's crazy. We don't want to take the chance that our baby will be crazy too.'"

"Whoa." It was all Olivia could think to say.

"Her social worker assured me that she is mentally stable." He paused. "Then I met her, and . . ." He left that sentence unfinished. "But, if you're interested, I can tell you which motel she's staying at, and you and Michael can meet her and make your own decision."

Olivia didn't hesitate. Alex was a great attorney and they'd known him for years, but Olivia knew he didn't often venture out of his own comfort zone. She wasn't worried about meeting this young woman. "We'd like to meet her. Let me get a pencil to write down the information."

❧ ❧

"What's her name again?" Michael asked Olivia as they exited the freeway in South Salt Lake. They were both nervous.

"Shanelle," Olivia responded.

"Shanelle, Shanelle," Michael repeated softly to himself. "I can remember that."

"Her social worker, Molly, said that she'll be expecting us."

Michael pulled into the nondescript motel that his GPS had guided him to. Its beat-up sign advertised room rates by the week or month. "Not exactly a four-star hotel," Michael noted.

"What did you expect?" Olivia asked.

Michael grunted, and then they were silent as they got out of the car and walked up the metal staircase to the door marked with a faded green number seven.

Olivia took a deep breath and whispered, "Here goes nothing."

Michael squeezed her arm, kissed her on top of the head, and then knocked on the door. They heard the rattle of a chain bolt being unfastened, and then the door opened a crack. Two dark brown, almost black, eyes peered up at them. They were beautiful, but . . . Olivia shuffled through her mind for the right word to describe them. Sad . . . scared . . . lonely. *Haunted,* she finally decided. When Shanelle swung the door open, Olivia was surprised at how young she was. Those eyes belonged in a much older body.

"Shanelle?" Olivia asked.

"Yeah," she answered.

"Hi," Olivia said. She almost reached out to shake Shanelle's hand but changed her mind at the last second and hugged her instead. This seemed to startle Shanelle initially, but to Olivia's surprise, she hugged her back. "My name is Olivia, and this is my husband, Michael."

Michael smiled and took the hand Shanelle offered him into both of his. "It's really nice to meet you."

"Yeah," she said again. Michael peeked into the motel room, but he couldn't see much. The curtains were closed and the lights were all off. In the glow of the TV, which seemed to be playing a soap opera, he could make out the bed and a door that must lead to the bathroom. The room was small, but looked clean. He could only see one chair pushed up against a small table that held a couple boxes of pop-tarts, a half-eaten loaf of bread, a jar of peanut butter, and a mostly empty bag of nacho cheese Doritos. If these groceries had been Shanelle's meals since she arrived here three days ago, she was probably ready for a change. Besides, Michael didn't want to sit stiffly on the edge of the bed for the entire visit.

"Do you girls want to go out for an early dinner?" he asked.

"Good idea, Michael," Olivia said, glad to have the silence broken. "Is that okay with you, Shanelle? Are you hungry?" Olivia added when Shanelle didn't respond.

With both Michael and Olivia looking at her, Shanelle finally spoke. "I ain't got no money," she mumbled.

"Our treat," Michael answered with a smile. "Do you need to get anything before we go?"

"Oh, well, okay," Shanelle stammered. "Naw, I don't need nothin' else." She stepped out of the room without turning off the TV and shut the door behind her.

"Don't you want a jacket?" Olivia asked, shivering a little in the cold November wind.

"I got my sweater," Shanelle said, buttoning a threadbare red sweater around her neck. It was too small to close over her very pregnant belly.

"Okay," Olivia answered. "Let's go."

As they drove to a Golden Corral that Michael had spotted on their way to the motel, Olivia tried to make small talk.

"So Molly tells me that you're from Chicago."

"Yep."

"And you're pregnant with a baby girl?"

"Yep. Least that's what the doctor told me."

"I'm sorry that things didn't work out with the other couple that you had chosen."

Shanelle shrugged without responding.

They rode in silence for a bit. Shanelle broke it. "You guys live in the city or on a farm?" she asked.

"We live in a city," Olivia answered. Michael saw Shanelle's reflection in the rearview mirror. She was disappointed.

"But it's a small city," he added. "Nothing like Chicago."

"Oh," was Shanelle's response.

A few more minutes of silence before Olivia decided to raise the question that was on her mind. "Are you still planning on placing your baby for adoption?"

"Course I am!" Shanelle shouted and Michael and Olivia both jumped. "Why else am I still sittin' out here when I need to be home tryin' to get my baby boy back!"

"Would you like to tell us about him?" Olivia calmly asked, thinking how glad she was to have dropped Hope off at her friend Heather's house before they came.

Shanelle started crying. "Joey's daddy—his name's Benjamin—he's the only one who ever loved me, and when those guys killed him . . ." She was really wailing now. "All I have is Joey, and they took him from me just 'cause I's tryin' to get him some food."

Shanelle grabbed the back of Olivia's seat and leaned forward. "That's why I got to get some of what Molly calls *livin' expenses* so I can get us a apartment and a bed for Joey and some food." She was bobbing her head up and down. "Then they'll see I can take care o' him and they'll give him back. That's what the judge said."

Michael had pulled into a parking space at the restaurant and turned to look at Shanelle. "Are you only placing this baby to try and get some money?" he asked gently.

"No!" Shanelle shot back. "It ain't like that. Molly's already been through this with me. But I can't find a job an' a place to live an' take care of Joey an' take care of a baby." She leaned back in her seat and buried her face in her hands. Her sobs were loud enough that they remained unmuffled. "There ain't no future there anyhow. 'Specially not for a baby girl. She'll just end up like me if I keep her." She looked up and her eyes were pleading. "But I gotta get my Joey back. He's the best part of Benjamin and the only thing I got left." She wiped her nose on the sleeve of her tattered red sweater. "He's the only one who really loves me," she whispered.

"Okay," Olivia said, patting Shanelle's arm. "Let's go inside and get something to eat and talk about this."

Michael and Olivia didn't say much while Shanelle downed two big plates of pot roast, mashed potatoes and gravy, corn, and several rolls. She finished her third glass of milk, looked straight across the table at them, and then said, "Can you get me those livin' expenses so I can get Joey back?"

Olivia looked at Michael. She was so glad that they'd budgeted wisely and been saving money throughout their marriage so that they were in a position to move forward with this adoption if it felt right. Michael answered for both of them. "If we all decide that you placing your baby with us is the right thing to do, then yes, Shanelle, we could help out with some living expenses for a short time." Her eyes lit up and he continued, "Once a decision is made, then we can go before a judge and get it all approved."

Shanelle's eyes narrowed. "No judge. I thought you said you can get the money to me."

"I'm sorry, Shanelle," Michael continued. "We have to follow the law on this, and we *can* help you with living expenses, but it will have to be approved by a judge. Our attorney is certain there won't be any problem."

Shanelle leaned back and crossed her arms, suddenly suspicious. "No. I ain't gonna see no judge." She was shaking her head emphatically and the beads in her long black braids made a clicking noise.

"You wouldn't have to see the judge, Shanelle," Olivia explained. "We can take care of everything and the money would be put into an account that you could use to get back on your feet."

"No." Shanelle's voice was rising, and several people seated near them turned to look. "I gotta get my baby boy back, and there ain't no way I can do it 'less I get some money."

"We want to help you, Shanelle," Michael explained.

"Then leave them judges and lawyers outta this!" she wailed.

"We can't do that, Shanelle," Olivia added quietly.

"I'm out here all alone." Shanelle was just getting started. "I ain't got no one. I ain't talked to my momma in more'n a week. I just gotta get Joey back! That's what I need, and you just wanna take my baby and then have the judge tell me that there ain't no money for me."

Everyone within earshot had stopped eating and turned to watch the exchange.

"No, Shanelle." Michael remained calm. "We do *not* want to cheat you. We want to help you." Shanelle's sobs were carrying throughout the restaurant.

Olivia decided to change the subject. "It must be very difficult being out here, all alone, so far from your home and family."

Shanelle looked up but just shrugged. "My momma ain't much good at bein' a mom, but she's still mine."

"Does she know where you are?" Michael asked.

"Yeah." Shanelle wiped her eyes. "Least she know I came out to Utah. She don't know exactly where."

"Okay," Olivia said. "Why don't we all get some dessert, and then we'll get you in touch with your mom."

Shanelle nodded and wiped her eyes as she stood up to go to the dessert bar. Michael and Olivia followed, and the rest of the customers in the restaurant turned their attention back to their meals.

Thirty minutes later, the three of them were walking through Walmart. Olivia was pushing a shopping cart. They had already picked up a prepaid phone card with sixty minutes on it. When they left Golden Corral, Olivia had offered to let Shanelle use her cell phone, but Shanelle hesitated and Michael had wondered aloud if she wouldn't like to call her mom from the privacy of her own room. Shanelle quickly agreed, and so they drove to Walmart and found the phone cards.

Olivia stopped at the maternity section and began looking through a rack of coats. Olivia picked out two coats and held them out to Shanelle. "Which do you like better, the red or the blue?"

Shanelle stood looking stunned before finally answering, "The red."

"Good choice," Olivia agreed and put the coat in her shopping cart. She turned and headed toward the groceries, leaving Michael and Shanelle to follow behind.

"Is there a little fridge or microwave in your room, Shanelle?" Olivia asked over her shoulder. "I don't remember seeing one."

"Uh, yeah, there is. In the closet."

"Good." Olivia grabbed two quarts of milk and some string cheese before leaving the dairy aisle.

She went to the soup aisle and got six different kinds of soup that could be microwaved and eaten right out of the container they were in. She then moved on to the bread aisle and got another loaf of bread. She grabbed a little jar of jam to go with the peanut butter she had seen on the table in Shanelle's room and picked up a bag of apples as well.

Olivia hadn't said a word since asking about the fridge and microwave. After grabbing a couple of bottles of Gatorade and arranging them in the cart so they didn't smash anything, she looked up at Shanelle with a smile. "Is there anything else you need?"

Shanelle stood there with her mouth open. "Really?"

"Sure," Olivia said.

"Um, maybe . . . well, no," she finally answered. "This all for me?"

"Of course." Olivia reached out and touched Shanelle's arm. "Are you sure there's nothing else you could use?"

"Well, maybe, if it's okay, I . . ."

"Go ahead," Michael encouraged. "What do you need?"

"Well, I been out of deodorant for two days, and my toothpaste's almost gone."

"I should have thought of that myself," Olivia said. "Come on."

A stick of deodorant, a tube of toothpaste, and a new toothbrush later, they were standing in the checkout line. While Michael paid for the groceries, Olivia pulled Shanelle aside.

"We'll take you back to your room, and then why don't you call your mom and talk to her." Olivia put her arm around Shanelle's shoulder. "Take as long as you need to make a decision about what you are going to do, and then give us a call."

"Okay, thanks."

Michael walked up to them carrying several bags. Olivia took the one that clearly held the new red coat. She took the coat out, carefully pulled off the tags, and handed it to Shanelle. She slipped her arms into the plush sleeves and smiled when she was able to zip it up over her belly. Shanelle's eyes filled with tears and she hugged Olivia. "Thanks so much," she whispered.

"Well, what do you think about her?" Michael asked as they drove home.

"She's not crazy," Olivia said. "She's a scared kid who's far away from home and just wants to get her little boy back."

Michael was nodding. "I'm glad that's how you saw it too." He reached over and put his hand on her knee. They rode in silence for several moments. To Olivia's surprise, Michael's voice was full of emotion when he spoke again.

"I met a few girls like Shanelle while I was serving in Detroit on my mission."

"What do you mean?" Olivia asked.

"Oh, just the big emotions and the loud opinions and the wailing and the drama." He swallowed hard. "She's not crazy. Life has kicked her down one too many times and she's just surviving the only way she knows how."

Olivia nodded. They drove on, and Olivia saw Michael swallow a few more times, trying to push back the unexpected emotion. She broke the silence a few minutes later.

"I guess I can see how someone *could* feel that way, though." Olivia suppressed a chuckle. "Did you see the looks we were getting in the restaurant when she started yelling?"

Michael laughed right out loud. "Yeah, I'm sure most of the people in there thought we were trying to buy her baby."

"Well, they'll all have a good story to tell when they get home." Olivia was laughing hard now, partly at the memory and partly in relief that the night had gone as well as it had. Michael kept laughing too.

"Maybe going to meet a potential birth mom was more stressful than I was willing to admit," Michael said when their laughter had finally subsided.

"You know, she's due in three weeks," Olivia said softly. She took a deep breath at the reality of what could happen. She squeezed Michael's hand that still rested on her knee. "It's very possible that in three weeks, we'll be welcoming a second daughter into our family." They both smiled the rest of the way home.

CHAPTER NINE

Olivia called Shanelle the next day to see how she was doing and if she needed anything. Shanelle mentioned that it had been good to talk to her mom for a few minutes but remained tight-lipped about how the conversation had gone. She thanked Olivia again for the night before and then told her she'd be making a decision about what she was going to do by Friday.

Olivia hung up the phone. It was only Wednesday morning, so she was just going to have to wait. Shanelle hadn't been overly friendly on the phone, but she hadn't seemed distant, either. On the one hand, they had had a great evening with Shanelle and seemed to have made a connection. Also, Shanelle's original pick for adoptive parents had turned her down. She might be concerned about finding another couple who was interested. On the other hand, Olivia kept reminding herself, an adoption is never a done deal until the final paperwork is signed.

Olivia sighed loudly. She would just have to keep the butterflies swarming around her insides at bay for a couple more days while she waited and hoped and wondered if their family was about to get bigger.

Friday morning finally arrived. Michael was spending the day at home in case they got any news. He was up in Hope's bedroom, pretending to be a bucking bronco while she tried to ride on his back, when the phone rang. Olivia ran to answer it and heard the laughter that was coming from upstairs subside as Michael obviously paused to hear Olivia's side of the conversation. She took a deep breath and noticed that her hands were shaking as she answered the phone.

"Hello?"

"Olivia?"

"Yes, Shanelle, it's me," Olivia answered. The blood was pounding so loudly through her ears that she had to really concentrate to hear what Shanelle was saying.

"I talked to Molly on Wednesday and again yesterday."

"Okay . . . ," Olivia said, unsure how to respond.

"I just wanna tell you . . ." Shanelle hesitated. "I wanna say thanks for all you did for me the other night."

"It was our pleasure, Shanelle," Olivia responded.

"Um . . ." Shanelle stopped and this time Olivia waited for her. "Well, see, Molly found some people in some little town named after a animal . . . Beaver, I think she said. An' they've been wantin' a baby for a long time now an' they live on a farm." She paused as if this should explain everything.

Olivia's mind started to swirl as she realized what Shanelle was trying to tell her. She stumbled to the couch and sat down.

"See, that's the whole reason I came all the way out here to start with," Shanelle plunged on when Olivia hadn't responded. "I'm from the city and there ain't no good for girls like me in a city." Words were just tumbling out now. "Cities jus' don't take care of girls like me an' like this baby. But I just thought if she could be in the country. Raisin' animals an' growin' vegetables. Least if you're growin' them you always got somethin' to eat." She chuckled nervously. "Anyway, they wired some money for a bus ticket and I'm leavin' this afternoon. Just got a doctor appointment to make sure it's okay for me to ride a few hours on the bus.

Then I'll be headin' down there to have this baby and goin' home to get my Joey back." Shanelle slowed down a bit. "I'm real sorry, Olivia. Real sorry." Michael had appeared at the top of the stairs and when he saw Olivia wipe her eyes and shake her head, he came down and put his arm around her.

Shanelle stopped talking again, and Olivia realized that she was waiting for a response. She sat silent, trying to think of something to say. When she finally opened her mouth, the words surprised her.

"Shanelle, do you have a ride to your doctor's appointment? Or to the bus station?"

"No, I'm gonna find a local bus schedule. Molly said it'll only be a couple dollars." Then more quietly, "That's all I got." Olivia could hear the scared teenage girl behind the forced bravado.

"What time is your appointment?"

"It's in a hour an' a half."

"I'll be there in forty-five minutes," Olivia responded. "I'll take you to your appointment and make sure you get to your bus." Shanelle started to protest, but Olivia said, "I'll see you soon," and hung up.

Olivia buried her head in Michael's shoulder and cried. Hope toddled down the stairs having grown tired of waiting for Michael to return. "What's wrong, Mommy?"

Olivia looked up and Michael handed her a tissue off the end table to wipe her nose. "Oh, Mommy's just a little sad right now, Hope," Olivia answered. "But I'll be okay soon."

"I can help you feel better, Mommy," Hope said. She climbed up, threw both arms around Olivia's neck, and planted a slobbery kiss on her nose. Olivia couldn't help but laugh.

"Thank you, sweet girl. That did make me feel better."

Hope beamed at her parents, and Michael said, "Head on upstairs, and I'll be up in just a minute to play Candy Land with you."

"Ya-a-a-a-y-y-y-y!" Hope squealed as she ran up the stairs as fast as her little preschool legs would take her.

Michael and Olivia both smiled at their daughter, and then Michael turned to face his wife. "Are you okay?"

Olivia sniffed, "I will be. You?" He nodded and wiped some moisture from his own eyes.

"You never cease to amaze me, Livvy. You know that?"

"Oh, really?" she asked with a grin.

"Why did you decide to do it?"

Olivia didn't have to ask what he was talking about. "She just sounded so scared and alone, and I thought—" Olivia's eyes filled with tears and her voice broke. "And I thought, 'What if it was Hope?' And I knew that I would want someone to help her, so . . ." Olivia cried silently for a minute and then wiped her eyes again. "She's somebody's baby girl," she added softly.

"I don't think that you being there will make her change her mind," Michael gently reminded.

"It won't," Olivia said matter-of-factly. "That's not why I'm going." She stood up and took her purse from the kitchen counter. "I'm going because," her voice wavered, but didn't crack, "because she needs help, and I need to help her."

"You're amazing, Olivia Ann," Michael said, taking her in his arms. He squeezed her tightly and then pulled back to look into her eyes. "And I love you more every single day." He kissed her softly on the lips. "Take your time. Hope and I will be here having a Candy Land tournament." He smiled and kissed her again.

"Thanks, Michael. I love you too."

Olivia pulled into the motel parking lot and offered a silent prayer that she could make it through the day before knocking, once again, on the faded number seven door.

"Coming!" Shanelle yelled from inside. A moment later she opened the door, a small, beat-up suitcase by her side and a large silver plastic purse slung over her arm. She was wearing the new red coat, zipped up to her chin against the cold wind.

Olivia hugged her. "Ready to go?"

"Yep." Shanelle hesitated awkwardly. "Thanks. You didn't have to come."

"I know." Olivia smiled. "But I wanted to." She reached down and picked up the suitcase. "Let's go."

Shanelle couldn't remember the name of the doctor but gave directions to the clinic where she had had an appointment shortly after arriving in Utah last week. They only got turned around twice, but Olivia parked the car, and they found the doctor's office inside the vast medical complex right on time.

Olivia sat down to wait while Shanelle checked in at the reception desk. She looked around. It had been nearly four years since she had been in an obstetrician's office. There was a fish tank bubbling away in one corner with a couple of toddlers crowded around it. Photographs of women holding newborn babies decorated the walls, as well as a few 3-D ultrasound pictures. Parenting magazines were scattered around the various coffee tables, and there was even soothing music playing softly in the background. And, of course, seated throughout the waiting room were women in varying stages of pregnancy.

Olivia felt her throat start to constrict as a wave of emotion swept through her. She tried to take a deep breath, but it caught in her chest. Hot moisture trickled from one corner of her eye, which she hastily wiped away. *Breathe, Olivia!* Shanelle had finished checking in and turned to find a seat. Olivia waved at her and stood up, managing to exhale, "I'll be right back," before darting out of the waiting room.

Olivia plunged into the hallway, gasping for breath. Ignoring the stares from an elderly couple walking down the hall, she remembered seeing a women's restroom near the front entrance to the building. She stumbled along, feeling her tears trace a pattern down her cheek. She pushed open the bathroom door, relieved that no one else was in there. Olivia made a beeline for the sink and turned on some cold water to splash on her face.

She braced herself with one hand on either side of the sink and looked at her reflection in the mirror. "What is the matter with you?" she whispered. "You've got to calm down." She focused on taking a breath in, holding it momentarily, and then exhaling, trying to force her pounding heart to slow down. She could feel her hands shaking and gripped the edges of the sink even tighter. Olivia realized she was still crying and was confused and overwhelmed by this outburst. She tried to focus on *why* she was crying. These weren't the tears of not having a child that she had shed so many times. She had Hope now, and she loved Hope. Loved her dearly. This reaction had been triggered by the sights and sounds of a maternity waiting room filled with pregnant women.

Olivia hesitantly reached down and touched her own belly. Flat. Firm. Some of her friends had joked that she was the lucky one, getting to have a family without sacrificing her body, but in that moment Olivia knew why she was crying. She *wanted* to have that experience. She wanted to feel the movement of her unborn child, knowing that she was keeping him safe and warm until he was ready to join the world. It wasn't that she thought she would love a biological child more than she loved Hope. That would be impossible. She was grieving her own lost opportunity to have the experience of a pregnancy and delivery.

She was grieving that the size of her family was completely out of her control. Would Hope be an only child? Would she never know what it was like to have a brother or sister? And she was suddenly feeling the full force of the realization that they had been *this* close to another child, only to have the baby snatched away from them because some couple in Beaver lived on a farm. She held on to the sink and quit trying to stop the tears and finally allowed them to come.

Over the past few years, Olivia had been able to push these feelings to the back recesses of her mind and keep them there, until the experiences of this last week brought them tumbling forward. She cried. When the sobs subsided, Olivia felt a little better. Now she needed to pull herself together.

She splashed some more water on her face and pulled two

paper towels out of the dispenser to pat her face dry. Her eyes were red and swollen. She ran the paper towels under the cold water and held the compresses over her eyes for a minute. That helped a little. She went into one of the stalls and pulled off a long sheet of toilet paper to blow her nose. That helped a lot. She wiped away the streaks that were the remnants of her mascara and dug around in her purse until she found some lip gloss which she carefully applied. She looked presentable again. Taking one last deep breath, Olivia returned to the waiting room.

A quick glance around told Olivia that Shanelle had already been called back and was with the doctor. She sat down in the corner and was relieved to see a copy of the morning newspaper. Olivia picked it up, glad that she wouldn't be faced with the choice of reading a pregnancy magazine or staring around the room at the pregnant women and pictures of babies everywhere.

Twenty minutes later, Shanelle emerged. Olivia smiled as she folded the newspaper and stood up.

"So, how did it go?" It sounded a little cliché, but Olivia didn't know what else to say.

"Good," Shanelle answered. "The doctor says I'm fine to ride the bus to that Beaver town. He thinks the baby'll be comin' in about two weeks."

"That's good," Olivia said, swallowing the lump that was trying to lodge in her throat. They stood almost long enough for the silence to get awkward before Olivia asked, "What time does your bus leave?"

"Twelve-thirty."

Olivia slipped her cell phone out of her pocket and checked the time. "We'd better get going then."

Shanelle nodded and followed Olivia out the door and into the car. They drove in silence for a few minutes before Shanelle started rummaging around in the large purse she was carrying. She finally found what she was looking for and held out the phone card that Michael and Olivia had purchased the other night.

"Here you go," Shanelle said. "I only used 'bout fifteen minutes, so there's plenty left on there."

Olivia put her hand on Shanelle's outstretched arm. "You keep it." Shanelle looked shocked. "That way you can call your mom again, if you need to." Shanelle nodded silently and slipped the card back into her purse.

Olivia glanced at the clock on the dashboard and then asked, "Are you hungry?"

"I'm okay. I got my last peanut butter sandwich here in my bag," Shanelle said, patting her purse. "The wife of this couple—her name's Susan—she says it's only three hours on the bus, and then they're gonna meet me an' take me to dinner so we can get to know each other." Shanelle's stomach betrayed her by emitting one big growl at that very moment. She laughed nervously. "Guess I better eat this sandwich right away."

"No, you save it in case you get hungry on the bus ride," Olivia said. "We've got time to swing by a drive-thru." She saw Shanelle's worried expression and clarified. "My treat."

"Thanks, Olivia," Shanelle said softly. "That's real nice."

"Don't worry about it," Olivia replied.

A few minutes later, Olivia spotted a Wendy's restaurant. "This okay?" she asked as she flipped her turn signal on.

"Great," Shanelle answered.

They pulled up to the menu board and Shanelle leaned over to study it carefully. "Order whatever you want," Olivia said with a smile.

Shanelle ordered a chicken sandwich that had cheese, bacon, ranch dressing—the works—with fries and a root beer; all large. Olivia ordered a single with cheese. She wasn't sure she could eat anything right now, but she didn't want Shanelle to feel bad, so she added an order of fries and asked for three bottles of water.

At the window, Olivia paid for the food and passed the bag to Shanelle. She opened her sandwich and took a large bite, then pulled a napkin from the bottom of the sack and wiped her mouth. "Mmmmm," Shanelle said. "So good. Thanks again."

"No problem," Olivia said, reaching over for a french fry and absently taking a bite. Shanelle ate without talking, intermittently taking large swigs of root beer and smiling at the sweet fizz that must have burned her throat on the way down.

They approached the large grocery store whose customer service counter also served as the ticket office for the bus line. Olivia was planning on dropping Shanelle off in front of the store, but when she turned to look at her, Shanelle was biting a fingernail and looking around nervously. "You think the money they wired got here?" she asked Olivia.

Olivia pulled into the nearest parking spot and turned off the engine. "Let's go in and make sure," she said. The relief washed across Shanelle's face and she nodded. Olivia grabbed Shanelle's suitcase out of the back seat, stuck the three bottles of water into her purse, and they walked into the store together. Olivia stood by her side while Shanelle asked about her ticket and the gray-haired clerk confirmed that the money had been wired and the ticket purchased.

"Bus should be here any minute," he told her, passing her the ticket. "Right out front, there."

"Thanks," Shanelle said.

Shanelle walked outside, and Olivia followed her, carrying the small suitcase. They sat down on a bench in the sun to wait. After a moment of silence, Olivia said, "I really hope that everything works out for you, Shanelle."

Shanelle nodded and swallowed hard but didn't say anything.

"Good luck with the delivery and placement," Olivia turned and looked right into Shanelle's eyes, "and good luck with getting Joey back." Shanelle's eyes glistened. "You're a good person," Olivia added. "Don't let anyone tell you otherwise."

Shanelle opened her mouth to say something but shook her head slightly and closed it again.

"Here," Olivia said, pulling out the water bottles that she had almost forgotten. "Take these. It's important that you remember to drink plenty of water. And," she reached into her purse again, "take this. Just in case you need something." It was a twenty-dollar bill.

Shanelle's eyes widened. She reached her hand forward, then stopped. Olivia smiled and nodded. "Go on, take it."

"Thanks," Shanelle mumbled as the water bottles and money disappeared into her big, silver purse. She blinked her eyes twice, then again.

They both saw the bus turning into the parking lot, and stood up. Olivia reached over and gave Shanelle a hug. "It was nice to meet you. Good luck."

The large gray bus eased to a stop in front of them and the door opened with a swish. Shanelle turned to climb the steps into the bus but hesitated. She turned back around and threw her arms around Olivia with tears running down her cheeks. "I can't believe you come and helped me all day. Even when you know I'm not having you adopt this baby."

"I care about you, Shanelle," Olivia said, tears forming in her own eyes. "You needed help, and I could help you." She shrugged her shoulders.

Shanelle wiped her eyes on her sleeve and reached down to pick up the suitcase she had dropped. Then her nearly black eyes bored into Olivia's blue ones. "I've never had anyone be so nice to me as you have. *Never.*" Then with one last squeeze, Shanelle turned and boarded the bus.

Olivia was frozen by the intensity of Shanelle's words, and she stood on the sidewalk and watched the bus drive away. She made it back to her car, climbed inside, and turned the key before the floodgates opened and she started to sob. The turmoil of emotions she'd experienced that week was still close to the surface, but she also recognized the truth of Shanelle's words, and she cried for the lonely, scared, yet strong girl who had briefly passed through her life and was now gone.

Michael met Olivia at the door when she arrived home. He wrapped her in his warm arms and kissed the puffy redness around her eyes. Hope came running over shouting, "Mommy, we made cookies!"

Olivia raised an eyebrow at her husband, who grinned. "Well, we bought the cookie dough at the store, but we did bake them."

Hope was tugging on Olivia's arm and leading her to the table. "We have milk too!" she squealed excitedly. As Olivia settled into a chair at the kitchen table, Hope passed her a plate of warm chocolate chip cookies, and Michael handed her a glass of milk. Hope looked up and softly touched Olivia's cheek.

"Are you sad, Mommy?"

"I was, Hope," Olivia said. Hope threw her arms around Olivia's neck and squeezed before Olivia added, "But you and Daddy have made me feel much better."

"Good," Hope said, satisfied. Then she kissed Olivia on the cheek and turned to Michael. "We did it, Daddy!" she whispered loudly and then grabbed a cookie and took a big bite.

Olivia laughed and she and Michael both reached for a cookie as well. Hope was talking a mile a minute about their adventure at the grocery store when Olivia caught Michael's eye. She mouthed the words, "I love you." He smiled.

"Love you more," he whispered.

CHAPTER TEN

Ally did a good job over the next few weeks of staying away from Riley. Shaylan and Holly did their best to convince her that she needed to talk to him, but Ally was certain that nothing good would come of getting even more attached than she already was. She skipped the next home game and volunteered to work the following Saturday so she wouldn't be home when Damon and Riley came over to watch that week's football game.

Ally was surprised when there was a knock on the door a full hour before the game was scheduled to start and thirty minutes before she had to leave for work. She retreated to her bedroom but cringed when she heard Riley's voice asking if she was home. A few moments later, Shaylan opened her door. "You can come out and see him now, or I can have him sit down and wait until you come out. Either way, you need to talk to him." Her arms were crossed and her eyes were blazing, and Ally knew there was no escape.

"Fine." Ally snapped. "I'll come out. Just give me a second." Shaylan nodded and turned around. Ally grabbed her coat and hat. She didn't want to have this conversation sitting on the couch with everyone around.

Damon and Holly had moved into the living room, and

Shaylan was gathering up some snacks from the kitchen cupboards. Riley remained standing next to the front door. Apparently he also wanted a little privacy for whatever was coming. Ally smiled weakly at him and said, "I have to leave for work in about a half hour." Riley nodded.

"Let's go for a walk," he said. Shaylan caught Ally's eye as Riley opened the door, and she mouthed, "Be nice." Ally rolled her eyes and followed Riley out the door. It was cold as they started down the sidewalk, but the sun was shining, and Ally closed her eyes and enjoyed the light on her face for a moment.

"I like sunny winter days," Riley said, breaking the silence. Ally opened her eyes.

"Me too." They walked on without saying anything more. After stepping off the sidewalk and onto a grassy area, Riley abruptly grabbed Ally's hand and stopped walking. She tried to pull it away, but Riley wouldn't let her go. She turned to face him, glaring and ready to storm away, but the turmoil in his bright green eyes stopped her, and her expression softened.

"Look, Ally. I don't know why you won't go out with me." She looked at the ground, desperate to look at anything besides the depth of his eyes. "And I thought that I would be okay with just being friends." His breath caught, and Ally looked up. "But, as it turns out, I'm really not."

"Riley, don't."

"Don't what?" Riley dropped her hand and shoved his fingers through his hair. "Don't tell you what is obvious to everyone around us?" Ally was shaking her head.

"I just can't, Riley," she said, turning her back to him.

"Ally . . ." Riley's voice was getting softer rather than louder, and Ally froze, not wanting to listen, but too afraid to miss a word. "I'm not asking for a commitment."

"Then what do you want from me?" Ally asked without turning around. Riley put his hand on her shoulder.

"I want a chance to get to know you. I want to find out if you are really as amazing as you seem, and how you got to be that way." Ally turned around but wouldn't meet his gaze. Riley gently lifted her chin. "I want to figure out why I can't stop thinking about you, and why you're so intent on staying away from me."

"No, you don't," Ally said, forcing the emotion out of her voice. "You don't really want to know me." She looked up and allowed herself to get lost in Riley's eyes. "And you don't even like me."

"Ally . . ."

"No, listen. You like the idea of me. But you don't know anything about me. Not really."

"That's not true. I know that you are smart and athletic and tough and hard-working. I know that you have a little dimple in your left cheek that appears when you smile." Ally blushed in spite of herself. No one ever noticed that tiny dimple. "I know that when you're happy your eyes are the smooth brown of melted chocolate, and when you're mad, they seem to get darker, almost black." Ally closed her eyes, unable to keep looking at Riley. "I know that you cheer harder at football games than any girl I've ever known in my life, which is awesome. I know that whenever I try to get close to you, you suddenly look sad, which makes me think that someone has hurt you before." Ally felt Riley's arm slip around her waist, and her heartbeat quickened. "I know that sometimes I catch you looking at me, and it makes me hope that maybe there's a chance you're interested in me, but then a wall comes up and I can't decide whether I want to hold you and protect you or just really shake you!" Ally could almost feel Riley's eyes begging her to look at him. When she didn't say anything, he went on.

"Ally, I said I'm not looking for any sort of commitment, and I'm not." She felt his hands move tentatively to her cheek. His fingertips brushed her skin lightly before they were gone, and he was no longer touching her. "But I am asking you to give me a chance." His voice was husky, and Ally imagined that his eyes were glistening. "Please, Ally. Just give *us* a chance."

Ally still hadn't opened her eyes, and she stood silently listening to Riley breathing. She fought against the impulse to throw her arms around him and open up to him, because he was right. She really did care about him. Sometime in the last few months, she had started to love him. And it was different than what she had felt for others in the past. This wasn't a crush or simply a desire to be together. She definitely felt excitement standing near him, but it was much more than that. This felt comfortable. Secure. Real. Was it?

Her thoughts drifted to Scott again, and the ache in her heart flared. *That had felt real too.* She lifted her eyes to Riley's, searching. There was nothing but goodness and concern in his gaze as he studied Ally, waiting for her answer. Her heart softened for just a moment. *No, I can't do it. I can't. Not again.*

"I'm sorry, Riley," she whispered. "I'm going to be late for work." She couldn't stop the tears from coming as she walked away. Riley didn't follow her.

CHAPTER ELEVEN

It's been a long time since I've been to church in this building, Ally thought as she walked into church with her family. She had been going to school year-round since she left, trying to make up for starting late, and although she came home to visit occasionally, she always went to the singles ward. She still had a hard time feeling completely comfortable here. The thoughtless remarks directed toward her when she was pregnant still lurked in the back of her mind. Ally shook her head as her family settled into the same bench that they had been sitting in since before Ally could remember. But today was a special day. It was Christmas break, and Charlie was leaving on his mission right after the first of the year. He would be speaking in church today. Ally couldn't miss that.

After she sat down, Ally furtively glanced around. No one was whispering. No one was pointing. In fact, many people were smiling at her, and a few even gave her a little wave. *Hmm. Maybe it's time to let all of those old feelings go.* Ally was startled from her thoughts when a hand came to rest on her shoulder.

"Well, Ally," came the familiar voice. "It's so good to see you."

"Hi, Bishop Jenkins," Ally responded. "It's great to see you too!" Ally truly meant it. She had been looking forward to a chance to talk with him.

He reached out to shake her hand. "How's everything going?" Ally hesitated just a moment too long, and Bishop Jenkins raised an eyebrow.

"Everything's fine," Ally said with a smile, "but I did actually want to talk to you for a minute, if you're free anytime this week."

"I've got time tonight. About five o'clock?"

"Thanks, Bishop. I'll see you then."

After the meeting ended, Ally was so happy to see Hannah, one of her best friends from high school, rushing up from behind. Hannah's gorgeous auburn curls were glistening as usual, and her eyes were even brighter. They hugged and Hannah said, "You look great! How's BYU?"

"So good," Ally replied. "I'm really enjoying it. How are you doing?"

"Great!" Hannah smiled. "I'll graduate in May, and . . ." Her eyes were still gleaming and her smile got even bigger as she lifted her left hand to show Ally a small, but beautiful, diamond ring.

"You're getting married!"

"Yep!"

"Oh, congratulations!" Ally hugged her again. "I'm so happy for you!" They turned and started walking down the hall.

"Thanks. Did you hear that Amy got married?"

"Yeah. My mom told me," Ally said. "Amy didn't send me an invitation, though." Ally sighed. "I was actually hoping that she would be here so I could visit with her for a minute." Hannah slipped an arm around Ally's shoulder and gave her a squeeze as Ally continued. "I mean, I know that we've all moved on from high school and that we don't see each other much." Hannah lifted an eyebrow and Ally laughed. "Or at all. But the last time I saw Amy, it was a fight, and I've always felt bad about that."

Hannah nodded toward the end of the hall. There was Amy. Her back was toward Ally, but the pixie-cut blonde hair was unmistakable. She was holding hands with a man who looked vaguely familiar to Ally, but she couldn't quite place him. They were visiting with another couple that Ally didn't know. "Looks like you'll get that chance," Hannah said. "I'll catch up with you later. My mom wanted me to help with her Primary class today."

Ally nodded at Hannah and smiled before continuing down the hall. As she approached the group, her heart started pounding and her hands got shaky. *Calm down,* she thought to herself. *It's just Amy. You've been friends with her since you were both five.* But she couldn't quite shake from her mind the last time she had seen Amy. It was several years ago, and she had been storming out of Ally's hospital room when she realized that Ally was still going to follow through with the adoption plan she had made for Hope.

Ally stopped a few feet from her friend. "Hi, Amy. It's great to see you again."

Amy turned slowly around, and Ally was relieved to see a smile. "No way! Wow, Ally. It's been a long time!" Ally reached out her arms, and they exchanged a slightly awkward hug.

"My mom told me that you got married," Ally said to break the silence that followed. "Congratulations."

"Thanks," Amy said, and then, "This is my husband, Jeff."

"Nice to meet you, Ally," he said.

"You might remember him," Amy continued. "We saw him once in a while at the church dances growing up."

"Oh, that's right," Ally answered. "I thought I'd seen you somewhere before."

"Yep," Jeff said. "I used to watch Amy at those dances but never got brave enough to ask her to dance. Then when I came home from my mission and ran into her at a singles activity, I took my chance."

Ally smiled. "That's really great, you two. I'm happy for you."

"Jeff, I want to talk to Ally for a minute." Amy gave his arm a squeeze. "I'll meet you in Sunday School."

"Okay, hon." He gave her a quick peck on the cheek. "See you, Ally." Ally smiled and waved, then turned to face Amy. The hallways were clearing out as everyone made their way to class, so the girls walked silently toward the foyer.

"You look terrific, Amy," Ally finally said. "Jeff seems great."

"Thanks. You look good, too." More silence. "Ally?"

"Yeah?"

"There's something that I've been wanting to tell you."

"Well, I'm all ears," Ally replied.

They had reached the empty foyer and sat down on the couch. Amy smoothed out her skirt. She cleared her throat. "I just want to tell you that I'm sorry."

Ally had been hoping to smooth things over, but she hadn't expected an apology. She was surprised to realize that her eyes were filling with tears.

Amy continued on. "I was too busy being caught up in my own world to realize that when you decided on adoption for your baby, you weren't judging my mom for raising me on her own or judging me for never having known my father. You were just trying to do what was right for you." Amy paused for a split second, then added, "And for your baby."

Ally nodded. "Thanks, Amy." She pulled a tissue out of her purse and dabbed at her eyes. "Of course I forgive you."

Amy threw her arms around Ally, and the earlier awkwardness was gone. "Do you ever hear from them? The family that you placed with?"

Ally wiped her eyes again and smiled. "I actually see them quite a bit. Usually about once a month."

"Oh, wow," Amy said. "I didn't realize that."

"Yeah. At first, I wasn't sure I wanted much contact, but Olivia and Michael are so amazing, and it's great seeing Hope so healthy and happy."

"I'm surprised that they would be so involved with you."

"Well, all adoptions are different, but this is working really well for us. Hope's mom and dad are really great." Ally sniffed away the last of the tears and tucked a stray hair behind her ear.

"Is it weird to talk about someone else as her mom?" Amy wasn't being callous; she was truly trying to understand.

"It's not," Ally replied, "because Olivia *is* Hope's mom. I gave birth to her, and I certainly love her and always, always will." Ally paused, trying to decide how to form her feelings into words. "But giving birth is only the very first part of motherhood. Moms are made day in and day out as they nurture and care for and teach their children; as they change diapers and stay up all night with sick babies; as they wipe sticky fingers and comb hair and kiss skinned knees."

"Wow, Ally." Amy was slowly shaking her head. "That's really amazing." Her eyes lit up. "That's probably why it all works out so well."

"What do you mean?" Ally wasn't following her.

"Well, your attitude. I mean, don't you think if you were acting like Hope was still *yours* that things wouldn't be so great with Olivia and Michael?"

Ally scrunched up her nose. Amy smiled. It meant Ally was thinking hard. "Maybe. I never really thought about it." She fingered the locket hanging at her neck. "When I placed Hope in Olivia's arms, and especially when she was sealed to them in the temple, she became *their* daughter. I knew that going in. It wasn't like I loaned her to them until she grows up. They're not babysitting her until I can come back and be her mom." Ally smiled and nodded her head once. "Hope will always be a part of me; a wonderful, special part of me. And I'm thankful that I get to see her and have a relationship with her, but she has a great mom. It would just confuse things if I tried to act like her mom. I get to fill the role of . . ." Ally paused searching for the right word. "I don't know, like a special friend or a favorite aunt."

"Ally, I'm really happy that things have worked out so well for you," Amy said, giving Ally one more hug. "I really, truly am."

"Thanks, Amy. That means a lot to me." They stood up and started walking back down the hall toward Sunday School. "It looks like things are working out pretty great for you too."

They opened the door to the classroom and Jeff spied Amy and flashed a huge smile. He pointed at the empty seat next to him and Amy smiled back. "Thanks, Ally. They really are," she whispered before she took the seat next to her husband.

Ally looked a second longer before she saw her parents and Charlie. They had saved a seat for her. She sat down next to her brother with a feeling of peace in her heart.

◦◦◦

Ally settled into the familiar chair facing Bishop Jenkins across his desk. "Wow, Bishop. Your office really hasn't changed one bit."

He laughed. "No, I guess it hasn't. I was a brand new bishop when you first came in to see me, and now I'm getting old and worn out." He laughed. "My hair may be gray now, but at least the office still looks good." Ally remembered those crinkly lines around his eyes that appeared. She smiled. He shifted in his chair and looked at Ally closely. "I was glad to see you here. It seems like you've been avoiding this ward over the last few years." Bishop Jenkins softened the words with a smile, but Ally still squirmed a bit.

"Well, that's because I *have* been avoiding this ward," she admitted. "I guess I just thought that it would be really awkward coming back and facing everyone here."

"And?" he questioned when Ally didn't continue.

Ally smiled. She had missed Bishop Jenkins. "And what?" she asked.

"And was it?"

"Actually," Ally began, "it wasn't at all." Bishop Jenkins nodded and smiled. "Everyone was really great. They asked about school and about how I liked living in Provo." She paused. "And I didn't feel like anyone was pointing or whispering about me."

"Time can heal a lot of things, Ally," he responded. "Especially when people are willing to be healed."

She nodded. "I guess so, because today was great." She paused and then added, "Amy apologized to me."

"Oh really? That's nice."

"Yeah, it was," Ally said, nodding her head.

"And did you forgive her?" This question caught Ally off guard.

"Of course I did, Bishop."

"Just like that?" He raised an eyebrow. Ally couldn't figure out where he was going with this.

"Of course, 'just like that.' I could tell she really meant it."

"Hmmm." Bishop Jenkins raised an eyebrow.

"Hmmm, what?" Ally demanded.

Bishop Jenkins leaned forward across the desk. "I'm just wondering why you were so quick to forgive Amy when you won't forgive yourself."

Ally automatically opened her mouth to argue, but it snapped shut when her eyes met Bishop Jenkins's penetrating gaze. She leaned back in her chair and crossed her arms, her mind shuffling through the last few months. She stared at the floor, seeing only the hurt on Riley's face the last time she had walked away from him. *He wouldn't like me if he knew,* Ally repeated in her mind.

Bishop Jenkins let her sit in silence for several minutes before clearing his throat. "Ally?" Ally looked up, her eyes wet. "Ally, you are clean. Your Heavenly Father has forgiven the mistake you made." He passed her the tissue box when she blinked and the tears ran down her cheeks. "But not only that," he continued, "He is very pleased with you. You are getting an education, you're improving your life, you're growing and progressing." He stopped. Ally wiped her eyes. "How is Hope doing?" Ally was surprised at the sudden turn in the conversation.

"She's great. She's learning and growing." Ally smiled. "Olivia and Michael are wonderful and they are a beautiful little family. Hope is happy."

"Of course she is. And, Ally, you can have that happiness in your life too." He studied her face closely. "Have you been dating much?"

"A little." Ally twisted the tissue around in her fingers. "But it's hard, you know?"

"Sure, sure." Bishop smiled. "Nothing harder than finding someone to date at BYU."

Ally smiled in spite of herself. "You know what I mean." Bishop Jenkins nodded.

"Ally, you need to go take a good look at yourself in the mirror and appreciate the woman that you have become." He took his glasses off and rubbed his eyes. "One thing I've learned while being the bishop is that life is hard, Ally. It's hard for everyone. And being successful and happy in life? Well, that's even harder. It's easy to sit back and watch life happen around you. It's easy to say that you're not going to reach out and trust someone because you might get hurt. The harder way is to try. To put yourself out there. To trust. Will you fail sometimes? Of course. We all do. Will you hurt occasionally? Absolutely. Will you feel angry and sad and frustrated and lonely sometimes? Without a doubt." Bishop laid a hand on the worn scriptures sitting on the corner of his desk. "But it's what we do with those feelings that matters. Do we cling to them so tightly that they become a heavy weight dragging us down? Or can we turn them over to the Savior and allow them to be a stepping stone toward making us a better person?" He shook his head softly and smiled. "Ally, you have a deeper understanding of love and sacrifice than many people three times your age, but you still cannot possibly fathom the depth of the love that your Heavenly Father and His Son have for you."

Ally nodded. It was impossible not to feel the truth of his words pulsing through her body. "They love you, Ally, and your family loves you. And somewhere out there Heavenly Father has prepared a young man who will also love everything about you and will appreciate the experiences that have molded you into the person that you are. Then together, you can continue to work on becoming the people that our Father in Heaven wants—and *needs*—you to be."

Ally didn't respond, and after a moment Bishop Jenkins asked, "Do you believe me?"

Ally inhaled sharply as she thought of Riley, and how she felt when she was around him. But then an image of Scott appeared in her mind, and she shook her head. "I don't know, Bishop, but I'll try to believe you." Ally wiped the tears that were once again trailing down her face and then stood to leave

Bishop Jenkins followed her lead. He shook her hand. "It was great to see you again, Ally. Stop in any time." She nodded. "And remember: don't be so afraid of losing something that you never get the chance to experience it in the first place."

Ally was helping her mom clean up from Christmas dinner. Emma and Elsie had been eager to go play with their new iPads, so Ally had shooed them out of the kitchen. At fifteen years old, the girls were easily convinced that they could take a break from helping with the dishes today. Charlie and Dad had helped for a while, but after each of them had snitched four or five bites of Mom's special "mud cake" dessert, she had laughingly banished them from the kitchen until further notice.

"Is everything okay?" Julie asked her daughter.

"Yeah," Ally answered. "Why?"

Julie smiled. "Well, you've been wiping that same spot on the counter for several minutes now. That's as clean as it's going to get."

Ally laughed and shot the rag into the sink like a basketball. Julie scowled, and then her eyes softened and she joined in laughing. "I used to get so irritated when you would do that as a kid." She shook her head and looked at Ally, her eyes filled with pride. "And now look at you."

Ally raised her eyebrows. "Yep, still treating the kitchen like a basketball court."

Julie walked over and put her arm around her oldest daughter. "No. Look at what a beautiful woman you have grown into. I know that I've had my struggles with, well, everything, but I want you to know that I am proud of you, Ally. And I'm proud of the person you are becoming."

Ally could only imagine all that had gone into those words. "Thanks, Mom." She hugged her. "Oh, I got a text from Olivia earlier." Ally pulled her phone out of her pocket. "Hope loves the princess you sent." Julie looked at the picture on Ally's phone of the beautiful curly haired little girl grinning widely and holding up a princess doll.

"You made a good decision, Ally," Julie said.

That caught Ally off guard. "About?"

"About Hope. About her family." Julie nodded again and swallowed the lump in her throat. "You did good." Ally didn't trust her voice, so she just nodded and headed down the hall to get the broom, a soft smile on her face.

She swept in silence for a few minutes while Julie dried and put away the last of the pots and pans. "Can I ask what were you thinking about a minute ago when you were trying to rub a hole into the counter?"

Ally hesitated, not sure if she was ready to talk about Riley. "Oh, you know. I was just thinking about the future . . . possibilities . . ." Ally shrugged. "Nothing too exciting." She finished sweeping the floor and emptied the dustpan.

Julie understood and patted Ally on the arm. "Well, I guess I'll go find your dad and Charlie and tell them that *now* they can have some dessert."

"I like the sound of that," Ally said just as her phone started to ring. She looked at the familiar name flashing on the phone. "It's Holly." She pressed a button and said, "Hi, Holly," before turning and whispering to her mom, "Make sure the boys save me some cake!"

"I'll do my best," Julie replied as she headed down the hall to Steve's office. She heard Ally's voice saying, "Merry Christmas to you too! Are you having a fun break?" before she entered Steve's office to find the boys looking through all of Charlie's missionary stuff. No sooner had she opened the door than both of them were heading straight for the kitchen. "I've been waiting *all year* for this dessert, Mom," Charlie said in response to Julie rolling her eyes. "You really should make it more often." Julie's response was cut off by a piercing squeal coming from the family room. "EEEEEEEEEEEE! Congratulations, Holly! I'm *so* happy for you!"

"Looks like it's official," Julie said. "Holly must be engaged."

CHAPTER TWELVE

Ally thought a lot about what Bishop Jenkins had told her, and by the time she was driving back to Provo to start the next semester of school, she had come to a decision. She had to talk to Riley. She didn't know what would happen from there, and when (or if) they would make it to the point where she would tell him about Hope, but it was time to quit running away. Now that Damon and Holly were engaged, Riley was sure to be around more than ever, and Ally would just look for a chance to talk to him alone. But as the first month of the semester dragged on without so much as a single visit from Riley, Ally's nerves were starting to get the better of her. She couldn't just wait for Riley to show up at their door some day. Damon was around all the time, as he and Holly were constantly working on wedding plans. Ally finally couldn't ignore it any longer and broached the subject with him.

"So, we haven't seen much of Riley since school started back up," Ally commented as innocently as she could one afternoon when Damon and Holly walked into the apartment carrying a variety of flowers.

"Yeah, he's pretty slammed this semester," Damon answered before turning to Holly. "I really like these purple ones. What are they called again?"

"Orchids," Holly answered. "They are really pretty and definitely something different than you usually see at weddings." She fingered through the stems of roses, carnations, great big daisies, and sunflowers. "What do you think, Ally?"

"I don't know. I'm kind of a softie for the classics. A nice bouquet of roses is perfect to me." Ally blushed slightly as she pressed the issue. "So Riley's been pretty busy? Is his internship taking up more time?"

"Hmm? Oh, yeah," Damon replied as he absently started picking petals from one of the larger daisies. "She loves me," he grinned plucking a petal, "she loves me not." He frowned and so did Holly. "She loves me . . ."

"Let's just end that right there," Holly said, planting a kiss on his cheek. "Right there with 'she loves me.'"

❧ ❧

"Hey, Riley, guess who was asking about you today?" Damon said, throwing his backpack onto the couch. Riley looked up from his stack of books, forcing his gaze to remain uninterested.

"Let me think. Holly was asking about what kind of a bachelor's party I'm going to throw for you?"

"Yeah. I came right home to tell you *that*." Damon shook his head. Riley ignored him and went back to studying. "Dude," Damon said, throwing a pencil across the room and hitting Riley in the back of the head. "Do you really not want to know what *she* said?"

Riley sighed and closed his book. "What, Damon? What did *she* say?"

Damon headed for the fridge, opened it, grabbed a gallon of chocolate milk, and drank four big swallows straight from the carton. He wiped the milk from his top lip before he began. "Well, she asked why they hadn't seen you around this semester." Damon was grinning from ear to ear, but his smile faded when Riley didn't respond.

"And?" Riley finally asked when it became apparent that Damon wasn't going to say any more.

"*And*," Damon continued, "I told her that you were really slammed and she asked if you were busy with the internship and I said yes."

"Is that it?" Riley was getting annoyed.

"Yeah. Then she went to her room while Holly and I continued the flower discussion." He shook his head. "I love Holly, man. You know I do, but this wedding planning is going to *kill* me!"

Riley grunted and opened his book back up. He still had several chapters of reading to get done tonight. He didn't have time for this. Damon took the hint and quit talking. He threw a frozen pizza in the oven, and ten minutes later slid it off the rack and back onto the box. He sliced it up and piled all of the pieces onto a plate. Before heading back to his bedroom to eat his pizza and watch TV, Damon turned and said, "I just thought you'd want to know that she noticed you weren't coming around. I thought that was a good sign."

Riley stared at the words swimming around on the page in front of him until he heard Damon's TV tune in to SportsCenter. Then he slammed his book shut and rested his elbows on the table, head in his hands. He had been trying for the past two months to get Ally out of his mind, but the more he tried to push her out, the more she kept creeping back in. Christmas break was usually his favorite time of year, with all of the football bowl games going on, but every time he sat down to watch a game, all he could see was Ally's face—her hair pulled back in a ponytail, and that headband, ear warmer thing she always wore to the stadium. He had tried and failed to forget the way it felt when that overly exuberant fan knocked Ally into him and he caught and held her close, their faces only inches apart. But whenever he found his mind lingering over the soft vanilla scent that always surrounded Ally, he forced the last image he had of her to the front of his mind: her back, as she walked away from him after he had just finished pouring his heart out to her.

"It's not happening, you idiot," he muttered to himself. "There are plenty of other girls out there. Forget about her." Riley closed his eyes and laid his head down on his arms. He knew that would be easier said than done. He decided to continue to stay away from her the best he could and hope that sooner or later he'd meet someone who would push her from his mind. After a few minutes, Riley opened his book again and made one last vain attempt at finishing the reading assignment before he packed up his books and went to bed.

BOOK THREE

CHAPTER ONE

Olivia stifled a yawn as her computer hummed to life. Michael was working in the home office tonight, trying to get all of his final papers graded. The end of school was just a week away, and Olivia was looking forward to the summer. Hope had turned three in February and Olivia had so much fun being with her. She had Hope all signed up for swimming lessons that would start the second week of June, and she was excited about the prospect of many summer days spent playing at the park and going to the zoo and visiting the nearby dinosaur museum.

Michael looked up from his desk in the corner. "You got Hope to bed?"

"Yep. And the kitchen cleaned up. I thought I'd check the emails before I settle in to read." Michael nodded absently as he went back to reading and marking the papers in front of him. Olivia logged into her personal account and quickly skimmed through the in-box. Nothing exciting: just some junk mail, which she deleted. She was anxious to get started on the new book she had checked out from the library today and thought about skipping her nightly check of their joint email account that was set up to go with their online adoption profile. She faithfully checked it every night, and there had never been a single email. Not one.

It'll only take two minutes, and then you won't have to think about it again until tomorrow night, Olivia told herself with a sigh.

She quickly logged herself out and then typed in the new password. She hit enter and was surprised to see a little red number one pop up next to the email icon. Her heart started beating faster, and her palms got sweaty. She looked up at Michael working busily in the corner and then back at the computer screen. It was still there. Just a tiny red number. Nothing to get worked up about. Olivia clicked the mouse and the screen showed one new message in their in-box. The subject line simply said: "hello." She clicked on the message.

> *Dear Michael and Olivia,*
>
> *My name is Nicole and I'm 21 years old, single, and pregnant. I am carrying a baby boy and am due on July 29. I have decided to place him for adoption and after looking at some online profiles, I have narrowed it down to three families, and you are one of those three. I would like to meet with you before I make my final decision. I have had a healthy, normal pregnancy. If you are interested in meeting with me, please email me back and let me know when we could get together.*
>
> *Best wishes,*
> *Nicole*

The air in Olivia's lungs felt heavy. Moisture filled her eyes. She read the short message once more before she managed to squeak out, "Michael?" The crack in her voice caught his immediate attention. He took one look at her sitting at the computer desk, pointing at the screen with tears in her eyes, and he was at her side.

"Wow," Michael said after reading the note. "Only about nine weeks to go." He rubbed his face. "She doesn't say where she lives or if she's already meeting with a social worker." Olivia shook her head. "Well, I guess you better email her back and tell her that we're definitely interested and ask her where she lives and when she would like to meet."

Olivia took a deep breath and tried to calm her shaking hands. "Here we go," she whispered as she began typing.

ও৩ ৩ও

Ten days and several emails later, Michael and Olivia were driving to Idaho to meet Nicole. As it turned out, she had started meeting with a social worker at LDS Family Services about the same time she sent them that initial email. Nicole told them that she had been planning on placing the baby from the moment her boyfriend walked out of her life the day she told him she was pregnant. She had grown up in the Church but hadn't been active since graduating from high school and going to college. Her parents lived in Colorado and they were supportive of her adoption plan. Nicole had graduated from the junior college she had been attending in Twin Falls and opted to stay there when she got offered a job running the front office for a dental practice.

That was the extent of Michael and Olivia's knowledge when they pulled into the parking lot of Maxie's Pizza and Pasta in Twin Falls. Hope was at home spending the night with Olivia's parents. Michael checked his watch, even though the clock on the dashboard clearly showed 5:28 p.m. Olivia smiled. He looked nervous. She was surprisingly calm. He cleared his throat. "Well, I guess we should go in."

Olivia nodded and they got out of the car and met in front of the headlights. She gave Michael a quick kiss on the cheek. "I really feel like if this baby boy is meant to be in our family, he'll make it to us." Michael nodded and they walked into the restaurant holding hands. Apparently the dinner rush hadn't arrived yet, because there was only one couple in line at the counter under the sign that read "Order Here." They were a middle-aged man and woman—clearly not Nicole—so Michael and Olivia asked to be seated, telling the waitress that they were waiting for one more to join their party—a young woman named Nicole—and that they would order once she arrived. The waitress told them they could sit anywhere and smiled before turning her attention to a pizza that was being passed to her from the kitchen. Michael and Olivia made their way to a nearby booth and sat next to each other without talking, Michael absently rubbing circles with his thumb on the back of Olivia's hand.

A sharp intake of breath from Olivia coincided with a tinkling bell as the door to the restaurant opened. Michael looked up. This had to be Nicole. She wasn't tall, maybe five feet four or five feet five, and she had dark brown hair that was cut short. She was very pregnant and looked around uncertainly. Olivia caught Nicole's eye and waved at her. She smiled, and Michael and Olivia stood and started walking toward her. Michael reached out his hand and said, "You must be Nicole." She nodded. "It's so nice to meet you," he continued as they shook hands. "I'm Michael and this is my wife Olivia."

The two women hugged. "I'm so happy to meet you," Olivia said.

Nicole flashed a beautiful smile. "I'm super excited that you're both here," she said. Her large eyes were nearly black, and the combined effect of her hair, eyes, and smile brought one word to Olivia's mind: *spunky.*

"You didn't bring Hope?" Nicole asked, glancing at the menu on the counter in front of them.

"No," Olivia said. "She's home with Grandma and Grandpa." She motioned to the girl behind the counter that they were ready to order. "She's been asking for a baby brother or sister constantly for the last year, and we didn't want to get her involved unless we have some good news for her."

"That makes sense." Nicole nodded. "She sure looks like a sweet little girl."

"She is," Michael agreed. "She'll make a terrific big sister one day. So, what's good to eat here?

Nicole made a few recommendations, and the waitress came and took their orders. The three of them returned to the booth that Michael and Olivia had vacated and they made small talk about their respective days. When the waitress brought their sodas, Olivia asked, "So, how are you feeling?"

Nicole smiled. "I'm actually feeling good. I had pretty bad morning sickness for the first trimester, but since then, it's been fairly smooth sailing."

"So you're due at the end of July?" Michael asked.

"Yep. July twenty-ninth." Nicole rubbed her belly. "My doctor says that everything is looking good. He's a healthy little baby."

"If I may ask," Olivia began, but paused. Nicole nodded for her to continue. "How did you come to the decision to make an adoption plan for him?"

"It just seemed like that's what I should do after my boyfriend took off." Nicole shook her head. "I should have known he wouldn't be up to this big of a commitment." She fiddled with the wrapper from her straw, tying it in a knot and then snapping it in half. "When I told my parents that David and I weren't together anymore, I think they were relieved." She laughed softly. "Until I dropped the bomb that I was pregnant."

"And now what?" Olivia pressed when Nicole didn't continue.

"Well, I think they were upset at first, but they handled it okay. Then when I mentioned adoption, they jumped right on board with that." She sighed and brushed the hair back from her face with her fingers. "I think it helps that I'm all the way up here in Idaho, and they're clear down in Colorado." She traced an imaginary circle on the surface of the table with her finger. "They're good parents, but we've never been very close. I moved away and came up here to make my life, and they've still got five kids at home to take care of. I visit them at Christmas and they come see me for a few days in the summer." She shrugged. "It is what it is." She looked up and flashed that smile again. "So, that brings us here."

The waitress arrived with their food. "The plates are hot," she cautioned as she set them down. "Let me know if you need anything else."

Nicole dug into her lasagna, blowing carefully on the first forkful before popping it into her mouth. "Mmmm," she said after swallowing. "This is my favorite place to eat."

Olivia smiled and cut a ravioli in two, eating one half. "This *is* really good," she agreed, and the three of them ate in silence for a few minutes.

Michael's thoughts were tumbling around like the rocks he always dumped in his little plastic polisher as a kid. He didn't want to push Nicole, but he had to know where she stood. He twirled the spaghetti on his plate and ate one of the meatballs. Finally he couldn't stand the silence any longer. "So, Nicole," he began, clearing his throat. Olivia shot him a sideways glance, which he ignored. "You mentioned that you had two other families in mind besides us." Nicole nodded but didn't say anything. She was chewing. "Have you already met them?"

Nicole took a long swig from her Sprite before answering. "Yes." She tucked her hair behind her ear. "Both of those couples live here in the valley, and I met them last week." Olivia swallowed hard and straightened up, touching Michael's hand under the table. "They were both really nice, but to be honest, I didn't really click with either of them." Olivia took in a quick breath. "So," Nicole continued, "I guess it's either you guys, or back to square one, searching through the online profiles."

"Fair enough," Michael said. Olivia smiled her agreement. "So, do you have any questions for us?"

The remainder of the evening flew by as Nicole asked them about where they grew up, how they met, and what sorts of things they like to do. Michael's apprehensions slowly melted away, and by the end of the night they were all laughing and talking about football (it turned out that Nicole was a big Denver Broncos fan), music, *Friends* reruns, and of course, Hope. As they left the restaurant, Olivia and Michael walked Nicole to her car, a royal blue Chevy Cruze. "Cute car," Olivia commented.

"Thanks." Nicole unlocked the doors with a click. "I got it about a year ago after I started my job." She turned to face Olivia and was engulfed in a hug. "It was great meeting you," she said when Olivia released her. "And you too," she added, briefly touching Michael's arm. Nicole stood there a moment longer studying them. Then her face split into a wide smile. "I'll talk to my social worker tomorrow morning and make it official, but I'd like you to be the family for my baby."

Olivia was speechless. Nicole laughed. "Don't look so surprised, you two." Olivia glanced at Michael, his eyes were wide and glistening. "You're both amazing." She patted her belly. "This little guy is going to be very happy." She gave Olivia one more quick squeeze before climbing into her car, latching her seat belt, and driving away.

Michael and Olivia watched her taillights fade and then turned to face each other. Olivia finally found her voice. "It's really happen-EEEEEEEEEE!" Her words ended in a squeal as Michael wrapped both arms around his wife's waist, picked her up, spun her around, and kissed her right there in the parking lot.

CHAPTER TWO

Allison dropped onto the worn sofa and let her backpack land on the ground next to her. She closed her eyes, took a deep breath, and slowly blew it out, a smile forming on her lips. Her last final exam for the semester was over. Not only was it over, but she also felt really good about it. She'd done well. She was scheduled to go into work at the campus floral shop after the exam, but as she was walking from the testing center over to the shop, her manager, Shawna, sent her a text telling her that it was really slow, and she could take the afternoon off, followed by: Do something fun!

Ally couldn't help but smile. Shawna was one of a small handful of people who knew about the whole Riley fiasco and how Ally really felt about him. Holly saw him quite a bit because he was going to be Damon's best man at the wedding, so Ally had been careful not to say anything about Riley in front of her. She had run into him a time or two during the semester, but they were never alone, and he always made some excuse to leave quickly before she could say more than "hi." Clearly he wanted nothing more to do with her, and Ally couldn't blame him after how she had walked away from him. Finally, she had given up on working things out, berating herself for not opening up to Riley sooner and giving him the chance he had asked for. Next time she met a great guy, she wouldn't make the same mistake.

And who says there's going to be a next time? Ally sighed and went to the refrigerator, poking around for the leftover Beijing beef and chow mein she knew were hiding in there from her Panda Express run a couple nights ago. She found the takeout container and pulled a disposable pair of chopsticks from the silverware drawer. She sat down at the kitchen table and started eating her cold leftovers for lunch. Her mouth was full of noodles when the front door opened and she heard Holly's voice.

"I really think it will be okay. I don't think she'll mind at all."

Damon responded, "Are you sure?"

"Of course I'm sure." Holly sounded convincing. "It'll be way more fun and a lot cheaper than if she drives alone."

"Holly, I told you. I don't think she wants to spend that much time with me." Ally froze. That was Riley's voice, and she could only hope they weren't talking about her.

"Oh, get over it, Riley." Holly laughed. "Ally agreed to be one of my bridesmaids and to come for the Disneyland trip the week before the wedding, all the while knowing that you're Damon's best man and would be there too." Riley tried to say something, but Holly overrode him. "She won't care." Ally squirmed. So they were talking about her.

"Don't fight it, man." Damon's voice floated from the entryway. "I've seen that expression before. This discussion is over."

"It's true." Holly giggled. *Ugh. She's so obnoxiously in love,* Ally thought with half a grin.

"Fine." Riley didn't sound very happy. "Let's just go play ball."

"I thought you wanted to come in and get some ice for your water bottle?" Holly was trying to smooth things over.

"I changed my mind. I'll wait for you in the truck, Damon."

There was a moment of silence and Ally guessed they were watching Riley stomp down the sidewalk. Then she heard a quick kiss and Damon said, "I'll talk to him. It'll be all right."

"I'm not worried," Holly said. "She really won't care." Holly must have stood in the doorway watching Damon leave because it was several long seconds before she closed the door and turned to walk into the kitchen. Holly froze when she saw Ally sitting at the table wearing an expression that clearly said that she *did* care.

"What was that all about?" Ally was struggling to keep her voice calm.

Holly faltered under her friend's stare. "Well, I was just thinking that it would be cheaper for everyone if the four of us—me, you, Damon, and Riley—drove down together." She waited for Ally to respond and when she didn't, Holly added, "In one car."

"I know what you mean," Ally said, but she didn't sound angry. She simply sounded tired. "What about the drive home?" Ally asked. "You and Damon will leave on your honeymoon, and I'm not sure I can face all those hours in the car alone with Riley."

Encouraged by the apparent absence of anger, Holly pushed on. "He's really not that bad, Ally. I don't know why you don't like him."

Ally was surprised by the emotion that sprang up in her eyes at those words. She looked down and pushed her fingers through her hair in an attempt to disguise her feelings. "Is that what he thinks?"

"Ally, that's what everyone thinks." Holly pulled up a chair and sat down. "He told Damon about you walking away from him back before Christmas." She reached out and put her hand on Ally's arm. "When someone tells you that he cares about you and wants to be with you and you turn and walk away, what's he supposed to think?" Ally looked up and Holly was surprised to see tears in her friend's eyes. "Is that *not* how you feel?"

Ally brushed at her eyes. "I don't know how I feel." She drummed her fingers on the table. "I know that I can't stop thinking about him. I know that every time you and Damon walk through the door, my breath catches until I realize that Riley isn't with you." Ally looked up and met Holly's gaze, and everything she was thinking just spilled out. "I know that it broke my heart to turn and walk away from him, and that once I got back here after

Christmas I was going to talk to him, but he never came around and the time wasn't right, and now it's too late and I missed my chance, and NOW you're telling me that I'm going to have to sit in a car with him for hours and hours?" She paused to take a breath. "I know gas is expensive, but maybe I'd better drive by myself. It might save my sanity."

"So, wait." Holly shook her head, trying to allow her jumble of thoughts to fall into place. "Riley is crazy about you, and you're crazy about him? What's the problem then?" Holly stared over Ally's head for just a moment and then understanding flickered in her eyes. She mouthed more than actually said the word. "Hope?"

Ally nodded. "No way!" Holly actually shouted and it made Ally jump. "He didn't tell Damon that part, so of course I just kept it to myself. I can't believe that Riley wouldn't want to be with you because of that. He's so lame!" Ally realized that Holly misunderstood, and she started shaking her head, but Holly hadn't noticed. "I'm gonna call him right up and straighten that boy out. No wonder he thinks you can't stand him. You have every right to be mad at him. What a jerk!"

Holly was pulling out her cell phone when Ally cut her off. "I didn't tell him about her."

"What?" Holly stopped searching through the contacts on her phone and looked up. She tried to read Ally's expression, but her head was down and her hair covered her face. "What happened then?" Ally tried to swallow the lump forming in her throat and shook her head. Holly didn't push it. If Ally wanted to answer, she could.

Ally brushed some invisible crumbs off the table. She wiped at the unwelcome moisture in her eyes. Finally she looked up. Holly's heart twisted at the sadness in Ally's eyes. "It's not that I don't like Riley, or that I'm mad at him." One tear escaped and traced a path down her cheek. "I've never felt this way about anyone before." Holly raised an eyebrow but kept quiet. "I mean, we haven't even gone out on a 'real' date and I'm already—" She shook her head, sniffed, and wiped her face. "It doesn't matter.

Back before Christmas I was too afraid of him rejecting me if I told him about Hope, like Scott did, so I rejected him first. Over the break I realized how stupid that was, and when school started again I was determined to tell him and then see where things went, but he went out of his way to avoid me, and I couldn't blame him for being mad at me." Ally shrugged. "And now it's too late. I just don't want it to be awkward, and I'd really rather not be two feet away from him in a car for all those hours."

Holly reached out and put a hand on her friend's arm. "I'm sorry, Ally. I . . ." She looked for the right words. "I didn't realize."

"Not your fault," Ally said with a humorless laugh. "But I think I'll drive myself, anyway." Holly nodded. "And please," Ally added, "don't tell Riley about this."

CHAPTER THREE

Ally was almost to work when her cell phone started ringing. She considered letting it go to voice mail but then looked at the name on her phone's display and answered it. "Hi, Olivia."

"Hey, Ally. How were finals?"

"I'm glad they're over," Ally said, laughing. "But I did well."

"Of course you did." Ally could tell by Olivia's voice that she was proud of her. "When are you heading to California?"

"Next week. I'm looking forward to the beach."

"Yeah, that'll be great! Are you still going to Disneyland?"

"Yep. The last time I went was the summer before my junior year of high school with my family. It should be fun."

"Oh, good." Olivia paused. Ally could tell there was something else she wanted to say. "So, we got some good news."

"Yeah?" Ally couldn't stop the smile that appeared.

"We're going to adopt a baby boy!"

"WOO-HOO!" Ally cheered. "Oh, Olivia, I'm so happy for you! Congratulations! When is he due? Is his birth mom from around here?"

"He's due the end of July, and his birth mom lives in Idaho. We're super excited!"

"Ahh, that's great, Olivia! Just great. Hope will LOVE being a big sister!"

"Thanks, Ally. We're really excited."

"I'll bet you are." Ally pulled into her parking spot at the flower shop and unbuckled her seat belt. "Hey, I just got to work so I need to go, but I'll talk to you in a couple days. Congrats again!"

"Okay. Thanks, Ally. Have a good day at work. Bye."

"Bye."

Olivia touched the "End Call" button on her phone's screen and smiled at Michael. "She's excited."

"Oh, good." Michael put his arms around Olivia and pulled her close, softly kissing her on the corner of her mouth. It had been several days since they met Nicole, but once their social worker, Kevin, confirmed that Nicole's worker had contacted him and it looked like the adoption would move forward, Michael and Olivia had started calling their families with the exciting news. Ally was the final call they would be making today.

"I thought you told Hope we were going to go shopping for baby boy stuff," Olivia whispered with a smile.

"We are," Michael breathed. He reached up and tucked Olivia's hair behind her ear with a soft kiss. "But the stores aren't going anywhere."

Hope walked in and squealed. "Ewww! Gross, Daddy! Why are you kissing Mommy?"

They both laughed and Michael gave Olivia another kiss on the lips. "Because she's my girlfriend and I love her." Hope giggled and Michael released Olivia before reaching toward Hope with his fingers wiggling. "And you're my baby girl, so that means I get to tickle you!"

Hope squealed and started running. "Only if you catch me!" She paused in the hallway to make sure Michael was, in fact, chasing her, before she ran into her bedroom, delighted to be playing one of her favorite games with Daddy.

Once Hope had been thoroughly tickled by Michael and then

"rescued" by Olivia, the girls ganged up on Michael. Olivia held him down while Hope wiggled her little fingers under Michael's chin and squealed, "Tickle, tickle, tickle!" Michael squirmed and hooted in just the way he knew Hope expected. Finally, Hope sat down on Michael's chest, put a hand on either side of his face, and said seriously, "Now let's go get some clothes for my baby brother."

Two hours later they were walking out of Walmart with a cart full of diapers, formula, sleepers, and the softest green, sky blue, and yellow blanket Olivia had ever felt. Since they wouldn't need to pay any living expenses for Nicole, there was some extra money in the budget and they bought new crib sheets with a cute jungle theme and an adorable picture with a giraffe and two zebras that matched. Hope surveyed the filled sacks as they loaded everything into the car and then announced, "Now, we're ready for him!" Michael and Olivia both laughed while Olivia buckled Hope into her car seat.

"Yes, we are, Hope," Michael said. "Yes, we are."

CHAPTER FOUR

Ally sighed. She hadn't felt this content in quite a while. She dug her heels a little further into the warm sand. She had purposely slid them off the end of the beach towel so she could feel the soft grit against her heels. "I could get used to this," she said quietly and closed her eyes to soak in the heat pouring down on her.

Holly hadn't been exaggerating when she'd told Ally that her parents had plenty of room for her to stay at their house. Holly had grandparents and aunts and uncles who all lived nearby, so the six bedrooms at Holly's house were kept open for Damon and Holly's friends who were coming in from out of town. Shaylan's parents lived only an hour away, so she was staying at home but would be joining the group on Monday for the week at Disneyland, followed by the wedding. Ally had wondered about Holly's parents treating Holly and Damon, along with the bridal party (Ally, Shaylan, and one of Holly's cousins, along with Riley and Damon's two younger brothers) to four-day Disneyland park hopper tickets until she saw their gorgeous home and giant manicured yard complete with a swimming pool. Ally had known that Holly was an only child, but shortly after arriving two days ago, she'd learned that Holly was the only *living* child her parents had, although her mom had been pregnant five times. After three late-term miscarriages and one baby girl being stillborn, Holly's parents could take no more and had assigned all of their time and love and energy into raising Holly and working. They were thrilled to be celebrating their daughter's wedding and could afford to do it in style.

Ally had just arrived the night before, after driving here on her own, and had managed to avoid any one-on-one time with Riley so far. She'd missed her chance to be with him, and although she longed for another, she didn't feel like he would appreciate her dragging up the past now.

Ally rubbed the tears that formed in her eyes and then instantly regretted it as they began to burn from the sunscreen that lingered on her fingers. She was fumbling through her beach bag, trying to find a bottle of water to rinse them out, when she was startled by the very voice she had been thinking about.

"Looking for something?" Ally paused, caught off guard by his approach and by the obvious answer to his question. Riley shook his head and shoved his fingers through his hair. "I mean, I can see you're looking for something. I . . . I just wondered if you needed some help."

"I got this stupid sunscreen in my eye, and I know there's some water in here somewhere."

"I've got you covered." Riley pulled a bottle of water from the large pocket on the side of his cargo shorts and sat down next to her as he cracked open the lid. Ally reached for the bottle, but Riley pulled it back slightly. "You've still got sunscreen all over your hands. You'll never get your eye cleared up if you do it." He reached his hand up and paused just before he touched her cheek, as though asking permission to proceed. Ally sucked in a breath and leaned forward a bit.

Riley gently, hesitantly touched the side of her face and she tipped her head to the side. Ally's eyes closed as his touch registered in her mind. Seconds ticked by. "You'll have to open your eyes if I'm going to rinse them out," Riley said softly, and Ally felt her neck and cheeks warm as she looked into his face so close to her own. He trickled some water on the inside corner of her eye and let it run off the other side and drip onto the sand. He repeated it a few more times and then rubbed the remaining water from her cheek. "Better?"

Ally nodded, unnerved by the cascade of butterfly wings fighting to get out of her stomach and the heat that lingered on her cheek where his fingers had been. They sat in a charged silence until Riley finally cleared his throat and started standing up. "Well, I didn't mean to bug you. I'll let you get back to . . ." He looked around. ". . . whatever you were doing."

Thinking of you? "Riley, wait." Ally reached up and touched his arm. "Can I talk to you for a second?" Ally scooted over and motioned to the beach towel next to her, suddenly very aware that she was only wearing her swimsuit. She grabbed the cover-up that she'd been using as a pillow and slipped it over her head as Riley sat down again.

"Look, Riley." Ally swallowed the lump that came to her throat. "I'm sorry about how everything went down before Christmas." Riley was shaking his head as if to wave off her apology.

"Don't worry about it. No big deal."

Ouch. Ally hesitated. Maybe Riley had moved on and didn't care anymore. *Just say it. This is your chance. You'll regret it if you don't.*

Riley was looking toward the water, watching the whitecaps break as they neared the shore. *It's now or never.*

"Well, I'm still sorry." Ally took a huge breath and jumped in. "It's not that I didn't want to spend time with you. I was . . . scared . . . or something." She shook her head. "You probably haven't given it a second thought, but I have. I've replayed that moment over and over in my mind, wishing there was a way that I could go back and just . . . just *not* walk away."

Riley turned and looked into her eyes, but his expression was guarded. Ally had no idea what he was thinking. She couldn't hold his gaze, so she looked down and began tracing the pattern on her beach towel with her finger. "Then school started again, and I wanted to talk to you, but there was never a good time and then it had been so long, and then . . ." Ally shrugged and it was her turn to stare out at the water. "I'm probably too late, but I just had to tell you that I'm sorry. I'm sorry, and I wish that I would have done things differently." She reached up to wipe the tears that spilled onto her cheeks, careful not to touch her eyes and get sunscreen in them again. She didn't dare look at Riley. Her heart was pounding in her ears, drowning out the sound of the waves.

Ally felt Riley shift next to her. *Will he stand up and walk away? It would serve you right, you know.*

"Ally?" His voice was barely a whisper. She turned her head slightly toward him but didn't want to look into his eyes and reveal the vulnerability she felt. The air squeezed from her chest when Riley's hand rested on her shoulder and a current shot through her body as he whispered in her ear. "Will you please look at me?"

She slowly turned and found herself inches from his face. He let his fingertips trail down her cheek, and Ally forgot that they were on a crowded beach. "*I'm* sorry that I gave up so quickly." He leaned closer, stopping just a breath from her lips, giving Ally the chance to pull away. She didn't. Ally clung to the moment, the thrill of anticipation charging her body. Riley closed the gap, brushing her lips with his. His breath caught as Ally responded to his touch, and then he *really* kissed her.

Ally reluctantly released him several moments later, and Riley slowly shook his head, trying to calm his breathing. He looked up at her and grinned. "I should have done that months ago."

Ally laughed right out loud. "I should have let you."

Later that night, when Riley sat next to Ally and put his hand on her back, Holly raised an eyebrow at her friend and grinned. Ally blushed and smiled and then thoroughly enjoyed a light-hearted evening of card games with Riley by her side.

The next day was Sunday. Damon, Holly, and her parents would be attending their family ward, but Ally and Riley decided they would sleep in a bit and go to the singles ward that met two hours later. They stepped into the crowded chapel with five minutes to spare and scanned the chairs at the back of the room until they found two empty ones. Ally was pleasantly surprised when Riley softly touched the small of her back and led her to the chairs, and a thrill ran up her spine when they sat down and he wrapped his arm around her shoulder.

Ally was trying to listen to the speakers but found herself paying more attention to the gentle pressure of Riley's fingertips against her shoulder. She liked how it felt sitting this close to him, feeling as though they belonged together, feeling that maybe he really did care for her and that she might be able to trust him with the truth. She snuck a glance at him, only to discover that he was looking at her too. The familiar warmth crept up her neck and he leaned over and brushed his lips softly along her forehead before turning and looking to the podium at the front of the chapel again. Ally didn't hear a thing that was said during the rest of the meeting.

After the benediction had been offered, Riley turned to look at Ally. "To Sunday School, then?" When they left that morning, they were still undecided on whether to leave after sacrament meeting so they would arrive back at Holly's parents' about the same time as everybody else.

"Fine with me," Ally said. She was enjoying this time with Riley. They stood up, and as a few curious eyes from around the room lingered on Ally, Riley reached up and took her hand. Sure, they had gotten caught up in the moment and kissed yesterday, but Riley had never held her hand before. She turned and met his gaze, eyebrows raised. Riley shrugged and grinned and squeezed her hand. Ally's joy escaped in a laugh, and she squeezed back as they followed the crowd down the hall toward Sunday School.

Ally settled in to enjoy the next forty-five minutes at Riley's side but was jerked back to reality when a bubbly girl with extra curly brown hair stood up and announced that today's lesson would be on the law of chastity. "As we all know, it's *super* important to keep ourselves clean and pure so that we can marry in the temple." She winked at someone across the room whom Ally couldn't see. *Ugh. This isn't going to be pretty.* Ally knew, better than most, the importance of the law of chastity. She started sinking lower in her chair, then caught herself and straightened. *No. I'm not going to let her make me feel bad. I faced my consequences, I repented, and I have been forgiven. Besides, I certainly have a deeper understanding and appreciation of the Atonement and love for the Savior than I had before.* She smiled. *Nothing she can say will make me feel bad.*

While caught up in her own thoughts, Ally hadn't noticed the teacher reaching down under the table, but Miss Super Curl was now pulling a beautiful, long-stemmed, red rose from a paper sack that was on the floor. She flourished it in front of the class before beginning her well-rehearsed remarks.

"When I was sixteen, my Young Women's leader presented an object lesson that has really stuck with me, and I wanted to share it with you today." She held the rose up a little higher and cleared her throat before continuing. Ally was slightly curious, in spite of her initial annoyance at the girl. "Would anyone in here like to have this beautiful red rose?" Three girls on the front row immediately raised their hands, and the teacher gave them a quick smile and a little nod.

Her roommates. Ally rolled her eyes. But once the first three hands were in the air, many others followed suit. Ally glanced sideways at Riley and was surprised to see that his eyes were firm, and his mouth was set in a tight line. He looked almost angry. She was a little unnerved by his reaction. *Maybe he knows something that I don't about this little object lesson.* Feeling her initial curiosity twist into a pit in her stomach, Ally turned her attention back to the front of the room.

"Of course we all would love to have this flower." Super Curl gently stroked the delicate petals. "It's lovely. It's perfect. It's fresh and untainted." She looked up and paused for effect. "You might even say it's pure."

She continued to caress the soft, red petal. "But what if . . .

oops!" Super Curl pulled a few petals off and crumpled them before dropping them to the ground. "Oh no. Now look what I've done." She painted a frown on her face as she passed the rose to her three minions on the front row. They each took a turn rolling the flower around in their hands, being sure to rumple the petals and break a few of the leaves. "What if we pass this rose around for a bit?"

The young man next to the three girls hesitated as the flower was passed to him, but the teacher nodded vigorously, and he took it. "Go ahead," Super Curl continued. "Keep passing it." The rose made its way from hand to hand, and Ally sunk lower and lower in her seat. Now she could see where this was heading, and despite her determination not to feel guilt, she felt the traitorous burn of tears in her eyes. She focused on her hands, silently begging Riley not to look at her.

How could you have been so stupid to think that you deserve someone like him? Ally peeked up and her eye was drawn to the flower as it moved from person to person. Some class members were squirming a bit, seeming a little uncomfortable with this display. They just carefully passed the flower along. Others took care to pinch, break, or further destroy the rose.

To Ally's relief, before the flower made it to the back row where she sat with Riley, Super Curl swooped over and grabbed the now dilapidated rose. She carried it back to the front of the classroom shaking her head in mock sadness.

"It's too bad," she crooned. "This rose was so beautiful. It had so much potential." Her voice rose in pitch and volume. "But now it's been used, soiled. Just look at it." She thrust the flower in the air, and Ally felt as wilted as the rose. "This flower is now ruined. No longer is it perfect and pure. Who could possibly want this rose now?" She made a motion to toss the flower aside when Ally was startled by Riley's voice.

"I want it."

Super Curl's arm froze as her head jerked up to locate the traitor. "What did you say?"

Riley raised his hand so that she could find him. "I said that I want the rose." His voice was firm, almost daring her to challenge him.

Ally couldn't help but turn and stare at him. *Could he really be saying . . . ? Does this mean . . . ?* Her thoughts were a jumble as she tried to sort through his words.

Super Curl quickly regained her composure as she held out the rose and wrinkled her nose. "Well, I guess if you really want a ruined rose, that's your bad taste."

Riley's voice somehow became more powerful without increasing in volume. "Everybody here knows that you're not really talking about roses. You're talking about people. About Heavenly Father's children." She opened her mouth to protest, but Riley overrode her. "If what you're saying is true, if a person really is *ruined* by making mistakes and should be tossed aside, then why are we all here? The whole point of the gospel is that because of Jesus Christ, all wrongs can be made right. Because of the Atonement, sins can be washed away . . . wiped clean."

The bravado behind the teacher's eyes faded just a bit, but then she gathered herself and tried to pick up the pieces of her object lesson. "That's all well and good, but *I* still don't want to marry anyone who has already been *used* by someone else. Do you?"

It seemed the entire class inhaled at once, and Ally held her breath, waiting along with everyone else, for his answer.

Riley folded his arms. "I suppose that you're entitled to your feelings, but if you're going to push the Atonement aside, then this class is no place for me." He slowly stood and offered his hand to Ally. She didn't look into his face, afraid her eyes would betray her if she did, but she reached up and took his hand and let him lead her toward the door. The class was silent for a split second, and then erupted into a buzz of conversation as the door closed behind them.

Ally's mind was spinning. *Did he answer her question? Super Curl just asked Riley if he would marry someone who wasn't a virgin. It kind of* felt *like he would still consider a future with someone if they'd repented, and he was clearly upset about the object lesson . . .* Ally searched her memory of the last moments in the classroom. *But he never actually* said *that he would be with someone who had already had sex with somebody else.*

Ally didn't realize that she was shaking until they got to the foyer and Riley ushered her onto the couch and sat down next to her. "Are you okay?" he asked. "I'm sorry if I embarrassed you in there."

Ally started to say that she was fine, but the words caught in her throat and the tears that had been threatening finally spilled onto her cheeks.

"What is it, Ally? What's the matter?" He searched her face and his gaze forced her to meet his eyes. There was only concern written there.

Tell him. Ally hesitated at the thought. *Tell him now and then let the chips fall where they may. It's time.* Ally thought of all that she had been through, and all that she had learned. She thought of sweet little Hope with her curly blonde hair, and the hope she had come to depend on from the Savior. Ally thought about her longing to truly be at peace with herself and her future. She thought about Riley and how it felt to be near him. She took a deep breath and looked into his stunning green eyes. "I'd like to tell you something."

After a quick text to Holly telling her not to wait dinner for them, Ally suggested they drive to the beach where they could walk. Riley agreed. Ally was silent during the fifteen-minute drive, and Riley followed her lead, only handing her a packet of tissues from the jockey box when she continued sniffling and wiping her eyes. They arrived, and after walking to the water's edge, Ally slipped off her sandals to carry in one hand while they walked along the shoreline. Riley was content to let Ally take her time, and they continued in silence for several more minutes. Finally Ally dabbed at her eyes with the crumpled tissue she carried, took a deep breath, and began. "I want to tell you about Hope."

The talk went better than she had anticipated with Riley. At least he didn't storm off the beach and leave her to hitchhike back to Holly's. They talked for several hours. Well, actually, Ally talked for several hours with an occasional "hmm" or "I see" or "keep going" from Riley as they walked side by side on the beach. Riley held her hand, but his eyes were guarded, a perfect poker face.

Ally knew that this was a lot to digest, and it was easier to say that you believed in the power of the Atonement than to actually apply it in your life with something this big. She'd faced the same dilemma when wondering if the Savior really knew and cared about her personally and would actually help her.

Riley was quiet on the drive back to Holly's house, and Ally was all talked out. When they pulled into the driveway, Riley reached over and took Ally's hand. He stared out the windshield for what seemed like an eternity before turning to face her.

"Thank you for sharing this with me."

Ally nodded. She didn't trust her voice.

"So all along, this is what was keeping us apart?" Riley swallowed hard. "This is why you walked away from me, and why I've been miserable since Christmas?" His jaw trembled but he tried to smile. The effort brought tears back to Ally's eyes. Riley took a deep breath.

"I meant what I said back at the church, you know." His voice was soft. "I believe in the power of the Atonement. I believe in repentance."

Ally touched Riley's arm, but before she could respond, he continued.

"I also know that there are consequences and feelings that have to be faced and worked through." Ally looked up at the sadness that had seeped into his voice. "All of this came between us once already, and it was almost more than I could take. How do we know it won't come between us again?" He looked up, his eyes searching hers.

Ally looked down. "I guess we don't know," she whispered. "Not for sure."

Riley let go of her hand and buried his face in both of his hands. He sat for a few seconds, before pushing his fingers through his hair and looking up at her. Ally's heart broke at the sight of his tears. "That's what I'm afraid of, Ally."

She nodded. What could she say?

Riley reached over and tucked a piece of hair behind Ally's ear. His hand lingered on the side of her neck. He leaned forward and rested his forehead against hers. Ally closed her eyes, wanting to stay connected to him, not wanting this moment to end, afraid of what might come next.

Too soon, Riley pulled back. "Will you tell Damon that I'm going for a drive and I'll see him later tonight?" Ally found herself nodding again. Why couldn't she seem to find her voice? "I just need some time to think, you know?"

Riley reached for his door handle. Ally knew he was going to come around and open her door for her. She didn't want to face the sadness in his eyes again, so she quickly opened her own door and jumped out.

"I'll tell him," she managed to choke out before stumbling up the steps to the front door. She didn't turn around as she heard Riley's car drive slowly away.

Damon opened the door, but didn't focus on Ally. He was watching Riley's car head down the street. "I thought I heard the car pull up, but where's Riley going? There's a ton of food in the kitchen." When Ally didn't say anything, his gaze moved back to her face. She realized that she was probably a mess. She combed her fingers through her hair and wiped under her eyes.

"Are you okay, Ally?" Damon asked.

Ally nodded and shrugged at the same time. She didn't know. "Riley said to tell you he'll see you later tonight."

Damon nodded and Ally headed for the stairs. She just wanted to collapse in the privacy of her room. Holly appeared as Ally started climbing the stairs. She touched her friend on the shoulder, and when Ally turned, Holly read her expression and gave her a hug.

"You need anything?"

Ally shook her head. "Just some alone time."

Holly released Ally, who walked up the stairs.

⁂

Ally spent a restless night and slept only sporadically. She was feeling it this morning. She let the hot water from the shower soothe her tight muscles. If only it was possible to let her tension run down the drain with the sudsy water at her feet. She turned her attention to the warm water pouring down and focused on rinsing the conditioner out of her hair. "Well, the worst part is over," she said to herself. *At least the part you've been dreading is over. Today will tell if that was the worst part or not.* She didn't hear Riley come in last night, but then again, it was a big house and she hadn't really been listening. The plan was for all of them to go to Disneyland today. Ally sighed. She wasn't sure she was up to several days of "The Happiest Place on Earth," but she didn't want to ruin Holly and Damon's week. *Well, you never know,* she thought. *It might be just what I need.*

Ally enjoyed the warm spray for a few more minutes before getting out and toweling off. She was glad that her bedroom had an attached bathroom so she didn't have to hurry out of anyone's way. She rummaged through her suitcase and found her favorite pair of denim capris and the olive green fitted T-shirt that she bought for this trip. It was casual, but definitely cute. She considered her strappy sandals—they would look the best—but instead pulled out a pair of ankle socks and her tennis shoes. *Whatever else this day might hold, at least my feet won't be hurting.*

Ally checked the clock and realized that her extra time in the shower had cost her. They were planning on leaving soon. She applied a quick coat of makeup, relieved that her eyes weren't too puffy after her long night, and pulled her hair back in a messy bun. It was an easy look, but Ally knew that it worked on her. *Hopefully Riley will notice.* She took a deep breath and looked in the mirror. "You can do this," she said. Another moment passed as Ally looked herself in the eye, reinforcing her words with a stern glare. Then she left her room without a backward glance and headed down the stairs.

The kitchen counter was piled with bagels and cream cheese, cinnamon rolls, and several gallons of milk. The kitchen itself was no less crowded. All of Holly's extended family had arrived, and everyone was excited about the day ahead. There was plenty of laughter to go along with the eating, and it took Ally a minute before she realized that Riley wasn't there. She scanned the room one more time, wondering if she had somehow missed him when Holly walked up behind her and lightly grabbed her elbow.

"So, I guess Riley got up early and headed into Los Angeles."

Ally's heart sank, but she tried to control the emotions on her face. "Oh?"

"I don't know anything except that he told Damon that he wanted to catch a session at the temple this morning, and that he would meet up with us this afternoon."

Ally tried to say something, but her throat was squeezing together and she had to settle for a nod.

Holly glanced up, but no one was paying any attention to them. Still, she lowered her voice. "You told him about Hope." It wasn't really a question.

Again, Ally just nodded, fighting against the burn in her eyes. *Get a hold of yourself. This is Holly's week. Don't ruin it for her by moping around.* Ally swallowed hard, forcing a smile. "I did. We were kind of . . . starting something up, and I wanted him to know."

Holly offered a sympathetic smile and cocked her head to the side in the universal gesture that says, *I'm so sorry, but I don't really know what to say to you.*

"Hey, it'll be fine," Ally continued with a pat on Holly's shoulder. "Mickey Mouse, here we come!"

Holly gave her friend a quick squeeze. "You're the best, Ally."

CHAPTER FIVE

Riley's plan to leave early before Ally got up was a success. He hadn't slept much the night before and his mind was still buzzing. He couldn't see Ally this morning. Not yet. He had guessed that she'd been hurt by someone back when she walked away from him at Christmas time. He wasn't a complete idiot. There was chemistry between them, and he had known she felt it too before he bared his soul to her. But the reality was that regardless of *why* she had walked away and wouldn't let him in, it *had* happened, and he hadn't thought there was any way to fix it.

Then he saw her fumbling through her bag there on the beach, and he couldn't resist talking to her. In fact, he knew she was down there and had gone out looking for her. Then before he knew it, he was kissing her. *Man, was it good!* Riley smiled at the memory. He had felt that they could work through whatever was bothering Ally and see what would happen down the road.

Then came that stupid Sunday School lesson. Riley had seen a similar object lesson when he was younger, and it bothered him then. He clearly remembered wondering why they were even at church if a person was "ruined" by mistakes, with no chance for healing. What was the Atonement even about if not that we can all be made whole? He had wished he would've said something back then, but he didn't want to cause trouble, so he'd stayed quiet. It surprised him how intensely his emotions boiled up when he saw yesterday's teacher pull a rose out of her bag and launch into the same sermon. He just couldn't stay quiet. In his mind, it was wrong to stand up in front of a class and teach that no one could possibly want a person who had made a mistake. The gospel centered on healing and forgiveness. Sure, there were consequences, but there was always hope. Always healing. The Savior was always there.

Riley hadn't considered that the discussion would come full circle so quickly. In trying to regain control of her lesson, the teacher had asked him, "Would *you* marry someone . . ."

Riley sighed. As it turned out, it wasn't just "someone." It was Ally. Knowing what he knew now, knowing the reason for her rejecting him, knowing the pain this had already caused in their relationship, could he move forward with Ally? Could he risk this coming between them again?

You're a jerk for even having to think about this. Riley slapped the steering wheel. "You don't have to decide right now whether you're going to marry her," he said. He chided himself for his thoughts moving so quickly to marriage, but then Riley's memory lingered on Ally's big brown eyes and the way it had felt to hold her hand, to kiss her. He thought about how he hadn't been able to get Ally out of his mind after months of trying.

You can't pursue this any further if you don't think it could lead to something. Riley knew it wouldn't be fair to either of them to get in deeper, if all of these emotions were going to come between them later. No, he didn't have to decide on marriage today, but he did have to decide if he was willing to risk the heartbreak that would come if Ally ever pushed him away again.

"Be honest with yourself," he murmured. "You're also wondering if you'll be man enough to never throw this back in her face." All of his uncertainties aside, Riley knew that he never wanted to hurt Ally, never wanted to say in the heat of an argument something that he didn't mean and couldn't take back. Marriage was difficult enough, but what about when there is this kind of pain and heartache in the past?

To be fair, Ally seemed very much at peace with her decision. The thing that was really bothering him was that instead of talking to him about this after he'd first told her his feelings, she just walked away from him. *She didn't trust you enough to tell you.* That realization stung. Then the thought carried on to completion. *She didn't trust you enough to tell you at first, but she has told you now.* She trusted him now. She trusted him enough to share something very important about herself. *Can you live up to that trust?* Riley shook his head. He just didn't know. He had to clear his mind or he was never going to figure this out.

Riley forced himself to focus on the GPS navigation voice that was directing him to the temple. He arrived and found a parking spot. He turned off the car and sat for a moment, letting the early morning sun warm him through the glass. *I'm scared.* It was hard for him to admit that. Even after his shoulder injury, when his whole world was turned upside down, Riley hadn't been scared. Confused? Angry? Uncertain? Sure, but never scared. Knowing that Ally's past was what lead to her walking away from him all those months ago before Christmas scared him. *What if this comes between us again?* Riley didn't think he could handle it. He wasn't sure he wanted to take the risk.

Underneath it all, that was what had pushed Riley out the door early this morning before he had to face Ally. He needed some time and a quiet place to think, and he needed to sort through how he felt about all of this before he could talk with Ally. He couldn't be afraid. This decision was too important to be made out of fear.

Riley had been to the temple many times before, but he'd never had such a desire for peace as he had today. He really hoped that it would come.

Two hours later, Riley felt calmer, but the peace he was searching for wasn't there. He finally walked outside and found a place on the temple grounds to sit down in the shade. He closed his eyes to think and slipped into a silent prayer.

Heavenly Father, everything I've always been taught is telling me that Ally's past experiences and my own self-doubt aren't an obstacle. That because of Thy Son and His Atonement, we can overcome anything with Thy help. Riley paused, waiting for the warmth of confirmation to flood through him. Nothing. *But I guess I'm just scared that something unforeseen will come up, and that this will be too big of a challenge if we try to build a life together. Maybe there is too much pain, or maybe I'm not equipped to help and support her the way she deserves.* Again he stopped, listened, and tried to feel something. Riley sighed in frustration when nothing happened. *Heavenly Father . . .*

So, do you believe it or not? The words came softly, spoken by the internal voice Riley thought of as his own.

Do I believe what?

Do you believe what you've been taught since you were a child? Do you believe in the Atonement? Do you believe that Christ can offer healing . . . or not?

Of course I do, but—

Do you believe it or not?

Well, this is complicated because—

Do you believe it or not?

I just need to be sure that—

Do . . . you . . . believe it . . . or not?

Riley squeezed his eyes tight and gritted his teeth. He dropped his head into the palms of his hands. Was it possible that it was that simple? There were so many variables. So much he had to consider. What were the long-term issues that they might be faced with? Would this come between them again?

Do you believe me, or don't you?

Riley dropped his hands into his lap and opened his eyes. The first thing he saw was the white line that snaked its way from the base of his thumb, across the entire palm of his right hand, ending just below the first knuckle of his pinky finger. He rubbed the scar with his left thumb.

Wow. I haven't thought about that in a long, long time. Riley closed his eyes as his mind wandered back to being eleven years old and how excited he was to go fishing with his two best friends, all alone. He'd caught a little six-inch trout and was eager to show off his newly learned skill of cleaning a fish. Instead of waiting to find a place to lay the fish down, he'd held the slippery creature in the palm of his right hand and opened his new red pocketknife with his left. As Riley pressed the tip of the blade into the fish's shiny skin, it slipped and Riley was left staring at an angry gash that stretched the length of his palm, watching bright, red blood land on the forgotten fish at his feet.

The boys remembered the first aid training they'd had at cub scouts a few months before, and one of them took off his shirt and wrapped it tightly around the bloody hand. Somehow they'd made it home where Riley's mom took one peek at it before wrapping it back up and hurrying him to the car where they sped to the emergency room. The wound was deep, and before the evening was over, Riley had been whisked away to surgery to try and repair the damaged tendons. It had taken weeks of painful physical therapy before Riley could use his hand properly, and even longer before he could use it without it throbbing and aching. It seemed to go on forever.

One day, after a particularly frustrating hour trying to weed the garden, Riley had cried to his dad. "This is never going to get better!" Riley hadn't thought about his father's answer for years and years, but now it came to his mind with perfect clarity. His dad had put down his rake, wiped the dust from his forehead with the back of his arm, and then knelt down next to Riley to take his hand where the scar was still a large, purplish welt.

"That was a terrible wound, and it's been a hard and painful road to get it to this point. I'd like to tell you when it will stop hurting, and that once that day comes, it will never bother you again, but that wouldn't be the truth." His dad sighed. "The truth is, I don't know how long it will take before the pain ends, and even then, a scar will remain. But instead of letting it bother you, you can use that scar as a reminder of all that this experience has taught you."

"I'm not learning anything except that I hate how this feels," Riley whined.

His dad just laughed and put his arm around him. "Sure you are. Did you learn not to try and clean a fish while you're balancing it in one hand?"

"Yeah."

"Are you learning that it takes time and patience, as well as hard work, for some wounds to heal?"

"I guess so."

"Are you learning that sometimes healing is painful?"

Riley rolled his eyes. "I get it."

"And sooner or later you'll learn that your hand will be perfectly fine again. It'll be every bit as good as it was before. Oh sure, you'll have a little scar there, but that will represent everything you know now that you didn't know before all of this. And then, the day will come when you even quit thinking about the scar and the things you've learned, because those lessons have just become a part of who you are, and you'll be a better person for having gone through them."

"All right, all right."

"Do you believe me, Riley?" His dad stood up and tousled his hair.

"Sure I do, Dad."

Do you believe it or not, Riley? Do you believe that the Atonement can bring about true healing? Do you believe that the lessons we learn along the way can be valuable and that we can grow because of them? Do you believe that with hard work and the Savior's love, everything can be made right? Do you believe that the Savior understands all that you are feeling and struggling with and that He can help you make it through? Do you believe that our scars can remind us of the things we've learned until eventually we start to become the people we need to be and we don't even look at the scars anymore? You've been taught this all of your life. Now it's time to take a good hard look at what you say you believe. Is it true? Do you really believe it?

Riley opened his eyes, and he looked first at his scar and then up at the temple. Tears filled his eyes. "I do," he said quietly. "I really do." The warmth and peace he had been trying so hard to find finally washed over him.

CHAPTER SIX

The entire group emerged from the infamous briar patch soaked and laughing. "Splash Mountain has always been one of my favorite rides," Holly said.

"Mine too," Shaylan agreed. Shaylan met them at the front gate that morning, and Ally had decided to enjoy the day with her friends and not worry about Riley. She was succeeding with her first goal, but the second was proving to be more difficult.

Ally's phone buzzed in her pocket and she pulled it out to check the text. *Riley.* Her heart started pounding and her hands were shaking as she opened the message.

Walking through the front gate. Where r u guys?

She forced the tremor out of her voice. "Are we heading over to Thunder Mountain next?"

Damon nodded as they continued walking. "Yep. Why?" Ally fell to the back of the group.

"I guess Riley's here and he wanted to know where to meet us."

Shaylan and Holly both turned and looked at her, but Ally just shrugged. She looked down and started texting.

Almost to Thunder Mtn. We'll wait for u.

It only took a moment for Riley's response.

Tell the others to go ahead. Can we talk?

Ally almost tripped. She had to remind herself to breathe. She typed one letter.

K.

When they reached the entrance to the mining-themed roller coaster, Damon scanned the crowd, looking for Riley. Ally's pulse was pounding in her ears. *Calm down before you pass out.* "Hey, Damon? Why don't you all get in line. I'll wait for Riley, and we'll meet you back here once you're done."

Damon hesitated, and then Holly touched his arm. "Yeah, let's go. They'll be fine." Holly turned and winked at Ally as they all headed down the path that led to the ride.

Ally spotted a nearby bench and sat down. Now that she was alone, she was shaking worse than ever, and she could hardly hear over the roar in her ears. *Get a hold of yourself!* She took a deep breath, pleading with her body to calm down. *What if he tells me that he doesn't want to see me again? Or worse, that we should just be friends? Ugh. Talk about a dagger. Breathe, Ally. You're making it worse.*

In spite of her panic, Ally smiled at herself. Riley would be here any minute and trying to guess how he would brush her off wasn't going to change one thing. She focused on the sounds of people around her, concentrating on pushing back the dizzying whoosh of her own heartbeat in her ears. She took a slow breath, then another. Her hands were still shaking, but she ignored them, intent on calming her mind. She closed her eyes.

Maybe you're underestimating him. He's not Scott, after all. Ally turned her thoughts back to the warmth and the hope that had flooded through her soul countless times during her pregnancy, her meetings with Bishop Jenkins, Hope's placement, and the years since then. *Nothing can change the past, but the Savior is helping you become the person you are meant to be. Michael, Olivia, and Hope are a beautiful family, and you helped create that happiness. You've been through a lot, but you've come out a better person on the other side. Don't underestimate Riley, but more important do not underestimate yourself.*

Ally opened her eyes. She could breathe again, and there was only a slight tremble in her fingers. "Thank you," she whispered, and tears pricked her eyes as her heart was wrapped in hope and love and peace. She looked up and saw Riley approaching. Ally brushed at her eyes, and then smiled as she motioned for him to sit down beside her.

"How was the temple?"

Riley smiled. "Good. Sorry I left without seeing you this morning."

"You don't owe me an apology," she said softly. "You don't owe me anything, actually."

Riley nodded and cleared his throat. "I know that, Ally." He stared intently at the fraying cuff of his khaki cargo shorts. "The thing is . . ." Riley looked up and saw Ally staring past him, her big brown eyes guarded. His voice caught. He slowly reached up and touched Ally's chin, asking her to look at him. Their eyes met, and he lowered his hand. "I'm sorry about yesterday. I'm sorry I dropped you off and drove away." He clasped his hands together. "I was really feeling overwhelmed."

"I can understand that. I knew you would be."

"But you probably don't realize that when you told me how all of your experiences were the reason you walked away from me before . . ." Riley pushed his fingers through his hair, and Ally couldn't help but smile. She had come to love watching him do that when he was thinking hard. "Well, honestly, I got scared."

Ally didn't know what to say. She hadn't expected scared. She waited.

"I know that sounds stupid, but I was scared that somehow Hope—"

Riley hesitated and Ally nodded. "It's okay to talk about her."

The corners of his mouth turned up ever so slightly before he continued. "I was scared that somehow Hope would come between us again, or that I wouldn't know how to support you in the right way, or that you would need more help than I would be able to give." Riley sighed and tentatively reached over and covered Ally's hand with his own. "I was scared that I would get hurt again, or that somehow I'd hurt you."

Ally didn't move. She could hardly breathe. "It's okay," she whispered. "I know it's a lot to wrap your mind around."

"Well, that's just the thing, Ally. Today I realized that I was trying too hard to wrap my mind around it logically, when what I really need to do is open my heart and think about it spiritually."

He took his hand off hers and started rubbing his right palm. "Ally, today I realized that it all boils down to whether or not I believe that the Atonement of Jesus Christ can heal all wounds and right all wrongs. Whether or not He can actually dry our tears and carry our burdens. I've said that I believe it for a long time, and I taught it on my mission, but today I had to ask myself whether I *really* believe it. Because if I do, then I don't need to know exactly how things will end up between us. I don't need to have all of my questions answered. I just need to believe. If it's true, then I need to have faith that the Lord is watching us and guiding us and that because of Him, I don't need to be afraid."

Ally met Riley's eyes, and she saw understanding shining back at her. "I do believe it, Ally. I believe all of it." Ally felt a tear slide down her cheek. Riley reached up and gently wiped it away. "I really care about you, Ally. I have so much fun with you, and when we're not together I can't stop thinking about you. You are strong and independent, and soft and vulnerable all at the same time. You obviously love Jesus Christ and probably have a better understanding of Him than I do. The things you have been through have made you the amazing woman that you are today, and I wouldn't change the person you are for anything."

Ally was crying now, oblivious to all of the people walking by, and Riley gathered her up in his arms and spoke softly in her ear. "I want to get to know you better, Ally. I want to spend more time with you, because I already care about you more than any girl I've ever known. Will you forgive me for not saying all of this yesterday, and give me one more chance?" Ally felt him smile in her hair. "I'm not scared, anymore."

Ally buried her head in Riley's shoulder and cried. He held her and let her cry. She looked up and smiled through her tears. Their faces were inches apart.

"Do I get one more chance?"

Ally nodded. "Of course."

Riley squeezed her even more tightly, and Ally laid her head against his chest as warmth and peace settled over her.

ꕥ ꕥ

The rest of the days at Disneyland passed in a blur, leading up to one magical moment on the last night they were there. The whole group was squeezed together on the ground watching the fireworks light up the sky above Sleeping Beauty's castle. Riley leaned close and whispered in her ear. "Beautiful!"

Although his breath sent a tickle down her spine, Ally didn't move her eyes from the amazing pyrotechnic display going on above them as she agreed. "Yeah, they are beautiful!"

Riley chuckled. "I wasn't talking about the fireworks, silly girl." She turned to face him and laughed.

"That was kind of cheesy, you know."

He wrapped his arms around her. "Yeah, I know. True, though."

She giggled. "Everyone is watching us."

"No they're not. They're watching the fireworks."

"No, we're watching you." Damon laughed from the other side of Riley.

"Well, I don't care if they *are* watching." Riley's eyes reflected the bursts of light surrounding them, and Ally's stomach flipped. "Ever since I kissed you at the beach, I've been thinking about kissing you again."

"So, are you going to kiss me, or are you going to keep thinking about it?" Ally blushed at her attempt to flirt.

"I was thinking," Riley toyed, "that I would kiss you right . . . now." And he did.

Ally couldn't imagine anything more perfect than that moment.

ꕥ ꕥ

The wedding went off without a hitch. Holly and Damon were so happy they seemed to glow, and when Holly took aim and fired her bouquet right into Ally's arms, Ally blushed right down to the tips of her toes. She spent the remainder of the reception dancing in Riley's arms and helping Shaylan and the rest of the wedding party decorate the happy couple's car with streamers, balloons, and plenty of shaving cream.

Holly and Damon left for their honeymoon, and Ally, Riley, and Shaylan crashed one last night at Holly's parents' house before they headed back to Provo. Shaylan insisted on driving Ally's car home so that Ally and Riley could ride together. They talked the entire way back to Provo, and by the time Riley helped her and Shaylan carry their luggage up to the apartment that night and then drove away, Ally was convinced that Riley would be a huge part of her life from now on.

CHAPTER SEVEN

"Are you sure you're ready for this, Riley?" Ally called as she frosted the last cupcake and set it on a tray with the others.

Riley walked out of the bathroom tucking in the red T-shirt with the United States flag on it that Ally had provided for him to change into when he arrived. "Of course I am." He moved into the kitchen and stuck a finger into the bowl of frosting. "I'm actually very excited to meet Hope." He licked his finger and then walked behind Ally and wrapped his arms around her waist. "Are you sure that *you're* ready?"

Ally leaned her head against his chest, liking how comfortable she felt with Riley. "I am." She nodded. "I really am." She surveyed her cupcakes and added red, white, and blue sprinkles to some of them. "Hope is the cutest little girl you'll ever meet." She turned around so they were facing and Riley kissed the tip of her nose. "And it's time for you to meet Michael and Olivia too."

Riley kissed her softly and pulled away with a sigh. "I love you, you know."

Now it was Ally's turn to kiss him. "Yeah. I know. I love you too."

Riley carried the cupcakes to his car, and they headed north on I-15. Before long, they were pulling up in front of Michael and

Olivia's house. They got out and the unmistakable scent of grilling meat greeted their noses. "Smells good," Riley commented as he balanced the cupcake tray in one hand and held Ally's hand with the other.

"Michael always goes all out on the Fourth of July," Ally said. "There'll be steaks, chicken, burgers, the works." She laughed. "Way more than the five of us will be able to eat."

"That sounds like a challenge to me," Riley said with a grin. Right then, his stomach rumbled, and they both laughed. "I can't wait."

Before they reached the front door, it burst open and a cute little girl, with blonde curls and a nose just like Ally's, came running out.

"Alleeeeeeee," she squealed and jumped up for Ally to catch her.

"Hey, kiddo! Good to see you. How's your summer going?"

Hope wrinkled her nose. "Pretty good, 'cept Mommy makes me do chores *before* I get to swim."

"Yeah, that's what moms do."

"Why?"

"Because that's their job."

"Oh."

Ally laughed and ruffled a few fly-away curls before setting Hope down and holding her hand. Riley was content to watch. *That's Ally's daughter. Wow.* Ally motioned Riley to follow them into the house.

"Come on in," a voice called from the kitchen.

"We are," Ally said. Riley followed them into the kitchen where a woman with brown curls to match Hope's was sprinkling something on top of some deviled eggs. Riley recognized her from the pictures Ally had showed him. *Olivia.* She wiped her hands on a dish towel and then gave Ally a big hug. Hope was eyeing the neatly arranged tray of eggs and Olivia handed her two.

"Here you go, sweetie. One for you, and take one out to Daddy."

Hope's eyes lit up and she threw her arms around Olivia's legs in a tight squeeze before grabbing the eggs. "Thanks, Mommy!" She shoved hers into her mouth in one bite and ran out the back door.

In that brief exchange, Riley's perspective shifted. Hope was excited to see Ally, and clearly loved her, but more as the cool, favorite aunt or something. The little girl certainly didn't look at Ally the same way she looked at Olivia when she squeezed her legs and called her Mommy. He corrected his former thought in his mind. *No, Hope isn't Ally's daughter. She's Olivia's daughter. Olivia's daughter who was able to join her family because of Ally.*

He squeezed Ally's hand, and her body tensed as she turned to look at him. Ally's right eyebrow quivered, a sure giveaway that she wasn't as calm as she appeared. Her chocolate eyes were searching his face. Riley was sure that Ally was looking for signs of panic or discomfort, but as he looked around from Ally to Olivia and out through the sliding glass door that Hope had left open, Riley realized how *right* this all felt.

Riley smiled and gave Ally a wink. He set the tray of cupcakes down on the counter and pulled her up next to him before whispering in her ear, "Thanks for bringing me here." Ally exhaled, unaware that she had been holding her breath and met Riley's smile with one of her own.

"Thanks for being here." Ally's eyes welled up with the realization of just what it truly meant to have Riley *here* with her. She gave him a quick squeeze before turning to Olivia, who had busied herself by rummaging around in the refrigerator. "So, Olivia," Ally began and Olivia immediately closed the fridge door and turned around. "This is Riley."

A fun afternoon filled with lots of laughter followed. Michael and Riley talked a lot of football and then moved on to basketball as they speculated how the recent NBA draft would affect their favorite teams. Olivia showed Ally the baby boy nursery they had all set up in a cute jungle theme. "Just a few more weeks, right?" Ally asked.

"Yep. Nicole's due date is in about three weeks, but her doctor says it looks like she might have him before that." Olivia tenderly fingered the tiny blue sleepers in the top drawer of the dresser. Tears filled her eyes as she closed the drawer. "I'm just so happy!"

Ally hugged her. "Congrats, Olivia! I'm so excited for you guys!"

"Thanks," Olivia said as she wiped her eyes. "Come on. Let's get back outside before the guys eat all of the food."

As the sun started going down, Riley and Michael disappeared to the front yard, saying that they needed to get everything ready for the fireworks. Ally and Hope followed Olivia into the kitchen where she produced a large box of fireworks from the cupboard above the fridge. "All right," Hope cheered. "I love fireworks!" She ran out the front door and Olivia and Ally followed her, laughing at her excitement.

Michael and Riley were trying to attach something to the oak tree in the front yard when the girls stepped out on the porch. "Hey, Livvy!" Michael shouted. "Could you come help us with this?"

Olivia nodded and both women started down the stairs. "Ally," Michael continued, "would you mind going to the trunk in the spare bedroom and grabbing a quilt that you girls can sit on during our fireworks show?"

"Sure." Ally went back inside and headed to the spare bedroom in the basement. *This has gone even better than I hoped for.* She thought of the ease with which everyone had accepted one another and of the relaxed conversations. Her stomach flipped when she remembered Riley holding her hand this afternoon and gently running his fingers up and down her arm.

After they had eaten, Michael and Olivia had gone inside to put Hope down for a nap. Ally looked up to find Riley studying her face with such emotion that she found it hard to breathe. When she asked him why he was staring at her,

Riley had kissed her. Even the memory filled Ally's body with warmth.

She shook her head, returning to the present moment, and laughed at herself. *I'm all in*, she thought. *I've let myself become totally in love with him*. She smiled. *But I'm so glad I did*.

Ally opened the old trunk in the corner of the room and found a denim quilt, which she quickly scooped up, and then she raced back up the stairs. She was looking forward to snuggling up next to Riley while watching the little fireworks show on the driveway. But when she walked out the front door, something was wrong.

Michael wasn't setting up the colorful, powder-filled cardboard cones on the driveway, and Olivia and Hope weren't waiting patiently on the grass. Instead, they were all gathered around the tree, and sparklers were everywhere. There were sparklers stuck in the grass around them, all three of them were holding sparklers, and there were even sparklers stuck to the tree. Riley was standing in the middle and his smile flickered in the erratic light of the sparklers.

"Ally, could you come over here? Please?"

Ally felt both frozen to the spot and somehow drawn to Riley. Something was definitely going on. She commanded her feet to move, and as she approached, Riley dropped to one knee and held out a small black box.

Ally's heart constricted, and she forced her lungs to drag in some air. Riley was looking up at her expectantly, longingly. "Allison Jane Campbell, you are the most amazing woman I've ever known. You are smart and funny and tough and sweet. You make me laugh and sometimes you make me want to pull my hair out." Riley laughed softly. "You are honest and kind and loving and independent, and the most beautiful woman on the planet."

Ally felt tears on her cheeks, but she was too mesmerized by Riley's voice to pay them any heed. "Ally, I love you. I love you, and I would be so honored if you would be my wife." Riley swallowed hard, and his emerald eyes continued to glow even as the sparklers started to fade. He opened the lid on the ring box to reveal a beautiful, round diamond flanked on either side by clusters of smaller diamonds. "Ally, will you marry me?"

Ally's face was numb, her hands were shaking, her heartbeat was pounding in her ears, and she had never felt so happy in her entire life. "Yes," she whispered. Riley's smile melted her heart. He slowly pulled the ring from the box and reached for Ally's left hand when a tiny voice pulled Ally back to reality.

"What did she say, Mommy?"

"Shh, Hope. Just a minute," Olivia whispered.

Riley slipped the ring onto Ally's finger, and she watched it reflect the flickers from the few remaining sparklers. She pulled her gaze from the ring long enough to turn to Hope. And Ally found her voice. "I said yes!" she yelled. "Yes, yes, yes!" Michael, Olivia, and Hope all started cheering.

Riley scooped Ally up and spun her around one time before whispering in her ear. "You've made me the happiest man in the world."

Ally sighed and looked up at Riley, and he kissed her with all of the passion and promise of their new life together. Ally lost herself in the warmth and potential of the moment, not even noticing Hope giggling and Olivia trying to shush her.

CHAPTER EIGHT

Olivia surveyed the completed stack of burp cloths on the dining room table as she packed her sewing machine back into its case. "Ten burp rags, finished!" she announced to no one in particular.

"Good job, Mommy," Hope said, running in and grabbing one of the soft flannel cloths from the top of the stack and rubbing it on her cheek.

"Do you think Baby Matthew will like it?" Olivia asked.

"He'll love it," Hope said.

"Yes, he will," Michael agreed as he walked in and put an arm around Olivia's shoulder. She leaned in and gave him a quick kiss before smiling and combing Hope's curls away from her eyes with a practiced hand.

"Thanks. I'm glad they're done."

They all moved back into the living room where Michael was trying to teach Hope how to play UNO. He flipped five cards in Olivia's direction. "Have you heard anything from Nicole today?"

Olivia gathered up her cards. "Nope. She called yesterday and said the doctor told her it could be any time now, but I haven't heard anything yet. Her due date's in five days, so . . ." Olivia let the thought trail off.

Michael nodded as Hope tried to play a red three on top of a green seven. "No, Hope, remember you have to match the color or the number."

"But I like red best, and I only have a three."

Michael laughed and scooped Hope up in a hug. "Who loves you more than your daddy?"

Hope laughed at the little game they always played before she squealed, "No one! No one loves me more than my daddy!"

Olivia's cell phone chimed, the signal that a text message was coming in. She moved her attention from her husband and daughter and went to the table to pick up her phone. Her heart almost jumped out of her chest when she saw the name on the screen. "It's from Nicole!"

Michael jumped to his feet. "Open it, open it!"

Olivia took a breath and forced her hands to stop shaking so she could press the right buttons. After a few very long seconds, Olivia opened the message:

> *Water broke. I'm at the hospital.*
> *Baby coming today. Please don't come.*
> *Sorry, but I just can't.*

The air rushed from Olivia's lungs and her knees swayed. She grabbed the back of the chair to steady herself. Michael was at her side in an instant. "What is it, Livvy?" His voice was rough with concern. "What does it say?"

She numbly passed him the phone as her lungs protested the lack of air and she started gasping. Hope stood up. "What's wrong, Mommy?"

Olivia shook herself. *Get a hold of yourself. Don't lose it in front of Hope.* She couldn't force any words out. *Heavenly Father, help!*

The color drained from Michael's face as he absorbed the text message, and he wrapped his arm around Olivia's shoulder to steady them both. "Come sit down, Livvy," he said softly as he led her around to the couch.

"What's wrong, Daddy? What's wrong?" Hope's eyes were wider than usual. She was scared.

"Come here, sweetie. Come sit on Daddy's lap."

Olivia still couldn't make her voice work, but her shuddering breaths had calmed. Tears streamed down her face, leaving streaks on her cheeks. Hope wiped at them. "Why are you crying, Mommy? Why is Mommy crying?"

Olivia sent a pleading glance to Michael. *Please tell her. I can't do it.*

Michael swallowed the lump in his throat, and Hope touched the tear that leaked out of the corner of his eye. "Well, Hope, Nicole is having the baby today—" Hope's eyes lit up and she started to clap, but Michael gently touched her arm and cut off her celebration, "but it looks like she's decided that she is going to be his mommy, so I don't think he's going to come to our family."

Hope's brow furrowed as she tried to process this news. "But Baby Matthew is 'sposed to be *our* baby." Her tiny voice cracked on the last word.

Olivia sensed Michael's pain in his silence.

"That's what we all wanted, sweetie," Livvy said softly, finding her voice so she could rescue Michael. "But it just isn't our choice. It's Nicole's choice, and if she wants to be his mommy . . ." Olivia couldn't continue and her sentence ended in a shrug.

Michael gathered his two girls in a hug and they sat on the couch for a long time, holding each other and crying. Olivia's cell phone rang a few minutes later, and Michael showed Olivia the caller ID before he answered. It was their social worker.

"Hi, Kevin." Pause. "Yeah, she sent us a text." Pause. "Well, you can imagine." Pause. "Okay, talk to you later."

Michael's eyes were flat as he hung up the phone. "Kevin just got off the phone with Nicole's social worker. She's changed her mind."

Olivia nodded. Any remaining chance was gone. Nothing was left. She felt empty. Hope looked up. She had been crying with them, but Michael was unsure whether she fully understood what was happening. "So, we're not getting a baby?" she asked.

"No, sweetie, we're not," Michael said, swiping his hand down over his face in frustration and pain.

Olivia choked back a sob as she thought of the hours of love that were represented in the nursery down the hall; of the unfulfilled dreams sitting stacked on the table near her sewing machine. The baby boy she had envisioned was gone. Just like that. Gone. And worse than that, her claim on him was gone. Ripped away before it had ever been given. He wasn't her Baby Matthew. He never had been hers, and now he never would be. She couldn't hold it in any longer and the pain broke free in a torrent of tears. Hope curled up next to her and Olivia clung to her, clung like she was her lifeline, and so she was in that moment. Michael held them both and tried to wrap them in love while his own heart broke.

"Are you sure you want to do this?" Michael pulled the car into a parking spot and turned off the key before looking at Olivia. "Are you sure you don't want to keep it all in the back of the closet in the downstairs bedroom?"

Olivia nodded. "I'm sure. I kept the tiny hat that Grandma crocheted for him, and the little sleeper I picked out the day after Nicole told us he would be ours." She dabbed at her eyes with the tissue she held in her hand. "The rest of this stuff needs to be used, and we can't use it."

Michael took her hand. "You're sure you don't want to save it for the future?"

Olivia nodded. "I'm sure. It will always remind me of Matthew and how he was almost part of our forever family. Almost."

Michael leaned over and kissed her cheek. "I love you, Livvy. You're amazing."

She smiled at the compliment but slowly shook her head. "I'm not so sure about the amazing part. It's been over a month now and I still cry about him."

"That's normal, Livvy. You lost a baby."

She nodded absently. "I wish people could understand that. I *did* lose a baby. Remember when Sister Preston's baby was stillborn and everyone rallied around her and supported her and helped them through?" Michael nodded. He had thought about the same thing. "Remember at the funeral when everyone talked about how she was still their daughter and they'd get to raise her one day?"

Michael nodded again. "It was beautiful, wasn't it?"

"It really was, and she seemed to draw strength from that knowledge." Olivia rubbed her forehead. "But what do I have? He's gone. I have no claim or right to him in this life or the next. And I loved him." Her voice cracked. "I really and truly did. I really do." Olivia stared out the window. "I just need a little time, you know?" Michael nodded. He did know.

"Are you mad at Nicole?" Michael had wanted to ask that in the weeks since the baby's birth, but the timing had never been right. He thought it was important to talk about, though.

"You know, the funny thing is, I'm really not." Olivia looked at Michael and he was nodding in agreement. "I totally understand that this was one hundred percent her decision, and she has every right in the world to change her mind. I mean, I can't even imagine how difficult it would be." Olivia shook her head and sighed. "But can I still be sad for me? For us?"

"Of course."

They sat in silence for a moment before Olivia cleared her throat. "All right, let's go. I already decided that there was no more sitting around wallowing." She tried to laugh, although it was a little strained. Michael loved her all the more for the effort.

"Let's do it," he agreed. They got out and opened the trunk of the car. Neatly packed inside were two boxes filled with tiny newborn clothes, blankets, burp rags, a couple packages of diapers, some bottles, and a package of pacifiers. Michael put his arm around Olivia's shoulder and gave it a squeeze. The boxes contained all of the personal items they had purchased or made for their new baby. They each picked up a box and carried it up the stairs and into the Neonatal Intensive Care Unit of the hospital, to be distributed and used as the nurses needed. Olivia's eyes were glistening as the head nurse thanked them profusely and promised that everything would be put to good use, but she was able to keep the tears from spilling over.

They walked back to the car holding hands in a comfortable silence. Michael opened Olivia's car door and then walked around and let himself in. As he was turning the key in the ignition, Olivia finally spoke. "Thanks for coming with me. I can't really explain it, but I feel lighter now. Better." Her face showed the hint of a smile. "Better."

"I'm glad, Livvy. Me too." Michael briefly touched her cheek before backing out of the parking spot. "Do you want to go get lunch?"

Olivia shook her head. "No, let's go home. I need to see Hope. And I want to give her the biggest squeeze of her life."

"Sounds like a great plan," Michael agreed.

CHAPTER NINE

"I love St. George in November," Olivia said as she walked through the parking lot toward the temple. Hope was skipping along between Olivia and Michael in the shimmery pastel green dress that Ally had sent especially for today.

"Me too," Michael agreed. "We need to leave the cold of Utah County to come down here more often. Don't you think, Hope?"

"Yep! Can we go swimming at the motel later?"

Olivia laughed. "Tomorrow, sweetie. Remember? Ally and Riley are getting married right now and tonight is their reception."

"That's the party, right?"

Michael smiled at the eagerness in Hope's voice. "Yes, that's the party."

"Okay." Hope reached up and Michael and Olivia each took one of her hands as they approached the street. "But I get to swim tomorrow?"

"For sure," Olivia said.

"Good." Satisfied that she would be spending tomorrow at the indoor pool, Hope turned her attention to the small group of people standing by the fountain outside the temple doors. "Who is Emma and Elsie?" Hope whispered as they got closer.

"Emma and Elsie are the two girls who are wearing the same color dress as you," Olivia replied.

"And I get to play with them while you're in the temple, and then you'll come right back out after the wedding?"

"That's right, Hope. It'll be fun," Michael said.

"Hi, Emma. Hi, Elsie," Olivia said as they walked up. "I'm sorry but I just can't tell you two apart." The two beautiful teenage girls laughed.

"It's okay. Nobody can," said one of them. "I'm Emma." She touched her hair. "Mom made me do my hair up today and Elsie left hers down so that everyone could tell us apart."

"And I'm Elsie," said the other girl.

They both had the same cute nose as Ally and Hope. *Must be a dominant gene*, Olivia thought with a smile.

"Hi, Hope," Emma said, kneeling down next to Hope, eyes glistening. "I haven't seen you since you were a tiny baby."

"I'm almost five now," Hope said.

"Well, you're certainly growing right up," Elsie said, reaching down to take Hope's hand. "Emma and I have been checking out all of the best flowers, and we found some great ones to show you."

"Can I go, Mom?" Hope asked.

"Of course," Olivia replied. "Have fun and we'll see you in a bit."

Michael mouthed the words *thank you* to Emma and Elsie before they turned and led Hope around the corner of the building. They smiled and waved.

⁂

Michael and Olivia sat holding hands in the middle of Ally and Riley's friends and family. Ally's parents had made them feel right at home by coming over and giving them a big hug and thanking them for coming. "We wouldn't have missed it," Michael said.

Once the wedding began, Olivia couldn't decide who looked happier, Ally or Riley. Neither of them could quit smiling, and when the ceremony was over, Riley kissed his bride so tenderly that it brought tears to Olivia's eyes. Everyone quietly congratulated the couple, and Ally and Riley thanked everyone for coming. "How are *you* doing?" Ally asked Olivia when it was her turn to hug the bride and groom.

"Actually, pretty good," Olivia whispered. Ally knew how difficult the past months had been for Olivia after the adoption plan fell through. "But today is about you, and you look beautifully happy."

Ally's smile got even wider. "I am. I just have this overwhelming feeling of"—Ally crinkled her nose as she searched for the right word—"of peace, you know? Like everything is working out the way it's supposed to."

"Good," Olivia said. "You deserve it." She gave Ally a big hug and then stepped back.

"Thanks again for coming," Riley said. "It really means a lot to us that you both are here."

Michael shook Riley's hand and patted his shoulder. "We're really proud of you." Michael reached up and put his other hand on Ally's shoulder. "Of both of you. Congratulations."

Later that night after the reception was over and Hope's exhaustion had finally overpowered her excitement, Olivia and Michael were visiting quietly on the little sofa in the sitting area of their hotel room.

"I've been thinking a lot about what Ally said today," Olivia said.

Michael was softly rubbing his thumb back and forth over Olivia's hand. "What was that?"

"About feeling an overwhelming sense of peace."

"Oh?" Michael smiled in the dim lamplight and put his arm around Olivia, pulling her closer to him. "What do you mean?"

"Well, the day that we found out Nicole changed her mind, I was devastated. I distinctly remember feeling like I had nothing left. Feeling . . . empty." Michael nodded, waiting for Olivia to continue. "But right when I was feeling that way, Hope snuggled into my arms, and you held both of us and in that moment that I didn't think I could go on . . . I did." Olivia looked up into Michael's face, her eyes sparkling. "I didn't recognize it in the moment, but I wasn't empty at all. I have you, and I have Hope." She laughed softly. "Even in a time where it seemed like He had let me down, the Savior *did* bless me. He *was* blessing me . . . with peace."

"You've worked really hard for that," Michael said.

"I have, but the funny thing is, the peace that Ally mentioned, that I'm finally discovering, has been there all the time." Olivia tucked her curls behind her ear. "Sometimes I just couldn't see it, or I allowed other influences to convince me that I wasn't good enough or didn't deserve it. But I've never truly been empty or alone, because . . . because I always made it through. Even when I couldn't see the way around the heartache or the pain, even when I didn't know the peace was there, it sustained me and carried me until I *could* see the way again."

"So do you know the direction you want to go from here?"

Olivia smiled. "Yes." She took a deep breath and walked over to the bed where Hope was sleeping. She tucked the blankets around Hope's chin and softly swept the ringlets from her face. Then Olivia bent down and kissed her daughter's cheek before turning and looking at Michael again. "I want to renew our adoption profile. I don't know what the Lord has in store for us, but I think that through everything that has happened to us since we got married . . . all of the ups and downs, the good times and the bad . . . I think that I've finally gained enough faith in Heavenly Father's ability to guide us that I don't need to know exactly what's going to happen in order to be at peace."

"Livvy . . ." Michael paused and swallowed the emotion burning in his throat. "I've said it before and I'll say it again. You're amazing. I love you . . . no matter what."

Olivia walked back to her husband and he stood and met her with a long, slow kiss. "I love you too," Olivia whispered. "No matter what."

ACKNOWLEDGMENTS

I'm so excited for this sequel to finally come to fruition! Thank you to everyone who read *Delivering Hope* and then emailed or messaged me to ask, "What happens next?" I was so touched by the many notes and messages expressing how the story resonated with readers and helped them work through their own trials and not feel so alone. I'm truly humbled to think that my words had a positive impact in the lives of others.

Thanks to my wonderful friends and family who kept encouraging me to continue when I would get frustrated or sidetracked. Your support means so much! I want to especially thank my mom. She is always telling someone about my book or giving them a copy. She's the best!

I owe a big thank you to Cedar Fort and especially to Alissa Voss for helping this book become the best it could be. Your comments and questions pushed me to think deeper and look more closely at the story. This book is better because of your efforts.

This book is dedicated to my three beautiful children. I'm thankful every day for the biggest miracles in my life and for the opportunity to love and squeeze and laugh and play with each of them. Isabella, Tyson, and Jay, you are more than worth every tear I shed in the journey to get you here.

Most especially, I want to thank my amazing husband, Shane. He is my best friend, my biggest fan, my greatest support, and the love of my life. He also knows precisely when I need a frozen yogurt or a Panda Express run, and he always, always believes in me.

Discussion Questions

1. Although Allison believes she followed our Heavenly Father's will when she placed Hope for adoption, she still faces a lot of pain and heartache after the fact. When we do what Heavenly Father wants us to do, are we always spared pain? Is doing the right thing always easy?

2. When Brandon apologizes to Allison for leaving her alone to deal with the pregnancy, she accepts his apology. Would it be easy to forgive someone who had hurt you in this way? How does forgiving Brandon help Allison?

3. Michael believed that once they adopted a baby, Olivia would be "cured" of the emotions associated with infertility. Did this happen? Did Olivia ever learn to work through those emotions? Are there other circumstances in life when an internal struggle continues, even after the external situation has been resolved?

4. Olivia made a split-second decision to offer service to Shanelle, even when her own heart was breaking. How did this decision help bring some peace to her life? When has

service (either that you provided or that was provided to you) blessed your life?

5. Riley had a moment when he had to decide whether or not he believed in the gospel lessons he had been taught his entire life. Have you ever had such a moment in your life? What did you decide? How has that decision affected your life?

6. The characters in this book are searching for peace in their lives. What does peace mean to you? How did Allison and Olivia discover peace for themselves? Have you found peace in your life? If so, how?

About the Author

Jennifer Holt was raised as a farm girl in Enterprise, Utah. An avid reader since age four, she always enjoys a good book. Jennifer graduated cum laude from Brigham Young University and shortly after, began her journey through infertility and the miracle of adoption. She lives in Boise, Idaho, with her husband, Shane, and their daughter and two sons. She enjoys wakeboarding and watching football with her family. You can connect with Jennifer on her website: www.authorjenniferannholt.com.

0 26575 14139 9